Bring It On

Shelley K. Wall, author of *Numbers Never Lie*

CRIMSON
ROMANCE
F+W Media, Inc.

This edition published by
Crimson Romance
an imprint of F+W Media, Inc.
10151 Carver Road, Suite 200
Blue Ash, Ohio 45242

www.crimsonromance.com

Dedication

TO MY HUSBAND, STAN, FOR SUPPORTING ALL MY DREAMS AND DESIRES THROUGHOUT OUR YEARS TOGETHER. SERIOUSLY.

AND TO MY CHILDREN, TYLER, KYLE, AND GRACE—DO THE THINGS YOU WANT TO DO, DREAM THE DREAMS YOU WANT TO DREAM, LIVE THE LIFE YOU WANT TO LIVE, BUT BE THE PERSON MOM WANTS YOU TO BE...OR ELSE. KIDDING.

Acknowledgments

My sincerest thanks to my friends, Cindy Davis and Carol Bland, for their fantastic advice and support. My appreciation to Jennifer Lawler, for taking a chance on an unknown author, and inspiring me to work harder.

My love and adoration to my parents, Bob and Agnes Kurtz, who have taught me what hard work, respect, kindness, and loyalty really means—and more importantly what it can achieve.

Chapter One

Kathryn Delroy was in her element. All those years of fishing with her dad and brothers had given her the background to be here. She wore a grin a mile wide as she watched the salmon leap through the water in their quest for a bed for their eggs. It was late June and right in the middle of spawning season. The air was crisp and the sun warm like a hot towel after a massage. She laughed at herself for comparing a trip to the spa to this more rustic experience. All the men in her group were taking wagers on who would get the biggest catch and deciding who would net, de-hook, and clean Kathryn's catch. She ignored them. Let 'em laugh. First rule of Team Building, never underestimate the power of your team members. Isn't that what they said in the conference? That was right before the guys all spent half an hour deciding where to go to happy hour. Ha, these guys hadn't got a clue.

Kathryn stood with her hands on her hips. The river rushed past, lapping white water waves at the shore near her feet. It kind of reminded her of her life, always in a hurry. She tilted her head up and closed her eyes briefly to bask in the sun's warmth. She was up for this challenge, more so than these guys knew. After all, she was sans one over-controlling fiancé and it was her time to take life by the horns. Yeah. Time to be her own person.

The lower Kenai waters churned so heavily that sometimes the water took on a pink hue from the multitudes of fish streaming by like soldiers on a crusade. Kathryn hadn't been salmon fishing before but she was more than ready to try.

"Where the hell is Tito?" James Wallace asked. James was a manager from their San Diego office and looked every bit the native Californian with his long straggly hair pulled back in a super-short ponytail and wire-rimmed glasses, obviously worn only to make a statement. He was wearing all the right outdoor gear and carrying a backpack over one shoulder. His look wasn't favored by the executives though, and he'd been given more than one "talk" about professional appearance, which he politely ignored. Apparently, his view was that California had their own rules, and he preferred to follow them. Since his office remained profitable and sales steadily stayed at the top of the list for their divisions, Kathryn assumed he was given latitude with his appearance. For now. She marveled at how different he'd become since he moved.

"Tito?" asked Zak, one of the manager trainees from L.A. "That's the new guy, right?"

"Yeah, that's me," said a voice behind them. And that's when Kathryn saw little Thomas Ryan, all grown up into a big boy coming down the bank, also with a backpack over his shoulder. "Hey Kathryn." Thomas grinned. "I heard you were going to be here."

Kathryn's mouth dropped open as the man approached. "Thomas? Thomas Ryan?" Could it really be the skinny guy that graduated with her brother and had been at her house most of his junior and senior year?

"Yep. Haven't seen you since you were playing softball with Dad's company team a few years ago in that fundraiser deal. How's things going?" he drawled as he walked up to the boat launch and dropped his backpack into the aluminum boat in front of them. He didn't listen for her answer before turning to the group. "Who's in which boat, gentlemen? How are we divvying up?" He glanced around at the six other people encircling them.

"Doesn't matter to me," one answered.

"Me either," came several replies.

"Okay, then." Thomas shook his sandy blond hair out of his eyes, and held a hand out to Kathryn. "Kathryn, you're here with

Zak, James, and me. The rest of you guys take that boat." Thomas pointed to the one in front of theirs and waited for Kathryn to take his hand and step in.

"I can manage," Kathryn mumbled as she stepped into the boat, disregarding his outstretched hand. The boat shifted to the side under her weight while the rumbling current tried to pry them from the dock. She held her balance but grabbed his arm without looking up. When did Thomas get so tall? And so hard? She hadn't seen him in what? Three years? No, it was five, but they had been kind to him. Very kind.

"I know, Kathryn. You were always good at managing on your own, weren't you?" He winked. "Try not to embarrass 'em too much this week, okay?" he whispered, out of earshot from the others.

Zak stepped into the boat behind Kathryn, and sat next to her on the bench; James took the seat by Thomas.

"So, where did the name Tito come from?" Zak asked.

"Long story. It's a nickname from college." Thomas nodded at the guide. "Line's free. We're ready." The guide throttled the boat away from the dock.

"Looks like we have plenty of time for stories," Zak said as the boat motor kicked into gear and slowly propelled them upstream.

"Not this one. It's probably not one I should tell right now, if you know what I mean." Thomas glanced at Kathryn, then looked out at the bank and promptly changed the subject. "Great day for this, isn't it?" Zak got the hint and left him alone.

That was the beginning of Team Building 101 for Stein Incorporated's leadership class. Everyone in this small group had been, or was going to be, management for the company at one of the various locations across the country and Thomas Ryan was one of them.

Kathryn had a lot of questions. Where'd he been all these years? She'd heard from his dad that he'd gone to work for a firm in Cleveland after he graduated. He'd followed a girl up there, or something like that. How did he get from that to here? She frowned at her inquisitiveness. Sans guy, she reminded herself. She was on her own for the first time in a long time and she had vowed to enjoy it. So what if he apparently still made her stomach flip? He did that to every girl she knew back then. High school was over.

"So, how have you been, Katy?" His quiet voice came from behind her.

"No one's called me that since high school," she said.

"Oh, sorry. Some habits are hard to break. What do you want to be called?" he asked as she turned around to face him. The air was chilly as the wind gusted past them on the water. He leaned into it with his hands shoved down into his coat pockets. His hair whipped back and forth across his face haphazardly as he smiled.

She sucked in cold air. *Okay, when did you get so good looking?* Kathryn had an uncomfortable reaction to that smile and looked down at the bottom of the boat.

"Up to you." She shrugged. As she swiveled to face forward, her cap caught the wind and flew off, sending her hair bursting out in every direction. "Whoops!" she exclaimed. She grasped after it, tumbling backward in the boat, slamming against Thomas' feet and legs. *And when did you get so built, Tommy?*

Their guide for the day was a man named Don Something. She didn't catch his last name and wasn't sure he had even given it. He was a big, burly guy with brown wavy hair and a thick, bushy moustache. When he spoke, the hairs of the moustache curled into his lip. Kathryn wondered how much food ended up on it when he ate.

"All right, we'll start here. There are a few ground rules I need to mention," Don Something said as he faced them. His arm was behind his back keeping the boat aimed steadily into the current.

He made it sound involved but the process was little more than throw your line in and wait patiently.

The experience of pulling in the fish was exhilarating. Kathryn smiled satisfactorily for several minutes as she looked out over the silver glitter of the sun on the water. She was in Alaska, fishing for salmon, and she'd just caught her first. The sun was shining, the air was cool, and she was getting paid to be here. What a great life. She looked at Thomas' backside in front of her. The scenery wasn't too bad either.

"So, what kind of exercises are we doing tonight?" Zak asked. The exercises he referred to were all work-related. Each day, the group was required to do some sort of team-building process together and then meet to discuss it afterward. Most of them were problem-solving routines, designed to make them think on their feet or avert some sort of disaster.

"I heard it was a rope thing, something to do with climbing ropes or walking them," James offered. "At least that's what one of the guys at the office said they did before." He slowly reeled in his line to check the lure and then threw it back in. They all watched as one of the guys on a nearby boat pulled in a nice-sized salmon.

"That ought to be interesting," Thomas chimed in. "Anyone ever walked a rope? Or climbed one?"

"Yeah, in gym class in high school," Zak said.

"You walked a rope?"

"No. Climbed one. Everyone had to do it. You were supposed to climb all the way to the top. We also had to climb the peg board on the wall. It was intended to make you able to lift your full body weight and part of our final exam."

"Oh. Yeah. I guess I did that too. This should be interesting."

"What about you, Kathryn? You done anything interesting with ropes?" She was certain James worded it that way just to get a reaction. His tone and expression were more than suggestive. Oh brother.

"Yeah," Kathryn played along, "but it had nothing to do with lifting my own weight." She was used to James's jokes. He'd used them a lot. His comments bordered on unacceptable. Once she had worked with him a while, she realized he did that with everyone. It was his way of joking around and fairly harmless. She winked at him, then noticed Thomas had raised an eyebrow in disapproval.

James wasn't done yet. He took her comment and ran with it. "Ah, tying people up?"

She laughed. "Let's just say I'm pretty good at knots."

Thomas still maintained his frown but chimed in, startling her completely with, "I can vouch for that, guys. She definitely is pretty good with knots."

Kathryn wasn't often caught off-guard but she found herself frozen in place, catching a sparkle in Thomas' eye she hadn't seen before. All three of the other men on the boat also hesitated, then laughed. Kathryn frowned, turned around facing away, her face starting to match the salmon's color. Everyone on the boat had completely misunderstood his comment. He wanted them to, obviously.

"Sounds like there's a story there that we need to hear sometime," James chided.

"No, not really," Kathryn answered.

As a teen, she'd spent summers at the lake. Her parents sprang for a boat. She'd become pretty adept at tying it up as well as driving it. Her brother Sam was pretty social and he'd take two or three friends along every time they went out, more often than not including Thomas. Being a good brother, he also let Kathryn tag along if she wanted to. But only sometimes, mainly when there was no one else to drive the boat except him. He wanted to make sure he got a chance to board also and without her, he'd be stuck driving for everyone else. The down side was she often got stuck tying the boat up and washing it when they returned, while Sam and his friends escaped to do something fun. Yes, she was pretty good with knots. She was also pretty good at washing down a boat, steering a boat, wakeboarding, fishing, softball, and a lot of other things. Things she seldom did anymore because she was always working.

Don dropped them all back at the dock. "I'll clean the fish and bring them up to the lodge in a bit. We'll send them over to be processed in the morning. There's a cooler up there for each of you. The processors will come by and take whatever you have every day. At the end of the week, we'll ship them to your address. You don't have to do anything. That's part of our job."

Excellent! That just took the hassle out of fishing. As well as the smell. Kathryn glanced smugly at the men who'd earlier complained about the possibility of having to take care of her fish. *So there!*

"Have a good night folks." Don waved a salute as they all traipsed back up to the lodge. "Dinner is at seven in the dining room. Don't be late or you won't eat. Get some rest now, though, as you'll likely be up late with the exercises."

The lodge they were staying at consisted of one large building, which was actually someone's home turned into the camp's kitchen, main dining room, a meeting room, and some smaller bedrooms for individuals. There was also a big open living room that was equipped with a pool table, a bar, television, and a stack of DVDs.

Outside the main building were six cabins. Each cabin slept two people. Except hers, of course. Kathryn wasn't sharing but the guys were doubled up. She doubted they'd all be happy with each other by the end of the week. It was comical if she gave it thought. How did one swear off men only to get isolated in the Alaskan wilds with a bevy of them?

Chapter Two

Thomas sat in the bar of the lodge watching the sports channel. Even though this week was dedicated to training, if he didn't get at least a few sports highlights while he was away, he'd go nuts. He'd enjoyed the fishing more than expected. Truthfully, it hadn't been the fishing. He enjoyed seeing Kathryn again. She had been pretty as a girl but there was something different now. More confidence, maybe? Polish. That's what it was. There was a little more polish to her, which was nice. He preferred the unpolished version though. Had his father known she was here when he recommended he attend? Doubtful, since she was the one person his dad never approved of.

Laughter erupted at the doorway as two other members of their group entered the room. He had yet to meet them but knew one was in sales at their Chicago office. He wasn't sure about the other guy. Both appeared to be in their early thirties, medium build, looking for a good time and planning a night on the town. Hardly a town. More like a pit stop.

Past the bar and dining area, the view was gorgeous. The room was surrounded by floor to ceiling glass windows that opened to a deck that encompassed half the lodge. The view of the river and the mountains on the other side was amazing. But the greatest part of the view had nothing to do with the river or the mountains. Rather one Kathryn Delroy, dressed in black athletic pants and a blue jacket, sitting on the rocks by the river. Her hair was different. It used to be brown, sort of a light brown. It was longer now and had darkened significantly and clung in cascades of waves to her back. It was banded in a tie of some sort at her neck. She laid back on the ground with her hands behind her head and closed her eyes. The action made him realize that Sam's little sister was a lot more than the little girl he'd known growing up. She was built. Damn, she was built.

"Kathryn's pretty hot, isn't she?" James asked as he walked into the room and noticed where Thomas was focused. "We dated once."

"Really?" Thomas turned his attention to James. In his opinion, she was way out of his league. But then, she'd flirted with him on the boat. "I thought you were in San Diego."

"I am. Now. I started in the Houston office though. After I'd been there a year, they transferred me to California to build up a new sales team."

"So, you and Kathryn dated?"

"What? Is that so hard to believe?" James pouted. "Officially, we went out to dinner once. After a happy hour thing for work."

"I wouldn't call that dating," Thomas said.

"We hung out for a while. She's a great kisser."

She kissed *him*? No way. Thomas didn't want to hear this. Not about Sam's sister. He frowned at James. "Does she know you say that to the people she works with?"

James shrugged. He went around the bar to get a glass, added some ice, and filled it with Scotch and water. That was Thomas's exit cue. He slid off the bar stool and headed out the door, then down the grass embankment. He did not want to hear anything more from James. Not about Kathryn. Anyone who started out a conversation that way was an ass. Okay, maybe if it was about someone else, he wouldn't care, but not about her. Take that back. His legal mind kicked in. Talking about coworkers like that can get you in trouble.

"Look at 'em. It makes you want to reach out and grab one," he said when he got close enough to see her breathing.

She arched her head backward, peering at him upside down. "Who?"

"The salmon." He pointed at the water where a steady pink stream of bodies moved just under the surface. Large strips of bright color flashed like fireflies in the murky green. Every once in a while, one arched in the air and landed with a splash.

"Oh, yeah." She lowered her chin onto her chest to see the water, then raised off the ground to a sitting position. She slid her legs up and wrapped her arms around her knees. A couple of leaves had hidden themselves in her hair and the wind caught them, flicking them around just like their lures had moved in the water earlier that day.

Thomas dropped to the ground next to her, lifted one knee and rested his arm across it. "James said you're a great kisser."

"What!" she choked out. "When did he say that?"

"Just a minute ago in the kitchen. So you guys dated?" He squinted into the sun at her, looking for a reaction. The light blinded him such that he couldn't really get a good gauge of her thoughts.

"No." She drawled it out slowly as if hesitant to explain. It had been stupid to mention but he found himself needing to know. The wind carried her scent to him. He switched his gaze to the water and waited. "It wasn't like that. More of a drunk, spur of the moment, one time, stupid, very stupid, should not have happened, thing." She turned.

When he finally decided to return her gaze, he stopped breathing for a second. Crystal blue. Her eyes were crystal blue. Her lashes soft like wisps of silk. Her lips and cheeks were rosy from the cool air. Even the tip of her nose was pink. He'd never noticed the eyes before—never in all these years.

"What else did he say? Should I be worried?" she asked.

He shook his head, more to focus than answer. "That's all, but I didn't stay to hear any more." *Especially when his first impulse was to punch the guy. Right in the nose.* Fortunately, he had never been the violent type. Still, a picture of her with James flitted through his thoughts. "I wonder what Sam would have done if he'd heard."

"Why? Are you planning on being big brother since he's not here? I don't need big brother looking out for me, and I don't need you to either." Those eyes matched his gaze with a fierce challenge.

He surveyed her face, taking in the details. He imagined what that hair felt like. What James knew about kissing Kathryn that he didn't.

Thomas shook his head again to clear that vision. "Don't worry. I don't feel very brotherly anyway right now. Want to get him back?"

A smile crept across her face. "What did you have in mind, Thomas?"

A gust of wind hit them. Her hair whisked off her back for a moment, the leaves still entwined in the strands. Without thought, he pulled her hair around with one hand. He worked the leaves out with his fingers then released the lucky leaves into the wind.

She watched the leaves flitter away. "Thanks."

"No problem. Um...where was I? Oh, yeah. Getting back at James." His fingers were still laced into her hair. He slowly let go and lowered his hand.

"What exactly did you have in mind?" She leaned toward him, wiggling her eyebrows. Her eyes rested on his mouth.

"I'll think of something. So, Katy." He used the pet name on purpose. "Are you?" He leaned toward her putting his forehead against hers. She didn't draw back, which made him nervous. Crystal blue eyes looked up at him. Nervous as hell.

"Am I what?" *Don't say it. Remember it's Sam's little sister, you idiot. The one you spent all those summers with on the boat. Shit. Yeah. Shouldn't have thought of that.* Visions of her pink and blue striped bikini flew through his brain, rendering him numb for a second. That was the first time he really took notice of Kathryn. Looking back, it was the first time he'd thought about what always seemed to pop in his head. Now, sitting with their heads touching, it was all he could think about as he looked down at her mouth.

"A good kisser." *Crap*. It slipped out like a spasm. And by the look on her face, she wasn't as surprised as he was about the thought. What did that mean?

"Tommy Ryan." Kathryn pulled her head back from his, gave him a scolding glance, then looked out over the water. "If I didn't know you better, I'd say you're flirting. Don't you think it's a little wasted on me?"

"Katy Delroy, I doubt you know me as well as you think." He sat still for a moment, then added. "About James...just play along when we do our team-building exercise this evening, okay?"

"Okay. I guess."

The sound of confusion rang in her voice. He wasn't sure whether it was about his question or about James. Maybe it was more apprehension than confusion. It was hard to tell.

"And I do know you," she added. "I know that, growing up, you chased almost every girl in school. As I understand it, that didn't change much in college. You made flirting a class of its own. From what Sam tells me, you would have had an A in it, if you'd been graded. It must have worked well for you. Apparently, you got laid so much you should have gotten frequent flyer points."

Ouch, Sam said that?

He bellowed out a good laugh, and clutched his stomach. "Yeah, right. Remind me to talk to your brother about his gossiping."

"So, don't think I don't recognize the moves, buddy."

"Are they working?" He gave her his best devilish grin. *Why was he doing this?* Kathryn was his friend's sister. Yeah, got to remember that. Thomas frowned, wondering why he was even considering touching her. Who cares? It's not worth it, he chided himself. Then she smiled back and those crystal blue eyes had him. *The hell it isn't.*

"Don't expect me to fall for that crap, Tommy. Besides, you couldn't handle the likes of me." With that, Kathryn hopped to her feet, dusted the grass off her tight little behind and marched up the embankment toward the lodge. When she reached the stairs to the deck, she glanced over her shoulder.

Yeah, I'm still watching. He smiled and flipped his fingers in a mock salute. "Try me," he muttered softly before following. For all his education and maturity, he realized he had ended up right back where he was years ago—wanting something that was out of reach. This time he decided there wasn't any reward in doing the right thing.

Chapter Three

Kathryn was a grown woman, more than capable of handling bad boys like Tommy. After all, she had dealt with a lot more than his playboy ass, hadn't she? No time for men. Or at least she told herself that before she meandered toward the group meal. In the dining room, they all sat together at the giant table where a foray of appetizers, mostly cheese and crackers, decorated the cloth surface. Dinner turned out to be—big surprise—salmon.

Kathryn did her best to avoid looking at Thomas. And talking to him. She sat at the opposite end of the table and tried hard to focus her attention on the conversation of the guys around her. It wasn't happening. Thomas Ryan had flirted with her. No doubt about it. Why? She stole a glance down the table. Damn. He caught her gaze and grinned. No, she wouldn't fall for that. He had a fan club that covers five states. It'd be a cold day in hell before she joined it. She wasn't a kid now. She'd been flirted with before. A lot. She could handle it. In fact, two could play that game.

To prove her point, she tilted her glass at him, licked her lips and smiled back. Her insides warmed when a shocked look passed over his face.

Yeah, Thomas. You might want to take cover. I'm not little Katy anymore. But then, she reminded herself, he wasn't little Tommy either.

Dinner was over. He rose from the table and walked outside onto the porch. He leaned both hands against the rail and surveyed the mountains. Through the glass, she admired the broad shoulders, the arms, the way the faded jeans hugged his behind, especially in certain places. His thighs. She bet those could do a number on her.

Whoa. Stop. She shook her head. This is Thomas. Sam's friend. At that moment, he turned and caught her staring. Again. Out came that damn grin as he leaned back against the rail, crossed his arms over his chest and leisurely soaked in the moment. Okay, maybe she should take cover instead. There was a challenge in that smile.

The chair legs made a loud screech as she forced her chair back to rise from the table. Somehow the thought of the cabin, with its quiet and safe solitude was suddenly appealing. Her stomach was all knotted up, must have been a reaction to the food. No way Tommy Ryan had anything to do with it. Kathryn eased toward the door with the hopes of a quick exit.

At that moment, Sean Goldstein, their host for the week, walked into the room with a clipboard held loosely in one hand. "Everyone, round up and meet outside by the campfire. Wear something comfortable that you can move in and don't mind getting dirty. I'd recommend tennis shoes or hiking boots. Your choice. Anyone who has any physical illnesses or disabilities that prevent them from climbing, running, or crawling, come see me." He looked around the room, waiting briefly in case anyone came forward, then confidently strode out to the fire pit.

"Our first exercise is the ropes and ladders course," Sean said without smiling. He held up the clipboard and checked the top sheet of paper for a second. "This will be done in teams of two. The sales guys will work together and the admin guys will pair up. When I call out your name and your team number, find your teammate and stand over by that path." He pointed toward an opening in the trees. "Team One, Zeiger and Flint."

He paused while the two men met, shook hands, and started toward the path. "Team Two, Cassidy and Wallace. Team Three, Hernandez and Billings. Team Four, Delroy and Ryan." Sean raised an eyebrow. "Anyone have a problem with their teammate?"

Kathryn thought his glance rested on Thomas a little longer than normal.

No answers came from the group as everyone listened for the next order. "This is going to be fun. Most people get a good laugh, which is why we start with it, it's sort of an ice-breaker. Okay. Follow me," Sean motioned as he passed the group. He led the way down the path, talking as he moved. "Before we get too far, I want to caution everyone. You're in Alaska now. You're a guest here. This land belongs to the bear, moose, and a lot of other critters. As long as you move slowly, stay close to the cabins and lodge, and don't do anything stupid, you won't have any problems. *However*, if you do happen to come across a wild animal, remove yourself slowly from it. Do *NOT* run. Bears will chase you. That's one race you'll never win. They're usually just as afraid of you as you are of them, so they'll make a quick exit if you don't get stupid."

He hesitated for a second to catch his breath, then added, "And don't go walking around out here in the woods by yourself. I don't want to have to come looking for you."

Sean moved off into the trees. The group fell into line behind him.

Thomas sidled up next to Kathryn. He grinned. "Ready for this, partner?"

"Can't wait." She smiled back with a hint of sarcasm as she fell into step. The path through the trees was only wide enough for one person to pass through, so Thomas held out his hand for her to pass before him. They trudged a mere hundred feet through the trees to a large opening, devoid of vegetation other than a few sparse tufts of grass. Sunshine glinted streaks of light through thick branches casting a bright haze over the troop. In the middle of the opening was an adult-size jungle gym that looked like something out of a reality show. Two large wooden beams bolted together spanned over the entire structure. One end had two ropes attached to it that hung to the ground. The ropes were knotted at one-foot intervals. Kathryn swallowed as she realized she was going to have to climb one of them. There was no other purpose for that kind of rope. Good thing she'd used the gym as a mental rejuvenator the past few months.

A platform protruded about four feet below the top of the ropes, sort of a lookout point. On the other side of it was a large mesh net that cascaded down at an angle into the dirt. Beyond the net, a big green plastic tunnel that resembled a drainage tube curled around and ended at the other side of the structure. Large wooden slats were nailed to a six-foot wide wall on the far end. The slatted wall rose up to the very top beams. The beams above the structure formed a platform less than a foot wide. It had a large rope stretched across that was about six feet over the entire contraption and anchored at each end to the supports. Another green tunnel structure hung from a platform next to the top beam. However, that tunnel angled to the ground like a water slide, where at the bottom was a large puddle of water.

Oh great. It really is a water slide. She frowned. She didn't mind getting wet, but didn't relish the mud at the bottom. The temperature was more than just cool, it was nippy. It would ruin the jacket she had on. The only jacket she'd brought.

"This should be fun," Thomas whispered in her ear. Kathryn couldn't help but tip an eyebrow up and look at him sideways.

"Okay, here's how it works." Sean spoke loudly to get everyone's attention. "Each team is going to wear one of these harnesses." He held up a rope—a leather contraption that bore resemblance to a medieval torture device.

"Really fun," Thomas interjected, his breath tickling her earlobe. He let out a short "Ouch" as Kathryn landed a solid jab to his ribs.

Unaware of the comment, Sean continued, "Each belt goes around your waist. You are going to be chained at the hips and also at the hands to your partner with a three-foot length of rope. Just one hand, not both. Your job is to maneuver the entire obstacle course," he waved at the jungle gym, "together without falling. If you complete it in ten minutes or less, you get twenty points. Fifteen minutes or less, ten points. Twenty minutes, five points. If you fall, zero. Each person is awarded the points individually because the teams change as the week goes on. The purpose behind each exercise is to teach teamwork, critical thinking skills, leadership, and decision-making. At the end of the week, the person with the most points will receive a nice perk."

Zak's ears pricked up at the last sentence. "What's the perk, Sean?"

"A roundtrip ticket to the destination of your choice. Stateside only. And an extra twenty-four hours of vacation time. But don't start planning your trips, guys. This is a lot harder than it looks. None of the exercises are a piece of cake. You're going to have to figure out how to work the structure together without knocking each other down. If one person goes down, you'll pull the other one off too. That's why you see the big air mattress underneath everything. More people fall than finish."

"Any hints?" Zak asked.

"Yeah, sometimes leadership means *not* leading." Sean moved over to the two ropes, signaled the first team and pulled his iPhone from his pocket. "I have a stopwatch on this thing so when I blow the whistle, you start. When I blow it again, you're done. I encourage you to be creative."

The first team successfully climbed the ropes, slid down the other side and crawled through the tunnel. That part was a little disturbing for two big guys trying to maneuver hands and waist with only three feet of rope space between them. They made it through and emerged the other side, faces red and sweating. They climbed back up to the beam, but when they started across, one of the guys lost his balance. The rope at the top swayed and the weight of the first took both of them down. They fell safely and rose off the giant bubbled air mattress, cussing and laughing.

The second team made it through the entire course but took nineteen minutes. They crawled out of the mud below the slide, panting with exhaustion. From what Kathryn saw, crossing the beam was the hardest part. The three feet of rope wasn't enough to get both people side by side moving on the beam at any pace. If the rope moved with one, both were affected and balancing was hard.

The third team fell when climbing the rope mesh and didn't make it to the beam. Thomas and Kathryn were next. They stepped up to the ropes. Kathryn looked at Thomas, expecting him to start giving directions. "Let's knock 'em dead, Katy," he said with a wink just before the whistle blew. They heaved up the rope, pulling their bodies by the arms and locking their feet just above the knots. At the top, they flung over to the platform and turned backward to climb down. Thomas placed his body on the side the ropes connected them so they had more room to work with. They watched each other move and kept their arms in sequence going down.

At the opening to the first plastic tunnel, Kathryn said, "You go first, I'll follow. We just need to keep the hands moving together." She held up the wrist that was tied to his.

"Katy, I don't mind leading but in this situation, I think it'd be better if you did."

"Just go, you're wasting time."

"No, not this time. I'll go first some other time."

She let out an exasperated sigh and heaved herself into the tube. The rope on her wrist threaded between her legs and became taut. She immediately realized why he didn't want to go first. Maybe that's why the other guys took so long. "Okay. I get it," she blurted over her shoulder as she crawled forward.

"Figured it out, did ya? I'd kind of like to keep certain things working as they are." She couldn't see his grin but felt it.

Once out of the tunnel, they climbed the ropes back up to the beam across the top. Her wrist was pinching but she kept pace with Thomas. He glanced sideways once in a while to make sure they were in synch. "You're doing great," he said.

"So are you," she responded.

Only two more things to go. The beam and the slide.

"Any great ideas on the beam?" she asked.

"Yeah, we need to face each other. Our weight will be counterbalanced that way." They were almost to the top.

"The beam's not wide enough for that."

"Yeah, it is." He heaved himself up on the beam and waited. When she sat next to him, he looked at her. "Okay, let's raise up together." They slowly stood then grabbed the rope. Kathryn was already facing down the beam and ready to go.

"Katy?" His hair was flying back in the cold wind as he spoke softly.

"Yeah, what?"

"Spread your legs for me."

He did not just say that. She shot a glance up. He had that stupid grin in prime form. She didn't move.

"What?"

She felt her face flush as Thomas slid one of his thighs between her legs and anchored the other one behind her on the beam. He then lifted the rope and wrapped it behind her so they were pelvis to pelvis as they stood on the beam.

"This is what you meant?"

"Yeah. What did you think?" he whispered. "Okay, your hand in front on the rope, then mine, then yours. Let's just slide along hands, feet, hands, feet." They started moving. Hands. Feet. Hands. Feet. Muscular thigh wedged against hers. Hands. Feet. Hands. Feet. Hard chest touching hers. Hands. Feet. Hands. Feet. Kathryn's stomach was knotting up again. Her hair caught the wind and started whipping around.

"Tommy, you said great the first time." She wasn't sure why that popped into her head at that moment. Maybe because she was facing him and his mouth was right in front of her. The warmth of his breath took the chill off her cheeks. Or maybe because the entire length of his body was rubbing against hers as they moved.

"What?" he sounded puzzled.

"You said James said I was a great kisser."

"You're thinking about this now?"

"When you asked, you only said good."

Thomas' foot slipped and his weight leaned backward. He teetered. Kathryn kept the hand with the rope anchored on the line over them. She reached out with the other hand, grabbed his shirt and yanked him toward her. His weight thudded heavily against her, crushing their chests together. As his chin struck her nose, he spoke for her ears only, "Sorry, my imagination had a problem with that picture." They only had five more feet to go and they were off the beam.

"You imagined it?" she asked.

Hands. Feet. Thigh. Oops. Hands. Feet. Hands. She had to stop thinking about everything that was pressed up against her.

"Kind of hard not to right now. Just remember—you brought it up." He looked down.

"Stop that, Thomas. You're doing it again."

"Doing what?"

"Flirting." They were at the end of the beam. The slide tunnel was next to them.

"You brought it up, Katy." They were still facing each other.

"Okay, down we go." He sat in front of the slide and jerked his hand to pull her down with him. "Time's a wasting." He shoved off and they lunged down the slide together, landing in the mud pit below. They surfaced—completely soaked in gray water, hair matted to their faces—and crawled out. The whistle blew as they stood up.

Thomas reached down and hugged her, pulling her off the ground as he swung her around. "Good job, girl." For a short moment, she was completely encased in warm, wet, muddy arms. When he set her back down, he wiped the mud off her face and cupped her cheeks with both hands. "I think we might have won this one, Katy."

Kathryn was dizzy. Not from being spun around. From being wrapped like a bear cub in those big arms. She barely noticed that he had unshackled them until he was gone, striding away, getting high fives from the other teams. Why did she suddenly feel like she'd been manipulated?

Chapter Four

Day two started as follows: Team One: Zero Points. Team Two: Ten Points. Team Three: Zero Points. Team Four: Twenty Points.

"Way to go, Kathryn," James congratulated as he pulled up a chair next to her at breakfast. "Smart move on the beam." He held up a hand for her to slap.

She clapped a hand against his and she responded, "Thanks! That was Thomas' idea for the most part. It was a little strange but it kept us balanced."

"Yeah, and we all need a little more balance in our lives," Thomas chimed in as he slid into the opposite chair and winked. "How'd everyone sleep?" he looked from one to the other.

"*I* slept fine. Those room-darkening shades work pretty good." Kathryn slid the empty plate away as the rest of the group trickled in.

"And James slept great too," Thomas confirmed, "See, I happen to be his cabin mate. Judging by the snoring going on, I'd say he's pretty rested."

"Hey! I don't snore."

"Yeah, and there's no bear in these woods either. Remind me to get some earplugs if we go anywhere today."

A muffled giggle escaped from Kathryn as she rose. She had an almost musical tone to it. He liked that. She filled her cup with coffee and doctored it. She'd put her hair in a braid today—to contain it, most likely. Even so, several dark strands around her face were slinking out of the braid and falling forward to caress her face and neck. As she lifted the cup to her lips, he admired the smooth line of her neck. Her swift turn toward the table suddenly made him need an extra cup of coffee himself. And he didn't usually even drink the stuff.

The night of restlessness was hard to hide. Between James' constant rumbling motor noises, and thoughts of Kathryn pressed up against him on the beam, he wasn't in the best of moods. Not by any means. No one should look as perky and rested as she did this morning. That was just plain rude. "Kathryn, just curious... do you snore?" Not sure why he asked.

"Not that I know of." She was preoccupied with a newspaper sitting on the cupboard next to their table.

"Good," Thomas said. "I'm rooming with you from now on." He thought he'd get a reaction. He expected her to be alarmed or something but no, she just ignored him.

Her bored voice responded while her hands flipped carelessly through the newspaper, "No, I don't think so. I like roommates with a little less baggage." She glanced around the room. "But there's a sofa right there if you need it." Without raising her head, a slender ringless hand gestured toward the area next to them.

"Yeah, that looks real comfortable for a guy my size."

The cook rushed in with a plate full of food presented so well that it would rival Martha Stewart. It was humorous considering her appearance was in complete contrast to the culinary icon. She waltzed around the room offering it to the guys. She started with Thomas, smiling brightly at him. Her cheerfulness was contagious. "Hey Rita. You look great this morning."

"Thank you. So do you." She flashed a smile and moved to the next group. Kathryn returned to her chair across from him, frowning.

"Always pouring on the charm, aren't you, Thomas?" Kathryn said.

"Just looking for a friendly face to lessen my bad mood." He was honest. Always had been. Most people hated that about him because he'd often be pretty blunt in the process.

"Why should you be in a bad mood? You won last night."

"*We* won," he corrected. "And I don't do well without sleep."

"Maybe *we* won, but I wasn't the one everyone was high-fiving. I'd guess you got a little praise for your methods, didn't you?"

"What methods? We chose the best approach to make sure we stayed balanced and moved quickly. Is that a bad thing?" He looked around the room and nodded at a couple of the guys that mumbled good morning to them.

James chipped in, "Yeah, and who wouldn't want to go hip to hip with Kathryn here?" Damn. Wish he hadn't said that. Kathryn's brows furrowed as she gave Thomas a "see what I mean?" look.

"Shut up, James. Inappropriate." He jammed his fork into the plate of food and stuffed eggs into his mouth. His cheek bulged as he continued.

"Hey, I'm just kidding around," James responded.

"It's not funny, jackass."

Thankfully, he didn't have to watch someone else wrapped around her legs. His thoughts jumped to the memory of her thighs locked with his. The visual brought a surge of energy. Why did he care what James said about Kathryn? She *was* hot. They all noticed. He was their new idol. He frowned. Yeah, but she's Sam's sister. And a coworker.

Sean marched into the room carrying his clipboard. "Good morning, campers!" he announced. "Are we ready for a new day?" No response. "Everyone saw the scores so far, right? The chart's on the wall over there. We'll update it nightly. Today's going to be kind of a free day. Your agendas for the rest of the week are in your rooms. We have a fairly nice combination of sightseeing and fishing activities, along with the team-building events. We have a short exercise this morning that's just filling out a questionnaire about yourself. Before we do that though, I wanted to talk about yesterday's exercise." He motioned for those standing to seat themselves and waited.

"Why do you think we chose the activity?" Sean asked. The room was unusually quiet. "No one wants to answer?"

"You wanted creative solutions," the Chicago guy answered.

"Your name's Kevin, right?" he paused for the nod, then answered, "Yes, that's part of it. The key thing we usually see in that type of exercise is a combination of slow decision-making along with lack of cohesiveness. Some people will try to automatically take the lead and in doing so, not be willing to follow."

"But the ones that did the best didn't do either one," Kevin argued.

"It may have looked that way, but in truth they did both. Leadership isn't about giving orders and waiting for everyone to follow you. It's about coming up with a plan, hopefully together, then supporting the plan by words and actions. Sometimes you're first down the line, sometimes you're last. And in the best case, everyone crosses the finish line together."

Zak looked puzzled. "What if you can't get your people to that level of cohesiveness? I have some staff that are free in giving recommendations, but don't want to follow someone else's idea."

Sean nodded. "That's common. Any ideas?" He surveyed the room.

The discussion became animated as everyone made recommendations. They continued talking over the exercise and its implications for another hour. Sean was good. Thomas appreciated his calmness and his no b.s. candor. They broke when the discussion ended with the instruction to complete their questionnaire and turn it in by noon. They were free to do as they chose the rest of the day. However, everyone needed to meet in the kitchen at five the next morning for their next excursion: halibut fishing on the Cook Inlet.

Thomas observed James' advance toward Kathryn. The guy's persistence and innuendo grated on his nerves. It was bad enough that his incessant snoring made it impossible to get sound sleep, but he was obviously obsessed with Kathryn. Couldn't stop looking at her or talking about her. Annoyance bubbled up in the form of heavy finger-tapping on the table as Thomas watched him talking to her. He didn't know what they were saying but she shook her head. He put his hand on her forearm, she pulled back.

"Katy," Thomas interjected from his seat at the table. "Got a second?" Relief swam across her face, loosening the tension around her lips.

"Sure." She extricated herself from James' company and moved to sit next to Thomas at the table. "What's up?"

"You okay?"

"Of course. Why?"

"No reason. Um...I thought I'd take a drive north. Do a little sightseeing. If you're not going somewhere with James, maybe you'd like to tag along?" He hoped she'd see it as the lesser of two evils.

She looked around the room. Most of the group had taken their conversations outside. A few of the guys had discussed more fishing. James waited as if ready to pounce the minute their discussion was over. Thomas stood, waiting hesitantly for an answer.

"Are you playing big brother?" Her gaze rested on his. Crap, he stopped breathing. Big Brother? Hell no. There was nothing that innocent in what his mind was conjuring up right now. Still, the thought of her hanging out with James was completely repulsive. He gave an exasperated sigh. James shot a frown his way, which he ignored.

"Okay but no funny stuff," she answered. She pushed her chair back and stood with him.

She agreed? Yeah, she did. "I don't know what you're talking about." He grinned. "I'll meet you at your front door in ten minutes. Is that enough time?"

"Sure. I'm pretty much ready to go." He looked at her face for a minute, contemplating the way her cheeks dimpled around her mouth when she smiled. Immediately, he regretted asking. A day with Kathryn was probably not a smart move. She was right, he probably couldn't handle her. He wasn't sure it was a good idea to try either.

Chapter Five

The rental was a soft-top Jeep. The wind roared over it as they drove the tree-lined highway, the stereo blaring. The trees whizzed by, interrupted periodically by a log home or narrow road in the thick forestation. Kathryn enjoyed the slight chill in the air. Thomas drove slowly, looking around at the scenery as they moved. "If you see anything you want to check out, just let me know," he said as he glanced sideways at her.

Kathryn turned toward him, lifting a knee up and wedging her toes under her behind. "Please don't call me Katy in front of the group." She liked him saying it but the others were starting to watch them. It made her uncomfortable.

"Oh. Okay."

"It's just that—it gives the impression there's a relationship here. Something between us. I don't want rumors going around at work." His hair hung into his eyes a little, catching the sun. The urge to reach out and brush it back was overwhelming. Luckily, restraint was one of her best character traits.

"Understood." Ten minutes of silence passed. "Maybe I should call you thigh-master. You know, judging by the way we were locked together yesterday." He chuckled.

"You call me that and you'll walk funny for a week!" Thoughts of his warmth against her ran fleetingly through her mind again.

"Ouch. You wouldn't wound an old friend, would you?"

"An old friend wouldn't call me that. An old friend would know how important it is to keep a professional image at work, and support that."

"God, you sound like an old maid, Katy. Lighten up." His

brows furrowed over his eyes. The car slowed, and Thomas made a quick turn onto a two-lane highway.

She thought he tightened his knuckles on the steering wheel. "Do you have a plan, Thomas? Or are we just taking random roads into the trees?"

"I have a plan. I always have a plan. My life is built on plans." There was a faint hint of acidity in his tone.

"Are you going to tell me your plan, or do I have to guess?" She couldn't stand looking at the hair in his eyes anymore. She gave in and reached her fingers up to lightly brush it to the side. His fingers snaked up and grabbed her palm as she began to retract it. He rubbed over her fingers gently, looking at the hand before she snatched it away.

"What happened to David?" he asked matter-of-factly.

She thought about that for a moment. What's a good response to someone asking about the ex? The guy that she couldn't bring herself to marry. "You know, the fiancé?"

"We're not—together anymore."

"I gathered that." He gestured at her hand. "What happened?" He paused. "I was there, you know."

"There?"

"Yeah, at your mom and dad's anniversary. Remember?"

She remembered. It was their thirtieth. She and Sam had put together a video of pictures they'd gathered over the years and played it on the screen above the dance floor. There was a band, a group of family friends that had assembled to play old rock and country. She'd asked David to come on a whim. They'd dated for about a year, but it was off and on. More off than on because he traveled a lot with his work. He was an advertising account manager. His territory covered the southwest: Texas to California. Had she known what he would do, she would definitely have gone alone.

"So you witnessed the whole thing?" she marveled.

"Yeah, I got there late—just as the toasts started. Right in time for all the excitement. I stood in the back." His hands tapped to the music on the radio. His focus remained on the road.

Kathryn pulled the hem of her shirt out and rolled it between her fingers as she answered. "Can you believe he did that? Proposed to me right there at the party? Right in front of everyone."

"You didn't like that?" He quirked a brow at her. "It seemed a little romantic to me."

"Every girl wants romance, but the party wasn't about us! It was about Mom and Dad. He just took something that was supposed to be their big day and once again made it all about *him.*"

"Hmmm. It sounds like there's more to that than you're saying."

"He always did that. No matter what was going on. If it wasn't completely focused on him, then he always said or did something to put himself right in the center. He craved attention. I hated that. We didn't even really know each other and he pulled that charade."

"I thought you'd dated for several months."

"Yeah, but he traveled all the time. Sometimes, we'd go weeks without seeing each other—sometimes not even talking. That's not dating."

"But you had sex, right?"

True Thomas form. Straight to the nitty-gritty. She didn't understand why he was frowning at her. Or, for that matter, why he was even asking that question.

"That's not really any of your business." She looked at him, embarrassed to be discussing this. "And don't you think about anything else?"

"Sometimes. Not really. So, you were mad at him for proposing at the party? Then why did you say yes in front of everyone?"

"I couldn't humiliate him. Yeah, he was being a jerk and forcing me to be involved in that display, but it would have been downright cruel to turn him down publicly like that."

"But it was okay to put you on the spot publicly? And you ended it later anyway. I don't get your logic. You were mad, right?"

"Of course. Mad as hell. But that was supposed to be Mom and Dad's day. Not mine—or his. I wasn't about to make a scene. At least not any more than he'd already made."

Thomas' voice was musical when he laughed. A deep, loud sound. "You're something else, Katy," he said when he composed himself.

"What's so funny about that?"

"Nothing. It's not funny at all. It's just so—totally—you. You always put everyone else first." He made another turn in the car and slowed to pull into a manned station of some sort.

"What is this place?" she asked.

"It's the tunnel to Whittier. I spent time talking to Sean last night over some beers and he mentioned it. This tunnel was built years ago as a route for the residents on the other side to escape bad weather—or war. The tunnel has a railroad track down the middle of it and the cars and the train share it."

"So, what's Whittier like?" It sounded interesting.

"As I understand, it's mainly just a marina, lots of boats, a few hotels and restaurants. The cruise ships stop there. It's supposed to be really a nice tourist attraction."

"Oh. That sounds fantastic! I can't wait." She looked at him, smiling. "What made you choose this over fishing?"

"I thought you might like it." He grinned again and reached over to squeeze her fingers, and her stomach did a hula dance.

*

Thomas put his hands above his head and clasped his fingers together as he watched Kathryn throwing Tostitos chips into the air for the seagulls. The marina was a beautiful array of varying types and sizes of boats tied up to wooden posts that were wider than he was. The arctic air was refreshing but cool and he was glad for the extra sweater he'd thrown on at the last minute. She looked up, laughing and ducking when the bulbous bodies of the seagulls swooped within inches of her head to get the crumbles she tossed. There was a sense of satisfaction in pleasing Kathryn Delroy, the queen of people-pleasers. Standing here, mid pier, as she flung her worries to the gulls, he felt the tug that kept surfacing. She was infecting him with her easy warmth.

"Come here, Tommy!" Her hand outstretched toward him, in an innocently provocative gesture—a come-hither invitation to enjoy the moment. The all-encompassing desire to be blanketed in that laugh was enough to suck him in. He almost skipped the remaining steps over the wooden slats to where she stood. Thomas stuffed his hand in the bag and grabbed some chips. He flung them up as he watched the hawk-sized seagulls dive down without any concern for their safety. When one came so close he thought it would graze the top of her head, he thrust his arms over her protectively and drew her against his chest. She laughed and dug her fingers into his sweater, cowering. "My hair is probably full of chips," she giggled.

"Just a tad." In truth, there were tiny shards of chips lodged all over her head. "If we don't get these out, you're going to turn into dinner." Using both hands, he started disengaging the slivers of chips and tossing them into the water next to them. The birds reacted accordingly and dove after them, competing with the fish for the prizes. Her hair smelled like cucumbers and felt like silk against his rough fingers. He leaned closer to breathe her in.

"Thomas, is your eyesight going bad?" Kathryn teased. "Surely you can see good enough to get them out?"

He grinned. "I can see fine, but you're covered in chips. You might as well have rolled in them. There. I think I got them all." He stepped back and her hands that were previously clutched in his sweater dropped to her sides. She shivered.

"Are you cold?" He asked.

"A little."

"Let's go up and walk around the shops there." He pointed above where the steps from the docks led to a plank-covered walkway. The warm spot on his chest where she had been faded.

"I'd love that."

Thirty minutes later, they were sitting inside a small seafood restaurant that overlooked the collection of boats, spooning into bowls of chowder with chunks of sourdough bread. The chowder radiated through his insides. He smiled, watching her clutch her chowder bowl to heat her hands.

"Kathryn?"

"Hmm?" She raised her eyes to his, a smile anchored deep in the gaze.

"Do you ever ask for anything? You know, tell people what you want?"

"What does that mean?"

"I was thinking about David. Did you ever tell him you didn't like what he did? Or tell him what you wanted? Did he know what bothered you? What pleased you? I never really thought about it until just a little while ago but I remember as a kid, Sam always brought you along to drive the boat so that he could board. You hardly ever asked to board too. The only time you went..."

"Was when you asked me if I wanted to, usually when we were about to leave."

"Yeah. Why didn't you ever say something?"

"Because it was Sam's outing with his friends. Not mine. So, it wasn't up to me."

"But how do you expect to have fun or get what you want if you don't ask?"

Her face scrunched up in an unreadable expression and she looked out the window. He followed her gaze and noticed a fishing boat slowly moving its way toward the bay. He wondered if the reason she'd been so athletic was because it was a way to stake her claim on her world. Her way of taking what she wanted without having to ask permission.

"I do have fun. I've had a lot of fun. Probably too much so in college." She grinned.

"Everyone did that. That's not what I meant."

"No, Tommy. Everyone doesn't do it the same way you did." Her voice held sarcasm.

"Look, don't believe everything your brother tells you, okay? I'm not a complete ass." He yanked his water glass up to drink, splashing water down his front. "Shit!"

"I never said you were," she answered calmly as she rubbed her napkin across his sweater like he was a child.

He pushed her hand away and leaned over the table toward her. "I don't want to know how much you partied in school. What I want to know is have you ever asked for the things that you want simply because *you* wanted them? Not because it's right for someone else, but because it's right for you. Or at least you think it is. You know," his eyes bore into hers, "like saying 'no, I don't want to get married' or 'I want to kiss you' or 'I want to wakeboard too' or 'No, I don't want to drive the damn boat for your friends' or 'Why don't you call me sometime' or 'I want to have sex with you.'"

He searched her face as she dropped her mouth open and stared at him. Her eyes rested on his mouth. Okay, maybe he went too far with that last comment.

Her neck hitched as she swallowed hard. "So, you have me all figured out, don't you, Thomas?"

"Not really. I have never understood you. I'd never let someone else drive my decisions for me. And if I saw an opportunity, I wouldn't hesitate to take it if I wanted it."

"I don't either."

"Maybe not at work, but in the important parts of life, is that true? When it's a matter of your heart or your future?" He looked at the empty bowls in front of them and suddenly had a need to get out of the restaurant. He needed the crispness of the outside air to lower his temperature and temperament before he did or said anything more stupid. He stood from the table, throwing down money for the bill. "Let's blow this place."

A soft, steady drizzle misted them gently as they walked back into the street. "Wow, I didn't expect that." Kathryn held up her hand to catch the dampness.

"Didn't expect the rain? Or the debate?" He let the stress flow out of him as she smiled back.

"Both." She looked over his shoulder, fixating on a point past him. "Tommy?"

"Yeah?"

"I want—to go kayaking." She lifted a slender finger and pointed. He followed the direction to a building on the pier. Over the door was a large wooden sign, painted in red with "Arctic Kayak Rentals." He laughed, glad to relieve the tension he'd caused.

"Come on, now," she urged. "You can't turn a girl down when she tells you what she wants, can you? Not after a speech like that." Her lips curled tauntingly.

"No. I guess I can't." Thomas drew her hand into his and pulled her toward the building. "I'm up for it if you are."

The rain cleared by the time they'd donned wet suits and rode the bus to their launch site, just a few miles up the bank. They were given brief instruction and told to work back toward the boat pier. They had four hours.

It was the best four hours he'd spent in months. They spoke sporadically, basking in the sun and water between conversations. He made sure not to bring up anything else that was controversial. The water was clear and they could see the fish moving below. An otter rolled in the water, circling like the rock tumbler he had as a kid. It periodically dove and then came up again, and lay on his back as if on a Barca lounger. The only thing missing was a beer in his paw. Above them, they could still see the snow-laden tops of the mountains around them, even the glacial ice on one of the peaks. It was damned gorgeous. Breathtaking.

"Smile!" Kathryn shouted from behind him. He turned to hear the click of the camera shutter as she snapped a picture.

"Let me get one of you." He paddled up next to her and reached for the camera. Her fingers, blue with the chill, slid against his hands and it startled him. "Kathryn! You're freezing."

"I'm fine. Just a little chilly." She rubbed her hands together hard.

"Give me your hands." He slipped the camera in his pocket and thrust his hand out to grab hers before she could maneuver away. The color returned slowly as he vigorously rubbed her small hands between his.

"We should have brought gloves," she said.

"Yeah." He lifted her hands and blew into them in an attempt to speed the warming process. She watched him, her eyes clouded with curiosity. Finally, she pulled back.

"I'm good. Thanks, Tommy." She turned her kayak and paddled toward the pier. She didn't see him pull the camera out and click away. He zoomed in, catching her silhouette. Then zoomed back out to get the full mountain view behind her. Then one more with the pier lurking ahead. It was frickin' beautiful. *She* was frickin' beautiful.

They drove back in silence. She leaned her head against the glass and closed her eyes as they went through the tunnel and kept them closed for a good while after. He wasn't sure if she was sleeping or just resting. She lifted her head for a moment and looked at him. "Tommy?" her sleepy voice queried.

"Yeah, Katy?"

"Thank you."

"For what?"

"For today. This was a great day." She smiled and laid her head back against the car door.

"Yes, it was. Thanks for sharing it with me." He squinted his eyes into the sun and drove the remainder of the way back, peacefully enjoying the company without any tension.

Chapter Six

"I need to make a phone call," Thomas said gruffly when the Jeep pulled up to the lodge and he cut the engine. "I'll see you at dinner." And he bolted out of the car, in a hurry to get into his cabin and apparently away from her.

Kathryn rubbed her eyes repeatedly until she could focus enough to get out of the seat, then opened the door and slipped off to the waiting cabin and threw herself onto the bed. She'd just spent the day with Tommy. Not little Tommy. Thomas. Big Thomas. Big, Burly, Sexy, Sweet Thomas. It had been beyond splendid. She'd enjoyed every second. And he couldn't wait to get rid of her when they arrived back at the lodge. She tapped her palm to forehead for thinking it mattered. *Get a grip, girl. You know who he is. He's a flirt. A chaser. The kind that carries a twenty-four pack of condoms everywhere he goes.* Like some guys carry a checkbook or their wallet.

Thomas didn't make it to dinner. Kathryn arrived late with creases in her cheek from her pillow. She was amazed at how much she wanted to sleep. As if she hadn't slept in months. It was good though, to finally feel rested. She surveyed the group, hoping to catch a glimpse of Thomas and thank him again. Perhaps he just didn't want to see her. He'd had all he could fill of Sam's little sis. Maybe he'd just humored her because Sam would have wanted him to. That pissed her off. Would he really do that? He said he was used to getting what he wanted, asking for it. The thought that the entire day could have been an act of appeasement rankled under her skin. She visited with Kevin and his friend, Chris during dinner, and when it was over, they invited her to go to the local bar with them. They'd found a pub in Kenai that many people recommended as nice and friendly.

The thought of hanging out in her room for a couple of hours sounded boring compared to a couple of hours on the town. She saw no harm in joining them for a beer or two. She surveyed them for the "ick factor" and decided they were safe. "Sure, when are you leaving?"

"We'll meet you outside at nine. Okay?" Kevin asked.

"Great. See you then." She went back to her room, showered, and put on the only clothes she had that were likely appropriate. She dabbed on some makeup and rebraided her hair, then twisted it into a knot at the nape of her neck.

Hooksetter's was deceptive from the outside. It was obviously a bar based on the blinking red Coors sign in the window and the fluorescent lights that could be seen through the glass. Other than that, the white painted exterior looked more like a repair shop than a place of entertainment. The building sat alone in a gravel parking lot, flanked by pine trees and bushes. Two light posts with single bulbs hanging from them graced both sides of the lot making the place a little eerie. If it were dark when they arrived, she'd probably have opted for a rain check. As it was, the sun was still shining and likely would continue to be for at least two or three hours. The lot was sparsely filled with vehicles, most of which were of the four-wheel drive variety. They crunched across the gravel to the door, listening to the blare of music from inside. Country music.

Kevin pulled the door back for her and, with mild apprehension, she led the group inside. Hardly anyone in the place saw them come in. The other patrons were all talking and drinking. Obviously enjoying themselves.

The three worked their way to the bar and eased into barstools, Kevin and Chris flanking Kathryn on each side.

"Cool place, huh?" Kevin leaned over the bar and gestured for the bartender to take their order.

"Yeah. This must be where all the locals hang out. I've hardly seen a soul on the road all day and now there's more here than I expected," she laughed. It wasn't exactly a mob crowd.

The lady behind the bar eased down and gave them a huge smile. "What'll it be, folks?" They all ordered a beer, something local that they'd never heard of, and she brought them within minutes.

"You guys here on vacation?" she asked as they took their first sip.

Chris lowered his glass. "Not exactly. Our company is doing a team-building thing at a lodge not far from here. We're fishing in between the exercises, though."

"Oh, that's weird."

"Yeah, I guess."

"The salmon are running good right now, so make sure you don't miss out. It'll be over in another week or so," she snorted as she moved away. Obviously, their appearance was of little interest.

"Wanna play pool, Kathryn?" Kevin asked.

"Sure." She hopped out of her seat and followed him to the pool tables, beer in hand. As she worked her way through the three tables of men she thought a hand brushed across her behind and she whirled around. The men at the table were talking to each other, ignoring her. She glared at them with no reaction and moved on. That was her first indication she probably shouldn't have come.

She won the first match easily. So, Kevin upped the stakes. "Let's make this worthwhile. Whoever misses drinks a shot. You game?" She didn't like the way this was headed. Suddenly, her prior assessment of safe was near retraction. Drinking in college had taught her a lesson about boys and shots. Kathryn had learned it the hard way. Two close calls made her wary of getting in that situation again. So, she shrugged and pulled her self-rescue game. "Sure, but I get to pick the liquor."

"No problem," he answered. She smiled innocently. Kevin thought he'd just had a big victory. *Idiot.*

"Great! Vodka, straight up, please. And I'd like a big glass of water as a chaser." She racked the balls and lined them up for the break while he went for the drinks. The cue stick rested on the floor, with both of her hands holding it in a relaxed grip. She analyzed her situation, trying to decide the best way to get out when it was time to do so. The lady at the bar handed Kevin the drinks and then gave Kathryn a concerned look.

The game began. Kevin broke and sank two before missing. He downed his shot and deferred to Kathryn. She hit one and missed the second intentionally. She downed her vodka. While Kevin rounded the table, she gulped half the glass of water, then set it on the shelf below the pool table. She'd reach for it periodically as needed. When the next round of shots came, she set her empty shot glass next to the water and poured water into it, bending low to hide her efforts.

Kevin made another shot, then missed the next and drank his vodka. Kathryn carried her shot glass of water with her as she looked for the best ball to hit. She missed and drank the water. Moving back to the end of the table, she refilled the shot glass again with water. Kevin doubled up the drinks, bringing two at a time. The woman behind the bar gave Kathryn a sympathetic look and said something to the bartender standing next to her as he carried the glasses away. They didn't see the water glass stashed under the table.

When Kevin circled the table for his next roll, a light pressure rested against Kathryn's forearm and she glanced around to see the woman next to her. "You okay, sweetie?" she whispered.

"Yeah, for now. Thanks for checking. Listen, if you see me wink at you, can you call me a cab?"

"Sure, honey. No problem." She cast a cursory glance toward Kevin and shuffled back to her place behind the bar. Good. Escape plan in place.

The game went on and Kevin, disappointed that she was still standing, challenged her to another. Half-way through the second game he began to stagger around the table and slur heavily. Kathryn was almost ready to signal for that cab. She searched for the woman's face over the bar. Suddenly a hand clamped down on her wrist and yanked her backward. She looked around, startled to see Thomas dragging her out. The cue stick clattered to the floor, with Kevin yelling after them. "Hey! Aren't you going to finish?"

"She *is* finished," Thomas spat as he maneuvered through the tables, his grip locked around her wrist with no chance of release.

"Thomas, it's okay!" Kathryn yelled out.

"No, it's not!" His shoulders shoved through the small clutch of people like they were dominoes.

"I have this under control."

"You do? Really? How many shots have you had?" When they were in the parking lot, breathing fresh air again, he whirled around to face her. "Do you know what he was doing?"

"Yeah, I know exactly what he was doing. And if you hadn't shown up, I'd be stepping into a cab right about now."

"Yeah, shit-faced with that sleaze bag."

"No, stone-cold sober. And alone." She laughed at him. "Did Sam put you up to this? Are you following me around to keep me out of trouble?"

"No. Sam didn't say a word."

"But you've talked to him, haven't you?"

"Sure, a couple of hours ago. That's why I didn't make it to dinner."

"He didn't tell you to follow me?" She clenched her teeth at her brother's interference.

"Hell, no. He didn't even know you were here until I said something. Why would he do that?"

"Thomas Ryan, are you telling the truth?" She bunched her eyebrows in that motherly, don't-make-me-wash-your-mouth-out look, waiting for an answer.

"Yes. I'm telling the truth. And don't give me that stupid look. James told me where you were and I thought I'd join in. When I got here, I knew what these guys were up to."

"How could you possibly know that?" She crossed her arms in front of her.

"I just did."

"I'll bet you did. Listen, I can take care of myself, Tommy." Her chin rose defiantly as she jammed her hands into fists at her sides. "I don't need you trying to be my babysitter. Am I clear?"

"Crystal." He looked over her head, watching a lone car pass on the highway, then added, "Now get in the car." He opened the Jeep door and shoved her in.

"And for your information, I drank twelve shots."

"Shit!" Thomas stomped around the car and opened the driver side door.

"Of water, Tommy. Of water. And one shot of vodka." She turned to him as he slid into the driver's seat, and grinned. "Do you really think I'm that stupid?" He dropped his hand from the key in the ignition and looked at her, stunned. He leaned closer and surveyed her eyes, then briefly glanced down. Appreciation flashed across his face, but he didn't smile back.

"Stay away from that guy, Katy," he growled before he started the engine.

"Why? Because he's dangerous?"

"Yeah, that's exactly why."

"And you're not? You're harmless, right? Perfectly safe because you're Sam's best friend and you aren't the least bit attracted to his gangly little sister. But you don't want anyone else to be interested either, do you? Apparently you don't think I'm smart enough to know what to do when the wrong someone does and don't think I know better than to be the girl everyone talks about at work? Geez, you are so ridiculously archaic." She could have dropped a penny on the stiffness in his shoulders at that moment. "Give it a rest, Thomas. You stay out of my business and I'll stay out of yours."

Minutes later, her feet couldn't fly fast enough to her cabin when she got out of the Jeep. She slammed the door. The heat from the room blasted her in the face and she yanked her sweater over her head to cool down. The cami underneath wrenched up around her waist. She tugged it back down. She marched into the bathroom and began brushing her teeth till they hurt. The pounding on the door brought her to a halt before her gums started bleeding.

"Who is it?" She half-expected Kevin to answer.

"It's me." Thomas.

She opened the door, toothbrush in hand. A flicker of a smile tugged at his mouth as he used a finger to wipe toothpaste from the corner of her mouth. He looked at it briefly, shrugged, then licked it off his finger and passed his tongue over his teeth.

Kathryn grimaced. "Do you always eat used toothpaste?" He stood there, staring at her. The cold air blew over her shoulders.

"No, but it seemed like a good time to." He grinned. "Are you gonna let me in or do I have to stand out here and watch you shiver in that little undershirt?"

"What do you want, Tommy?" She didn't even try to mask the impatience when she dropped her hand to her hips. "To make sure Kevin didn't follow me home? Or maybe James? Here." She stood back and gestured toward her queen-size bed. "You want to make sure the bed's empty?"

He came in and kicked the door shut behind him. "Kathryn, I'm not harmless," he blurted.

"What?" She didn't understand. He edged toward her, backing her against the wall by the door.

"I'm not safe either." He put his head down and looked at her, his mouth inches from hers. "And as far as Sam's gangly little sister, I don't know who the hell you're talking about, but there's nothing gangly about the woman in front of me right now." He hesitated as his eyes took in her black cami. "What do you want, Kathryn?"

His body was inches away. She could feel her back arching toward him, his mouth pulling her in. It wasn't fair to pose a question like that when he was this close.

"I don't know." She gasped. "You're confusing me."

"Yeah, you do. You know."

She splayed her fingers across his chest and his jaw clenched. He started to back away. Then she pulled on his shirt, trailed her fingers up his neck, and cupped his cheek. She gently raised her fingers farther and swiped his hair away from his eyes.

"Okay, I guess I do," she whispered as he moved his mouth closer. She wasn't sure if he got there first or she did. They met somewhere in the middle. She had dropped her hand to his chest and pulled him into her. His lips settled softly on hers at first. When she pressed against him and ran her hands up into his hair, he sucked in sharply as if she'd slapped him. He lifted his head. "I know," she said. "Bad idea, right?"

He shook his head and grinned. "Not from where I'm standing. I just wasn't expecting that."

He braced his arm on the wall and leaned into her. This time, his mouth wasn't soft at all. The pressure increased and he forced her mouth open. He moved to wedge his leg between hers, pressing her into the wall. She sighed as his tongue brushed inside her mouth and rubbed greedily against hers.

"Wow, Katy," he muttered against her lips, drawing his hands down to wrap them tightly around her waist. She pushed back into him, sending him off balance. His lips didn't leave hers as his butt landed with a thump on the table by the door. She wanted to crawl up onto him. Slither inside his sweater, against his chest. Instead, she backed off, embarrassed that she'd knocked him down. That she'd jammed into him like a linebacker.

"Where are you going?" he asked huskily. He snaked an arm

out to pull her back to him. He looked into her face and stroked the hair away from her forehead before he kissed it briefly then returned to her lips. This time, more insistent, more demanding. His hands moved across her shoulders and trailed up her neck to frame her face.

She was kissing Thomas. Tommy Ryan. And God, could he kiss! He wasn't kissing her senseless. Her senses were totally functional and completely involved. She was completely aware of his mouth on hers. She felt his tongue thrusting against hers, demanding a response. Her pulse pounded and she heard ringing in her ears. She pressed deeper into him and felt the burning sensation return to her stomach. Smelled his deeply masculine cologne. His palm spread against her back and clutched the cloth of the cami. She heard voices outside and ignored them. Her cell rang and went to voicemail. She was in complete control, and damn he was a good kisser. Scratch that. Great kisser. It wasn't until she looked down and saw she had her hand under his sweater, resting against the bare skin of his chest that she realized her control was wavering. When she became keenly aware of Thomas' hand, which previously clutched the material of her cami, had somehow ended up on her breast inside the cami, she caught her breath.

"Tommy. Wait," she spat between breaths.

"Huh?" There was a dazed look in his eyes as she saw him struggle to slow himself down. He moved his hand to her waist. "Oh, God. Katy. I'm sorry." He closed his eyes and looked up at the ceiling. He continued to hold her against him, his hands anchored on her hips.

"We can't do this," she whispered against his lips.

"Yeah, I know. I know." He tugged her in and pressed his lips against her neck, nipping gently against her collarbone. "We can do this though, right?" He looked up at her, teasing. He trailed his mouth over her ear and tugged on the lobe with his teeth. "And this?" With measured patience, he slid back to face her, searching her eyes. "And this? What about this?" He pressed lips to hers and plunged his tongue into her mouth, entwining it with hers, and she groaned. His answering groan made her catch her breath again.

Yeah, we can do that, Tommy. We can do that all day. Wait. No. Where had the control gone? Where was the steely reserve she'd planned to have?

Who was she kidding? She wanted Tommy Ryan. She wanted him bad. And right now, at this moment, he wanted her. She knew it was weak but she didn't care. She knew he wasn't the kind to hang around. She would deal with that later. She wrapped her arms around him and clung on for dear life. *We can do this,* she thought. Wait. Did she say that out loud? Yikes. She did.

She struggled to regain consciousness when he shook his head and pulled her arms from his hair. He held her arms down and caressed his thumbs along them, smiling into her eyes. He remained there for the longest time, as if trying to decide what to do. Then he lifted off the table, pulled his sweater back down over his jeans and reached for the door.

Chapter Seven

When Thomas was safely outside, he turned around and faced Kathryn. His hands trembled as he plunged them into his pockets to keep from reaching for her.

"Katy." He hesitated. The limbs of the trees moved in the wind behind the cabins creating a loud rustling that filled the silence. "I want this. I *really* want this. But, well, let's not start something we'll regret later." He kissed her on the forehead and started backing up. Or at least he was trying to back up but his feet wouldn't move. "Oh, and if you don't want people to think there's something between us, you might want to stop calling me Tommy. And don't answer the door the next time I knock."

He flashed a smile to break the tension and somehow regained control of his legs. He turned quickly. If he didn't leave immediately, all bets were off. Her face was luminous with her lips all red and swollen from his whiskers. He jumped when the door slammed behind him. Wonder how many people heard that. He looked around at the other cabins. The curtain on his own moved and he realized that at the bare minimum, James had. Screw him. He headed to the lodge, and decided to make use of the couch she'd mentioned the day before.

He grabbed his cell out of his pocket and tapped on speed dial for Sam's name. When Sam's voice spoke hoarsely into his ear, he began, "Hey man, it's Thomas again. How's Texas?"

Sam cleared his throat. "Do you have any idea what time it is right now?"

"Oh, yeah. Sorry about that." Thomas shrugged, "Listen Sam, you remember that deal we made when we were seniors?"

"Huh? What deal?"

"You know, right before the summer ended of our junior year. Before football started. I promised I'd leave Kathryn alone."

"Yeah, as long as I didn't tell your parents about the DUI." There was silence on the phone. "What about it?"

"The deal's off." He hung up the phone and made his way inside. He was a damned attorney now. Sure he still had a way to go, but who cared what happened when he was eighteen? They probably already knew anyway. It was public record. He'd done his community service, never had any trouble since, and never so much as looked back. Except about her.

*

Five a.m. came way too early. The guys turned on the blaring lights over his head as everyone made their way to the dining room for breakfast. His pants and shirt lay in a crumpled pile on the floor. His leg tingled in a painful cramp from the awkward way he had slept. An afghan retrieved from one of the chairs was draped over his waist, barely covering his torso. He'd kicked it off when it got too warm during the night. The damn thing was thick as carpet. He rubbed his eyes and stretched. "Good morning, guys." He waved sheepishly. He flung the small amount of covering back, picked up his clothes, and pattered barefoot toward the door in his boxers. He lowered his shoulders in relief when he saw that Kathryn hadn't made it to breakfast yet.

"Rough night, or new dress code, Thomas?" Her voice came from behind him.

He stiffened and glanced back again. She was sitting behind the pine column between the sofa and the table, completely blocked from his earlier view. A cheerful smirk crossed her lips and she turned back around.

"Both," he muttered as he shoved out the door, anxious to get feeling back in his legs, and for a shower.

Kevin's smartass voice called after him, "You might want to shave, man." A volcanic eruption of laughter followed. Thomas had no idea what he was talking about. He felt his chin and yes, it was stubbled, but he could carry that for a couple of days before it was noticeable. Five minutes in the shower and back to the dining room was all he needed.

Thomas' jaw dropped as he looked in the mirror, post-shower. His upper lip was completely covered by black lines, a drawn-in moustache, complete with handlebars on each side. Obviously, the artwork of one slightly pissed off Kevin.

"Shit!" he roared and grabbed for the soap again. He soaped and scrubbed his face trying to get it off. No success. He vaguely remembered seeing a Sharpie marker on the coffee table.

"You ass," he muttered at Kevin as he re-entered the dining hall later. His face was raw where he'd unsuccessfully tried to wash it off.

"Suits you, Thomas," Kevin responded. "All you need now is the white horse to go with it and you'd look just the part."

At that moment, Thomas noticed the pallor in Kevin's face and the sweat beaded on his forehead. It pleased him. The guy was miserable, his plan had backfired and left him with one full-fledged killer hangover. Probably been up all night praying to the porcelain god. Kathryn had really done a number on him with the shots. *Good for her.*

"What do you think, Kathryn?" he asked. "Does my moustache flatter me as much as the vodka vomit stains flatter Kevin here?" He quirked his lip a few times to get the handlebar moving and she burst out laughing, followed quickly by the rest of the group. Kevin frowned, then succumbed to the bile overflow that was working its way up to his throat. He ran out of the room, holding his mouth.

"You wear it proudly, Ryan," Zak offered.

"Thanks, man." Thomas sat at the table and ate as much as he could gulp down before Sean came in and hustled them off to a small bus out front.

"Wait!" Kathryn yelled after she'd already taken a seat on the bus. "I forgot something." She darted off to her cabin and returned seconds later. As she vaulted into the bus, she looked at Thomas and giggled. Despite his embarrassment, he warmed at the lyrical skips it caused in his chest. When she dropped into the seat next to him and said, "Look at me, Cowboy," he felt stupid turning his black-stained face to her. "You remind me of a young Sam Elliott with blond hair right now."

He wiggled his eyebrows and grinned. "I'll take that as a compliment." That squeezed a full laugh out of her. He held his hand to his chest to stop the next round of skips. *What the hell?*

Kathryn pulled out a silver nail polish remover pouch and ripped it open. She took the pad out and started rubbing his lip with it. Her free hand held his jaw steady as she slathered away with the other. The smell made his eyes water and his lip was so raw from the earlier scrubbing that the remover stung on contact. He silently thanked Kevin for the opportunity to be touched by Kathryn in front of everyone. Her hands warmed his face as she worked away. The prick thought it was payback. Thomas thought it turned out pretty good. Better than if he'd planned it.

"There you go." Kathryn sat back and admired her work. "Much better. Except for the redness."

"Thanks, Katy-Kathryn." Her lips looked a little raw this morning too. Prideful amusement surged through him as he realized he'd put the rawness there. He turned back around toward the front of the bus and looked out the window. The undeniable desire to kiss her lay like a gauntlet between them.

She lifted herself from the seat to move back where she'd started, but he placed an arm on her and pushed her back down. "You can sit here." He paused. "If you want to, of course." She glanced nervously around the bus at the others, then shrugged and settled into the seat.

Chapter Eight

The seas in the Cook Inlet had one of the most impressive tide changes on record. The waters moved up to twenty-seven feet between low and high tides. So much, that warning signs were plastered all along the embankment discouraging tourists from entering them. Every year, people ignored the warnings and ventured in, only to lose their lives or end up in the hospital.

The sunlight cast an iridescent polish across the top of the water. It was calm today, with barely any wind. Those conditions created a perfect morning to pull in some halibut. The bus drive was long and quiet. Since the road hugged the shoreline most of the way, they were able to see the water for a couple of hours before they arrived at the launch site.

"Too bad your drinking buddy didn't make the trip," Thomas teased. "We would have been able to sneak in a lot more pit stops on the way."

"I have a feeling we would lose our patience with that after about two stops," Kathryn answered.

"My patience was gone last night, just in case you didn't notice. It's really a good thing he didn't come today. You would have seen my worst."

Kathryn raised an eyebrow and made a tsking sound. He wondered what that expression meant.

Even though the morning was intended to be recreational, they had received an assignment before entering the bus. Sean passed each of them a stapled bundle of papers, which was a compilation of questionnaires from all the attendees. They were to know it before the afternoon return to the lodge. The group spent the three-hour bus ride studying the pages so they could enjoy the remainder of their excursion. For Thomas, he was done in forty-five minutes, but kept the pages held loosely in his hand. He had acquired a photographic memory over the years, something that had really helped out in law school. Being able to permanently store away case names, dates, and decisions was a monumental plus for passing the Bar exam.

"Want some help?" he asked Kathryn when she frowned at the papers. "I'm pretty good at this type of thing."

"Yeah, so I've heard."

"What does that mean?"

"Sam told me you could remember the most minuscule details. That if he ever needed help on tests, you were the guy."

He paused. "It helps when you practice law. And for other things too. If we play any memory games on this trip, I'm your guy. You won't want to be pitted against me."

"I would imagine not." She glanced out the window and then blurted, "Look!" Her hand slipped in front of his cheek and pointed out the window.

He snapped around to follow her gesture and saw a young bull moose trotting away from them toward the trees. "Hey! Good eye!" He caught the briefest whiff of her scent from the hand in front of him and his mind conjured up images from the night before—his mouth against her neck, her hand inside his shirt. He let out a small groan.

"You okay?" She peered at him with concern.

"Oh, yeah. Just remembered something." He looked down at the papers in his hand. "So, tell me what Chris' last name is and his hobbies."

He'd deftly changed the subject. He quizzed her until their bus slowed and pulled off the highway.

At the boat launch, they were greeted by a leathery-skinned man with short gray hair. He introduced himself as Charlie, and then a first mate named Danny who looked to be around fourteen. Charlie was their boat captain and host for the day. Charlie made idle conversation as they cruised for almost an hour to get to a good spot. No instruction was necessary. They threw in their lines, let them sink to the bottom and waited. Pulling in a halibut was like lifting a car hood off the ocean floor. They were big, heavy, and didn't fight much.

They were on their way back to the shore four hours later with a full catch. Kathryn stood on the back of the boat as they headed for the shore. The temperature had improved with the heavy dose of sunshine that blessed them. She stood in her running pants and long-sleeved Under Armour shirt, watching the water glisten behind them.

Chapter Nine

"Pretty, isn't it?" Thomas said as he leaned against the rail next to her and gazed out over the water. "If it were like this all year, people would flock here like it was Florida."

"It's nice," she agreed. Her shoulders tensed as she clutched the rail. Being in close proximity after last night was torture. He'd practically sucked the life out of her with those kisses, then just walked casually out.

He looked around at the others, all grouped in the boat's cabin drinking coffee. She felt his arm as he shifted around and leaned back against the rail, his arm still touching her fingers just slightly. He whispered but she could barely hear him over the wind as it fought to erase his words, "Katy, we should probably talk about last night."

She wasn't sure if she'd heard it right, it was so soft. "I'm sorry?"

"I said, we should talk." He looked at her for a second and the wind grabbed his hair and tossed it into his eyes.

She quelled the urge to push it back as she glanced at him with forced nonchalance. "Why? I don't see any need. We're adults. Those things happen. No big deal. I haven't slept with you." She shrugged.

"No, you haven't done that." He paused. "So, you're okay with it?" He quirked his brows for a brief moment. She tightened her lips and met his gaze.

"Sure. It's not like we're still kids. There's no reason for drama. Besides it was just a kiss."

"More like a mother lode of kisses."

Kathryn closed her eyes and felt the sun sinking into her skin.

The warmth was relaxing. She didn't answer. *A mother lode of kisses. Yeah. Hot. Heavy. Full mouth. Tongue. The whole bit. She shivered at the thought and licked her lips. Don't look at him. Or his mouth. Or those hands.*

"Kathryn." She jolted her thoughts back to reality as he continued, "Just curious. Did you kiss James like that?"

She narrowed her eyes to slits. "Did you really ask me that?"

At that moment, James joined them. "Hey guys."

"Hey. We were just talking about you," Kathryn said with a smile, noticing Thomas' instant frown.

"Good things, I hope."

"Of course. So, did you enjoy it?" She waved her hand at the box of fish.

"Yeah, pretty cool stuff. I'm not much of an outdoors buff, but this was nice. What'd you think?" He leaned back and sat on the metal box filled with fish.

"It was awesome!" Kathryn exclaimed. "I could stay out here all day. There's something about the sea air that just...drives me crazy. It's invigorating. Rocking back and forth in the boat. Basking in the sun. Getting all sweaty pulling in these big old boys. Kind of stimulating, don't you think?" She tapped the top of the fish hold. Both men looked at her, stunned. She thought she would have to pick their jaws off the deck. "What? Don't look at me like that."

"I'm out of here," Thomas blurted as he tromped into the cabin with the others.

"You okay?" James asked, watching him go.

"Sure. Why do you ask?"

"I don't know. Just thought..." He nodded after Thomas, hesitating briefly. "I'd be careful with him if I were you."

"That's funny, coming from you. Don't you think?" She smiled.

"Well, from what I understand, Tito can be pretty cold."

"Tito. What a stupid nickname."

"He didn't get it for no reason. Nothing to do with the liquor by that name either. Something about a girl with big tits and a comment he made when they hooked up. Or, at least that's what I heard. I don't know."

"Really?"

"Just be careful, Kathryn. He's not the kind to hang around."

"Who says I want him to? He's my brother's friend. I've known him since high school. You don't need to worry about me. Besides I'm like a kid sister to him."

"Yeah, right. That doesn't mean he's a good guy."

"And it doesn't mean he isn't either."

They changed the subject to work and talked for a while about one of their customers with whom James had trouble. After a few minutes, he went back in the cabin. Shortly after, they made it to land. People climbed from the boat and observed their catch as it was unloaded. Charlie and Danny hung all the fish up on hooks for the packing folks to gather and process.

Everyone left thoroughly exhausted and satisfied. Kathryn sat in the back of the bus on the return trip, cautiously avoiding any conversation. Thankfully, Thomas received a phone call as they boarded the bus and spent the first twenty minutes talking on the phone with someone. He lost signal after that and she saw him frown and try repeatedly to call back.

Chapter Ten

"Folks, we've already had one casualty," Sean spouted upon their return. "Kevin's gone to the airport and will be headed home in a couple of hours. Something about a crisis at the office."

"Sorry to hear that. I liked that guy." Thomas' faked sympathy brought a roaring laugh from the entire group. The sarcasm just popped out without his consent but he enjoyed the reaction.

Sean suppressed a smile and spoke, "Let's meet out by the fire pit for today's exercise. Everyone report there in thirty minutes."

The freshness of the cool gusts that blew around them energized Kathryn. The fire flickered angrily among the large boulders of gray stone that surrounded it. She inhaled the pine and smoke as she thought of past camping trips with her family.

"Kathryn, come on." Chris patted the smooth polished wood of the bench next to him. She hesitated, glancing around the group to evaluate the dynamics. She felt a small pang of regret for automatically judging Chris by the company he kept, but still wasn't sure whether she should trust him or not. She'd only seen him with Kevin. After their night at the bar, she balked at taking the seat. The bench next to Thomas was free, but he was deep in conversation with Sean and seemed to ignore her arrival. She smiled and plopped down next to Chris, slipping her hands between her thighs. He spoke first. "I'm sorry about Kevin. I wasn't paying attention."

"No worries. I can take care of myself. It turned out fine—at least for me. Tell me about you, Chris. How'd you get to know him?"

"I don't really. He and I talk a lot on the phone because we have to. We move inventory a lot to fill orders. He's a good salesman."

"I know nothing about him. I haven't talked to him much since I'm in I.T."

"We don't talk personal things, just business. The other night, I spent most of my time at the bar, drowning myself and watching the game on television. Sorry about that—I should have paid attention to what he was doing. My wife called and I was preoccupied with what was going on at home."

"So, you're married. That's great." She paused. "How long?"

"Almost five years." He opened his wallet and flipped the plastic-enclosed photographs in it until he found what he wanted. He pushed it toward her. "Here's a picture of her with our son, Adam."

Kathryn surveyed the picture of the pretty blonde woman and tow-headed boy and grinned as she returned it. "You must be proud of them." It was inspiring to see a new dad excited about family life and fatherhood. She listened briefly as he told her details about his wife and son and, after hearing it out, decided that Chris was a decent guy after all. She had lumped him into the same category as Kevin simply by association.

"Family is everything," he said. "If I hadn't met Sharon, I'd be a mess right now. Adam has only made things better. It's funny how it works out. When you're by yourself, you do all sorts of stupid things to have fun and enjoy life. It took me finding Sharon to realize you can enjoy the life you have without doing the stupid things. Some people figure out themselves. I didn't."

Chris was a bit melodramatic.

"Okay. Let's get started," Sean cheerfully began. "I've gathered details about each person here from three different sources: themselves, their bosses, and their family or friends. You guys have studied what each person wrote about themselves. What you don't have is the rest. This exercise is a chance to see how much you've learned about the people in our organization so far. The purpose is to show how important it is to get to know your staff and coworkers. They can make or break your success. Everyone's names are at the top of the list. Below you'll see lists of five characteristics. Match a name to each list. You'll be awarded points based on how many you answer correctly. Fill them out, pass them back and then we're all going to dinner."

After dinner, Sean went over the results, then did a fairly lengthy monologue about the dynamics of managing people. They were done by nine p.m. "Who wants to go out tonight?" he asked. "I'm taking anyone who wants to go to the town's best, and only, watering hole. Meet back here in fifteen minutes if you plan on going."

He surveyed the group and walked back into the lodge. Thirty minutes later, they all piled from Sean's van into the same place Thomas had yanked Kathryn out of the night before.

Kathryn stood outside looking at the peeling white paint on the building. Thomas strode by, brushing her shoulder as he passed, much as he had done when they were teenagers in high school. "Back to the scene of the crime, huh? Try not to put any other poor guy in the hospital with alcohol poisoning tonight."

She watched him stride to the door and wondered what would happen if he did happen to drag her back again. The last time ended in some pretty hot and heavy kisses. He hadn't let it go farther then, would he stop again? Was it all a mistake? She sighed and stepped in behind the others as they passed through the door.

Apparently, Wednesday was open-mike night at the rat-hole bar of Kenai that was better known as Hooksetter's. Four musicians clambered around on the stage setting up their equipment while Kathryn's group searched for seating. The place was packed. Standing room only. She followed everyone to the back where a table stood with not a single stool or chair around it.

As the band banged out their first song—a pop-rock tune of their own making—Thomas made a drink run for everyone.

He pushed through the crowd, elbowing between two women at the bar that couldn't seem to take their eyes off his butt. As the bartender that had potentially been Kathryn's savior from the prior night recognized him, she panned the crowd for Kathryn. When their eyes met, the woman gave Kathryn a cheerful hand waggle. She pointed to Thomas and joined her fingers in the world-renowned gesture for "Okay" and flashed a wink and a smile.

Kathryn gave her a wave back in polite agreement as Thomas glanced over his shoulder and caught her thumbs up. She dropped her hand quickly.

One of the women next to him placed a hand on his arm and said something into his ear. He grinned and said something back then turned and carried four glasses to their table. "First Round. I'm going back for the rest," he yelled over the music.

"I'll get them. Stay here," James shouted as he patted Thomas on the back and headed for the gap between the two women whose eyes had been glued to Thomas' jeans pockets. James struck up a conversation and it was another ten minutes before the remaining beers made it back to the table. "The girl in the black shirt wants you, Ryan." James gestured with his shoulder as he lowered the beer glasses to the table, sloshing generously. "The other one said she'd be happy to play third wheel or even double up." His comment seemed to question if Thomas wanted in or not.

Thomas shrugged, lifted his glass to his lips and drank heavily, then answered, "Not my type."

Hmmm. That wasn't the Tommy Ryan that Sam had talked about all these years.

"Well, they're certainly mine." James swaggered back to the bar with his beer glass.

"What exactly *is* your type?" Chris asked.

He glanced around the room as if he were looking for someone. Maybe someone to use as an example. "Not them," was all he said.

The first band played three more songs then released the floor to another band. The second band played similar music but had a female lead singer who practically licked the microphone as she sang. The guys all watched in awe.

Their enrapture gave Kathryn an opportunity to survey the crowd. An interesting array of locals and vacationers, mostly dressed quite relaxed—as if they'd just hopped out of a salmon boat. A lone man sat in the shadows at the corner of the bar. His back was braced against the wall and a light swath of beer foam nested in his beard. He looked up and caught her glance. She vaguely remembered him watching in amusement as Thomas had yanked her out of the bar last night. He looked young but his face was covered in hair so it was hard to tell age. The lead singer brought a round of cheers when she ran her hand down her breast to her crotch as she finished her first song. This was going to be a long night. Seven men drinking beer, a singer that will sing them all into oblivion in their minds, a ride home on a bus with seven drunk, horny men. *Whoopee.*

Thomas pushed his chest into the small gap next to her. Without turning, there wasn't any mistake who stood there. His scent gave him away. It was pretty hard to miss since she'd thought about it for the last twenty-four hours. "It's burning up in here— want to go outside for a bit?" he shouted into her ear.

"You don't want to drool with the rest of the fan club?" She pointed to their group standing on the other side of the table, eyes riveted on the stage. The singer turned her back to the crowd in her tiny skirt and ran her hand down her butt-cheek then trailed it back up again, ending with a slap. Her words were indistinguishable as her lips mashed into the microphone, leaving red lipstick stains. No one seemed to care.

"They've got it covered. Besides, there's nothing up there I haven't seen before." He spread his palm across her back and rotated her toward the door. She had little choice but to comply. The strong, masculine hand on her shoulder, hard chest muscles against her back, pressed her forward without any possibility of resistance.

Kathryn inhaled the fresh air as they crunched on the gravel of the parking lot. She had thought he was going to the bus, but he passed by and sat on the low iron fence rail surrounding the lot.

"Band's pretty good." She tossed her head in a gesture toward the bar.

"Yeah, if you like the show and not the voice. She can't sing worth a shit."

"No one seemed to notice or care. Since when did you not like to watch the show?"

He smirked. "I still like to watch but it kind of depends on who's in it. Speaking from a guy's perspective, truth is, make us think you'll have sex with us and we'll follow you anywhere—even if you can't sing." His lips twitched into a smile for a moment then sobered up. "Kathryn, can you sing?"

"No. And I wasn't asking you to have sex with me, either."

"You weren't?" His eyebrow arched but he didn't look at her. His face was fixated on the shadows of the trees behind the bar.

She glanced in the direction of the shadows. "No. I wasn't," she confirmed with little confidence.

"Guess I read that wrong then, because I thought those hot and heavy kisses were...something else." He stroked his hair back with his fingers and dropped his hand on her arm. "That's strange. I don't usually get it messed up."

Kathryn's throat went instantly dry as his hand stroked up her arm, his thumb grazing against the inside of her elbow and upward toward her shoulder. He was teasing her. Toying with her.

"Those hot and heavy kisses—were—just kisses. Not an invitation. Just kisses."

"Just kisses. So, you did kiss James like that too?" He frowned.

"No. And why do you care? I can kiss whoever I want, *dear brother*."

"Katy, I promise you, I don't have any brotherly feelings toward you. I thought we'd already cleared that up." He lifted his butt off the rail and turned toward her, pressing her to the back of their bus. "And I don't think you're feeling exactly sisterly toward me either. Am I right?" His breath felt like the fire from their fire pit against her neck. He dropped his mouth down and kissed her lightly on the shoulder as he trailed fingers to move her shirt to the side. Her neck instantly hunched up in tension.

"You said you wanted to come outside for fresh air."

"I did."

"I thought you didn't want to do anything you might regret?" She fixated on his mouth as he hovered in front of her, pinning her to the cold metal bus with his hands on both sides of her head.

"I said we, not me," he mused, "I don't ever have regrets. I was talking about you."

"That's a complete flip-flop from before. You seemed pretty concerned then." Kathryn was confused. He had extricated himself from her clutches just the night before as if he couldn't wait to get away. Now, he was back in front of her, taunting her.

"Okay, maybe I do have regrets but only because you scare me." He brushed his fingers against her cheek and she clenched her jaw. "In an exciting kind of way."

"I scare you, Tommy Ryan? Me? Your friend's little sister? That's a laugh."

"Yeah, well I don't find it all that funny."

"So, this is scared? You don't seem all that scared. More like hot in pursuit." She was relieved to have the bus behind her. It was the only thing keeping her from puddling to the ground.

"I'm scared. Take my word for it. I guess it's kind of like sticking my fingers in the flame to see if I get burned. I know it's about to sting but I can't stop myself." His last words were just breaths as his lips brushed against hers once lightly. Twice. The third time, he kept one arm braced against the bus while the other pulled her into him and ran down her back. And then she was doing it again. She couldn't stop it. Her hands were on their own, feeling their way inside his shirt, clutching tightly into his skin. Only this time it wasn't a sweater. It was a cotton shirt. There were buttons and somehow, she'd managed to get inside them. Her mouth opened on its own when his tongue started trailing its way across. Yes, her control was really admirable where Tommy was concerned. Admirably non-existent. It was forty-eight degrees outside and she was sweating like she was on the beach in Texas.

"Quick question, Tommy," Kathryn huffed as she nipped at his ear. "Which one of us is the fire again? And whose fingers are in the flame?"

He lifted his head to the sky and laughed softly. "Right now, I don't give a shit. Just don't run away. Okay?"

He groaned as her teeth grazed his ear and nibbled down his neck. "I don't have my running shoes on," she mumbled.

Thomas pulled her chin back up to him and planted his mouth firmly against hers causing a shudder all the way to her toes. How the hell did he get her wound up like this? His tongue was burning her up, hot, wet and searching against the inside of her mouth. She smelled him and it made her eyes close tightly as she soaked him in.

"Katy?" he rasped out.

She looked up, bleary-eyed. Then there was movement from the corner of her eye.

A voice to their right growled, "Where the hell are you?" startling them both.

Kathryn recognized the bearded man from the back of the bar. He jolted as he saw them when he passed by on his way to his car. His mouth was glued to his phone; he nodded with a grin as he slid into the seat of an old Ford, coaxed it to life, then sped out of the lot.

Kathryn shook her head. "What, Tommy?"

"Just to make sure," he hesitated. "Are these just everyday kisses? Or the kind with an invitation at the end?"

She felt his pulse thud against her, his jeans cut into her waist as he pressed against her. She looked down at her hands on his chest and realized she had completely opened his shirt and it was flapping loosely in the night breeze. He dropped his hands to rest on her hips, one finger of each hooked into her belt loops, clutching painfully into her as he waited.

She marveled at the red finger marks on his chest. "Wow, did I do that?" No, it was just the cold air, she thought. It made it look that way.

"Yeah." He laughed. "And I'm not complaining, but would you answer my question?"

"Oh, okay. Uh..."

A car sped by and someone yelled out. "Get a room!"

Thomas looked after them, his eyes dark and smoky. "Well?"

"Definitely not every day kisses, Tommy." She slipped her hands inside his shirt and slid them around his waist. He responded by delving those big hands inside the back band of her jeans and cupping her butt, pulling her hard up against him.

"Then we need to get the hell out of here before I jump you right now," he breathed. His lips trailed her temple, warming her forehead. The fog lifted off her passion-covered brain and she realized they were in a parking lot on the side of the street with cars passing by. Okay well, one car passed. But more could come. And their entire team was inside. All people she knew and had to talk to at work. Get a grip, girl.

"We can't. They'll know. We can't just leave."

He kissed her neck again. God that felt good. His breath was an oven against her cool skin. "Sure we can. I don't care if they know."

"I do. The whole company will know. They'll t-talk," she stuttered.

Did she want everyone to know Tommy had done it—made her part of his fan club? Another win for the Ryan team.

His lips stopped moving and he flung his head back to look her in the face.

"Exactly *who* are you concerned about knowing, Kathryn? Everyone in there? The whole company? Or maybe just James?" He stepped back and shoved her hands away.

"Does this embarrass you?" He lifted hands to clasp briefly behind his head, his shirt gaped open showing every muscular line of his chest. His fingers that had been stroking her skin only seconds earlier ran through his hair as the heat of anger warmed his voice. He turned her toward the bar and gave her a push. "Go on. Get in there."

She stumbled toward the bar door.

Chapter Eleven

Thomas buttoned his shirt, watching her go. The crunch of those slender feet on gravel increased the distance between them. The knot in his chest from the night before returned. He had thought it was just a fluke when he felt it then. The altitude or something. He'd struggled for breath when she clutched into him, climbing him like a cat climbs a tree. It shocked the hell out of him.

He didn't want her to waltz back into the club as if it didn't affect her. Like she'd just made out in the parking lot with a complete stranger and shrugged it off. Had she kissed others like that? Was that what James meant when he said she was a great kisser? Shit, that pissed him off. Kathryn hadn't grown up to be that kind of woman, had she? He didn't want to think about it.

Did it matter anyway? She was in a completely different city now. It wasn't like they'd really see each other again. Except at their parents'. That would be awkward—but manageable. Still, she had dug into him with unexpected passion and he found himself hungry to finish it. Her fingers had kneaded his back and chest with blatant, hot, desire and it was so frickin' arousing. She stimulated every nerve in his body then left him standing there wanting more. Wanting to get her back in the cabin. To yank off her clothes and stroke those muscles that had outrun half the state of Texas in track, as well as everything in between. She wanted it too. He saw it.

"Damn it, Kathryn," he muttered as he stuffed his shirt loosely back into his pants and followed her back into the bar.

He had to readjust his eyes to the darkness when he entered. It was so strange to be at a bar at eleven thirty at night and still have to shake off the sunlight. She had gone to the counter for a beer and was carrying it back to the others when he caught up to her and stepped in front. "Kathryn, don't go back to the group yet."

She darted him a scowl. "Thomas, don't do this. You don't need to prove anything by being with me. You've already had enough."

"What the hell are you talking about? I just wanted to tell you your shirt's undone." He pointed at the zipper that was displaying a thatch of her black lace bra.

He'd already had enough? Enough of what? What did she think he was trying to prove? "You wouldn't want to go back to the table like that, would you? If you want to hide what you've been up to—that'd be pretty obvious."

The neon beer light in the window didn't glow as red as her face at that moment. "Oh," she gasped, "Thanks. Here, hold this." She handed him the beer and turned toward him and pulled up on the hook with her thumb. His jaw tightened briefly as the black lace and lines of her breast disappeared under the zipper. She grabbed the beer and whirled around toward the group. Disappointment hit him hard when the distance increased like a chasm between them. He headed to the counter himself. His eyes collided with a cold stare from James, but he ignored it as he leaned both elbows on the smooth surface, waiting for his beverage. It would take more than beer to calm these jets. In fact, the only thing that would soothe him right now wasn't going to happen. She had just kicked him to the curb. No one had ever done that.

"She's a looker, your girl there," the woman behind the bar stated as she motioned toward Kathryn. "A good head on her shoulders too."

"Yep, that's for sure, but she's not my girl," he returned.

The lady sized him up. "That's a shame. Don't waste your time too long, honey. Girls like that don't wait forever. Someone else might just snap her up first."

Waste his time? He took the beer from her and turned away.

At one a.m., everyone cheered and whistled the third bands' final performance then tumbled out to the bus. Another band was getting ready to play but Sean had pulled rank and gathered everyone to leave. They had to be up no later than nine for the next round of exercises. Tomorrow—or by Thomas' watch, today—would be a long day. Their last full day together as a group. And Sean had a lot planned.

As he drove the bus toward their home away from home, Sean called back to the group. "I need to know everyone's return flight times this weekend so that I can make sure we get you out of here on time Friday. Who's leaving Friday afternoon?" Chris and Zak raised their hands.

"What time?"

"Six," Chris answered.

"Me too." From Zak.

"Okay, you need to leave no later than two. So, we'll finish up our final work together before noon. What about the rest of you?"

"I'm on a six a.m. flight Saturday morning," James piped, "I was planning to drive over to Anchorage Friday night."

"Okay. That'll work great. Kathryn? Thomas?"

"I had given myself an extra day up here to go look at the glaciers and maybe fish a little more," Kathryn responded. "My flight leaves Sunday morning so no need to worry about me. I was just gonna make a leisurely drive of it."

Thomas listened, remembering how they'd spent the afternoon together kayaking. Kathryn loved the outdoors and it showed. It didn't surprise him that she wanted to draw the trip out as long as possible.

"Good. I'll give you some brochures tomorrow then."

"I'm on a late flight Saturday," Thomas spoke.

"Sounds good." Sean concentrated on his driving as he spoke. "Everyone needs to make sure they give the fish-packing folks the correct address to ship their fish. If they haven't already done so."

The bus pulled up to the lodge and Sean turned off the engine. It sputtered reluctantly into silence and they all stepped out and went to their cabins, offering "goodnights" all around.

Thomas lay on his bed in the cabin, mulling over this thing with Kathryn. He couldn't keep his hands off her. Why? That scared the shit out of him. He'd kissed more than a few women and some of them had been pretty needy or clingy—especially if it went all the way to sleeping with them.

This wasn't like that though. It was more warm, more open, more everything. As if someone had shot adrenaline into his veins and his nerves were in overdrive when she touched him. Obviously it didn't affect her the same way. She didn't want anyone to know. That one little fact bothered him—it should have been the ideal situation—but it just made him angry.

So, this was simply recreational? Maybe so. He smiled into the darkness of the room. Kathryn was amusing herself with him? Surely not. But what else could it be? It was a novel idea—someone using him for entertainment. What more could a guy ask for?

A slow grumbling snore came from James' side of the room. Thomas turned on his side and rolled his pillow over his head as a muffler, then forced himself to doze off.

Chapter Twelve

Eric Cantor's Ford bounced up the freshly graveled road to his cabin around midnight. The drive from Kenai was slow. He used to take it at warp speed but two near-misses with moose and one not-miss taught him to temper his impatience while driving. The last time, he'd clipped a cow moose as she ran across the road in front of him. It had put a dimple in his fender. One that he hadn't bothered to fix—a constant reminder that he needed to be careful. This area was perfect for what he needed. Perfectly remote. Perfectly hard to find. But also perfectly rustic.

Perfectly remote. Yeah, probably so. Still, he was restless. He had another job to do and needed to get moving. He intended to finish it by next week in order to get home in time for his daughter's theater performance. It saddened him how the passing of time had made it so easy to slip farther and farther away from her. His work had taken him all over the country. Actually to be correct, all over the world.

When he married his wife, he made an attempt to get out. To leave it all behind. Unfortunately, the calls kept coming and his clients grew more and more impatient. When the inference that his clients would come after her if he didn't comply occurred, he reluctantly stepped back into his business. He'd kept it to only a few jobs a year then, trying to stay as close to her as possible. Trying to keep his dream of a normal life alive. It was easy to rationalize that he did it all for her; to keep her safe.

When their daughter, Emily, came into their lives, he rationalized that he had to do more jobs to ensure her safety. In truth, as much as he loved his daughter, he had no idea how to deal with her. He'd never changed a diaper, never stayed up all night holding her when she cried. He missed her first teeth and her first steps.

For all the things he had missed in Emily's life, the one line he drew was at her performances. He would not miss any of those. Sure, there was some hypocrisy in missing all the daily important moments that crop up on the fly, and only making her stage performances. He knew his wife hated him for it. He'd tried in earlier years to soothe her, to make it up by bringing flowers and presents. After a while, no amount of gifts could make up for being gone. And no amount of evading calls could keep his clients from tracking him down.

He had considered gathering up the two of them and escaping. In fact, there had been a job in Europe years ago where he thought it through. He spent three weeks tracking down his subject and waiting for the right moment. During long periods of waiting, he had passed the time by plotting out such an escape. He'd gone into significant detail in his mind; where they would go; what their new names would be; what new profession he would take on; what their new home would be like. He'd even thought about the schools Emily would attend.

The dream had been a short-term obsession for him. It was over when he finished the assignment and realized there was no way he would ever be able to explain away these jobs to his wife and child. They would never be able to accept what he had done. And unless he could explain it, they'd never willingly leave with him. He wasn't embarrassed by his work though. He knew it was necessary—even required, to help maintain certain world infrastructures or resolve whatever conflict or crisis was prevalent. Yet, most people would have difficulty accepting it. Hell, he couldn't really accept it himself.

He rolled down the window and gasped when the cold night air bit into him. A quick flick of the finger sent his cigarette tumbling out into the darkness. The ember flared then darkened before it hit the pavement behind him. His wife had always jumped on him for dropping cigarettes out the window. He knew it was a fire hazard and he had witnessed the damage it could do. Still, it was a habit he couldn't seem to break. An involuntary reflex to the burning ash on his fingers.

Eric flipped the lights to high beam and turned into the drive to his cabin. It was a worn gravel and dirt road, hardly visible from the main thoroughfare. In winter, it was completely covered with snow and he didn't bother trying to clear it. He just used a snow machine to get back and forth. The cabin sat far enough off the road to be relatively invisible to passing traffic, and provide sufficient warning of pending company.

He parked the Ford behind the truck in the shed. He was greeted by the huge black dog that had adopted him a few months earlier. It just showed up in the back yard one day, scrounging through his trash for food. No collar, nothing. He fed it in a momentary lapse of judgment and from that point forward the damned varmint would not leave.

"Hey Gypsy." He reached down to scruff its head. "How was your evening?"

The dog wagged its tail and graced his hand with a lick of saliva.

It surprised him that the dog had survived so well with all the large wild animals around. He half expected it to be a snack for a wandering bear or perhaps trampled by a moose at some point. The dog had irritated him in the beginning. Didn't he know he was hanging around with death and devils? After a few days, the animal's persistence and acceptance seemed to signal something. Eric hoped it might be a sign of a pathway to redemption. A way out of this decade-long hell. Unlikely, sure, but at this point in his life he desperately needed something to believe in and hope for. Even if it was a fantasy.

Thus began Eric's devotion to a big, furry dog he named Gypsy. The name fit the dog's appearance. He would feed it and keep it in when the weather got below freezing. Despite its wariness, the dog had to eventually be lured inside to eat so that predatory animals wouldn't be attracted to his food. Eric realized that once trust was won, the dog did not revoke it. Or at least he hadn't yet. Even when left alone for a few days.

He had gotten into the habit of talking to the mutt since there was no one else around. Telling him things was therapeutic. There was no judgment involved so he could say whatever he thought. Tonight was no exception. He vented about how tired he was and the frustration in waiting all night for Smitty to show up, only to get a call that he wasn't coming. The dog listened attentively as if Eric was giving him praise.

"I'll have to go back down tomorrow, bud," Eric explained. "Smitty will likely be here then and I'll be able to finish this project. Won't that be nice? I can make Emily's play and bring you back some pictures."

Chapter Thirteen

At seven the next morning, a soft tap sounded on Kathryn's door. She had been up for a while, even walked over to the lodge to get coffee. She had connected to her work email and was briefly sifting through the messages, replying or deleting as necessary when she heard it. She ignored the tap and continued working.

A ding signaled a text message on her phone and she glanced down.

Are you up? She didn't recognize the number, but it was from their Dallas office so she typed in a response.

Of course.

Meet me at the obstacle course.

Who is this?

Tommy. Who'd u think?

Wasn't sure. U never txtd me before.

Meet me?

Ok. When?

Now.

She thought for a minute. *Give me 10 minutes to dress.*

Come as u are. I won't mind.

Sure, Tommy.

Ten minutes.

OK, I tried.

The smell of pine needles engulfed her as she moved. She nervously glanced around as she made her way through to the opening they'd visited on the first day. Sean's lecture about the wildlife remained firmly in her thoughts. The excitement she'd felt then was a distant memory. Birds chattered busily in the trees. A massive one with white tipped wings flitted across in front of her just as she stepped into the clearing.

"Hey, beautiful." His voice came from above. She raised her head to see him sitting comfortably atop the beams they had traversed together, both legs dangling. His hands rested comfortably in his lap. Small puffs of steam rose into the air from cups at his side. "I brought breakfast." He motioned to the cups and a white paper bag.

"Don't say that." She closed the gap slowly, measuring each step.

"You don't want breakfast?"

"Not that. Don't call me—" She stopped at the bottom, set her hands defiantly on her hips.

"Beautiful?" His brows furrowed.

"Don't call me that. It sounds like you're talking to—"

"Come up here, Kathryn." He patted the wooden platform and waited.

She hesitated. Did she really want to do this? After all that had passed between them, was it a good idea to spend any more time around Tommy before she left?

"Don't worry. You know I can't touch you without us falling."

She climbed the rope ladder with ease and stepped across to him, placing her feet like a gymnast on a balance beam.

"You make that look graceful," he said.

She lowered herself next to him and took the steaming cup. He held out a small wrapped paper. "I brought you a breakfast burrito."

"My favorite." She smiled. Did he remember that or was it the only thing he could find in town? "You're up early this morning. Still having trouble sleeping?"

"I'm a morning person. I'm usually out of bed by five and head straight to the office. I can get a couple hours of work done before anyone else is even moving."

Kathryn opened the burrito wrapper. The rustling sound echoed in the stillness of the morning. She bit into the food and smiled a thank you at him. An uncomfortable silence suspended in the air for a second.

"So, what's scaring you about me, Katy?" he asked.

She shrugged. "Come on. Are you forgetting who you're talking to? You've had a revolving door of women since the time you turned seventeen."

He arched his right eyebrow. "I did not. Sam was the one they all followed around."

"He said he just hung back and picked up the pieces when they realized you weren't boyfriend material."

Tommy flinched and searched the tree line.

"Why are you always looking at the trees when we talk? Am I that boring?"

He darted back to her and opened his mouth to speak. He said nothing, then gazed down. "I was watching for bear or moose. I was up here a few years ago with my dad and one surprised us. I'm kind of nervous about it now. Especially with food around."

"A bear? Or a moose?"

"Bear."

"Really? What did you do?"

"It left us alone but it was weird. Kind of like we were all watching each other—wary of what the other would do."

"How close was it?"

"Too close for me. I had bad dreams for months after that."

Kathryn laughed, startling him.

"Exactly why is that funny, Kathryn?" he frowned.

She put her hand on his arm to reassure him. "I'm sorry. I wasn't laughing at you. It's just that—you've always seemed the predator-type. It seems strange that you would be—afraid."

"It's not fear—not really—more a recognition or maybe respect for the strength of the animal. And, wow. You really don't think much of me, Kathryn."

He shook his head and sipped from his coffee, then rolled up the empty wrapper from his breakfast and dropped it back into the paper bag at his side.

"That's not true. There are a lot of good things about you." Her cheeks warmed. "But let's be honest—you wouldn't have even looked at me on this trip if there'd been any other women here. You've always been good at—all that."

"All that?" he questioned. "All what?"

She shrugged. Okay, let's clear the air and level the playing field. Might as well just keep going. "The casual fling."

"Are you serious?"

"Of course. Only thing is—I've gotten fairly good at it myself now," she lied. No need to let him know that the kisses had jolted through her like lightning. It was impossible to stop thinking about it. She brushed her teeth earlier and instantly remembered his tongue glazing over the enamel and...*crap*. "So, that routine—the one that worked for you all these years...it's not going to be quite as effective on me." Her stomach knotted.

She wondered if he could see through the charade. They practically grew up around each other. She was a lot of things in high school, slut wasn't one of them. Could she make him believe she was more sophisticated now? She needed to, for her own stupid pride, if nothing else. She wanted him to think all of the kissing and clutching meant next to nothing. That she had grown up since then and could handle it.

"This is interesting. Why won't it be effective on you, Katy?"

"Because I know what you're after."

"And what would that be?"

"The win. The conquest. Kind of like another trophy."

"Wow." He snatched the bag up and crumpled it in his hand. The color in his face darkened. "Bullshit. Have I ever once talked about any women in front of you? Have you ever heard me say a derogatory word about any girl at all? Or talked about them in any way, good or bad?" He gritted his teeth.

She thought for a few minutes. No, she hadn't actually heard him talk bad about anyone, girl or guy. He talked sports, food, school events—but not people. Still, she remembered how some of the girls tried so hard to get his attention and he totally ignored them.

She was startled by his anger. *This bothers him?* "I don't know. I didn't l-listen. I just watched. I s-saw," she stuttered.

"You watched and saw what? A girl talking to me. Me being polite and talking back. Girls talking to me at school or wherever. Me being polite and answering," he scoffed. "What else did you see? Or imagine."

"Flirting. Lots of flirting."

"Not just me being polite? And having a good time?" He quirked a brow.

"There was that too," she admitted.

"Look, I'm not going to have this discussion with you. Why do you care anyway? It's not like I need your approval for the way I lived." He was scolding then. She'd hit a nerve.

"No," she agreed, "you certainly don't. Tommy, why did you ask me here this morning? And why all the other stuff. The kissing and groping. You don't really need to do that with me. I liked you just fine before all that."

Tommy scooted backward and flung his leg over the beams they sat on so he could straddle them to face her. He moved closer and wrapped his hands around each of her arms, clutching her forearms. "But you don't like me as much now? I asked you here because I wanted to. You don't get it, do you?"

She looked down at the ground below them, trying to keep the dizziness from taking over. "Get what?"

"Look at me, Katy." He shook her roughly. She slowly raised her eyes and met his. There was something there she didn't recognize. Something unfamiliar in the way he surveyed her face. "This is just the two of us. It's not about a conquest, a trophy, or a contest." He raised both hands and waved them at the trees. "Who am I going to impress here? The 'kissing and groping' as you called it, wasn't just me, and you know it. You participated just as actively as I did. And it was hot as hell. Don't try to pretend you were just playing along. You were as surprised as I was."

"And *you* weren't just *being polite and having a good time?*"

"Having a good time? Yes. Being polite? *Screw that.*" He reached out and yanked her toward him. He silenced her next words as he smashed his mouth to hers, yanking her off balance and throwing her against his chest. "I've got you." He murmured against her lips while he reached down and pulled her legs side-saddle onto his to balance her weight on the beam.

She let him kiss her, trying to stay calm. Then the most random thought suddenly popped into her head. "You know what?" It seemed relevant for some stupid reason.

"Hmmm?" His lips were still against her, his breath warming the wetness he'd left on her swollen mouth.

"You've kissed me every day we've been here, other than the first. Don't you think that's a little too much?" she whispered.

"No. Not too much. Not enough." He pressed his lips to her ear. "Nowhere near enough. Get closer." He slipped his hands down to her hips, turning her into him. One palm reached for the inside of her thigh and pulled her leg over the beam to straddle it. Then he grasped both thighs and worked them back over his, yanking her onto his lap. She gasped as she felt him against her. A surge of heat went through her abdomen and coursed its way through her veins.

"Mmmm," he moaned while tasting her lips again, "now this is what I call breakfast." His arms went around her hugging her tight. "Want to meet back here for lunch?"

"This sounds vaguely like you're planning to eat me alive," she teased.

"You're a little obsessed, you know. That fear of being eaten." He smiled into her eyes, resting his forehead against hers. "Maybe there's a bear in your dreams too?"

She smiled back weakly. *Yeah, a big blond one with arms that could crush a girl, eyes that could drown her, and thighs that make her think all sorts of perverted thoughts.*

"I thought you said you wouldn't touch me because we'd fall."

"I didn't say I wouldn't. I said, you know I can't touch you without us falling." He shrugged. "Guess I was wrong."

"You planned this, didn't you?" she scolded.

"Would it make you mad if I did?"

"Maybe a little."

"Then no, I didn't plan it. The thought didn't even cross my mind until you walked out of the trees." His forehead against hers made her dizzy. She reached up to stroke his cheek and pulled her head back.

"Liar."

"No." He clenched her against his chest. "I just wanted to talk to you again. Clear the air so to speak. Figure this out. Until I saw you." He stroked her hair. "I have an idea, Kathryn."

"What's that?"

"Let's leave here at the same time, drop your car off at the rental place, and spend the rest of the time up until my flight leaves in the mountains. I've always wanted to do the glacier tour. What about you?"

"You mean together?" she had a nervous twitch in her gut.

"Sure. Why not?" He smoothed a hand up and down her hair and she couldn't think straight. She knew he meant a lot more than just checking out the glaciers. After all, she'd ended up in this same place, these same arms, at least once a day for the past three. It had to lead somewhere. Right?

"Thomas Ryan, are you trying to get me into bed?" she chastised.

"Kathryn Delroy." His voiced dripped sarcasm. "Why would I do that? I'm just your brother's gangly friend. You'd never be interested in someone like me. I'm safe, remember? Harmless."

"Sure you are. Just like that bear you keep looking for in the trees."

Chapter Fourteen

"Okay. Maybe I'm not harmless," Thomas admitted. "I haven't exactly kept it simple, but I'd rather not spend the rest of the trip by myself. So, I can behave if you can." The words were a challenge.

"In other words, you don't want to be alone?" she jabbed.

He rubbed his thumbs up and down her sides, enjoying the feel of her skin. The sexual tension between them could be shattered like a crystal, it was so sharp and clear. He felt the weight of it knifing into him. In truth, he hoped she wouldn't behave. At all.

"No." He glanced at the tree line briefly. "I'm not that hungry. Or desperate." Silence.

"I'll go with you," she uttered. "But it's still casual. Okay?" She brushed his hair back from his forehead with her fingers as if he was a kid. As if she was trying to put him back on the shelf to get some distance. He half expected her to pat him on the head too and tell him how cute he was.

"Sure. Totally casual." He wasn't going to make it easy though. He slipped his hands upward to cup her face and melted his lips against hers again, trying to increase the tension. She leaned into him, pushing him backward. For a moment, her hands clung to him for balance. He was pleased when a soft moan escaped her lips. He answered it with his own voice, then rushed his hand up the front of her shirt and encased her breast with his fingers, squeezing until she gasped his name. Totally casual. You bet, Kathryn. He suppressed a smile.

"We'd better get back for the exercises today or they'll come looking for us," he whispered. His jeans were cutting off his circulation. It hurt like hell. As much as he liked the embrace, it wasn't physically possible to do what he wanted to on this damn beam. The thought of trying was pretty amusing though. "Damn," he blurted as the image came into his head.

"What?" Kathryn raised her head.

"Nothing. We just need to get back before we lose our—balance." She was doing that thing again. Her hands sneaking into his clothes, kneading his skin like bread dough. Too bad she didn't answer the door earlier. He really wanted to know what came next. After all the clawing and squeezing. Kathryn had completely rocked him with the way she dug into him. He would have thought her to be softer, less demanding of a man. It was amazing how she pulled and pleaded and licked at him like he was a gift to be ripped open and possessed.

"You might want to get your hand out of my shirt then." She looked down at his palm on her skin.

"Yeah, right." He didn't budge. "You first."

Kathryn eased her hands off his chest and slid them down his abs. He thought she would pull them away, instead she slipped two fingers of each hand into the waistband of his jeans. He sucked in his breath. "Damn it, Katy. That's not fair." He shuddered. "Don't tell me to keep it casual and then do something like that. That's just plain cruel."

"And what you're doing is any better?" She raised her eyebrows and nodded at his hand under her shirt.

"I wasn't the one setting the rules." He grinned and dropped his hand.

"No, just the one breaking them. Nothing new in that is there?" she teased and pulled her hands back, then slid back away from him. He instantly felt the cool air against his chest as she continued, "Give me one good reason why I should consider it safe to be around you the rest of the weekend? You and I both know this can't go anywhere."

Her expression was scolding. He admired the spackling of freckles across her nose and cheeks. He'd forgotten about those. All these years remembering everything else. He'd forgotten the way they made her smile sparkle, and her anger soften. It's hard to look menacing with those, no matter how much she furrowed her eyebrows.

"Sorry, Katy. I can't give you any good reasons. You'll have to figure that out on your own." He turned his back to her and started edging his way toward the rope netting so that he could climb down. He glanced back. "I want you to come with me. Casual or not. You decide. I don't have any rules here." Her shirt was still hiked up from where his hand had been and he took a fleeting look at her skin before climbing down. She pulled the fabric down and followed him. He waited for her, admiring the way she moved. As her feet touched the ground, she pushed herself away from the ropes and turned toward him, frowning.

"So, what if I said not?" she asked.

"Not?"

"Not casual."

"What are you saying?"

She hesitated, then stepped past him and started walking toward the path to the lodge, picking her way across the grass. "Don't worry, Thomas. I'll be long gone before you. I was just asking. It didn't mean anything."

He walked toward the path behind her. What the hell did that mean?

Chapter Fifteen

Eric sat on the front porch of his remote cabin, scruffing Gypsy's ears. The dog was certainly loyal and eased the quiet and loneliness of his lifestyle. Some birds frolicked around in the branches of the pine trees that flanked the property, chattering away. He lifted the coffee mug that sat at his side and took a sip of the stiff brew.

He briefly pondered calling to check on Emily. A glance at his watch shut that thought out of his mind. She would still be asleep, dreaming of theater performances, no doubt. He took a drag on his cigarette and reached for the tennis ball that lay a few feet away. With the cigarette hanging from his lips, he gestured with the ball toward the grass. As soon as Gypsy noticed, he started twirling in circles, his tail fluttering furiously. Eric tossed the ball into the yard and the dog bounded after it. A few seconds later the ball dropped at his feet, covered in dirt and slobber. He tossed it again and again. Emily would have liked Gypsy. Hell, Gypsy would have liked her better than he, himself. She had more energy to keep up with the stupid mutt.

He crushed his cigarette into the saucer he used as an ashtray and lifted off the porch. It was time to make a trip into town and call Smitty. If Smitty didn't answer, he'd go by Brenda's and see if she was up for breakfast. Brenda worked the bar at Hooksetter's. He'd spent a lot of time there lately chatting with her. He knew she had no choice but to listen to him. He sat at the bar, sometimes the sole customer, killing time and watching the television in the corner. Still, whenever he said something, she always had a lively response—something that spurred discussion, rather than silence.

He knew she'd be there soon, cleaning up from the night before and getting ready for today's crowd. Eric smiled at that thought—crowd. The only huge crowd he'd ever seen in the place was on band night. On that night, the place was wall-to-wall people. Other than that one night a week, there were seldom more than a small group of people at any one time. He was certain they made enough on the band nights to cover their expenses for the remaining slow times. He didn't particularly enjoy those crowds but it did give him an opportunity to socialize, even without any interaction.

The couple the other night had certainly been entertaining. He had watched the girl dupe the scheming idiot at the pool table. She was pretty, not what anyone would call beautiful, but something about her definitely made a person watch. She looked healthy, and strong. Maybe that was it. He and Brenda got a good laugh watching the girl swap the drinks for water without his knowledge. The guy thought he was destined to get lucky and she was totally working it. Then the big blond guy came in and pulled her out, probably thinking that he was saving her. He, too, was obviously underestimating the woman's intelligence. She didn't need saving. The hero thing worked for him, apparently, since he showed up for band night with her. And then the guy was in her clothes and lip-locked to her in the parking lot when he left. If he hadn't walked by, they probably would have done it right there. Hell, maybe they did. They didn't seem too bothered by his presence. Lucky bastard.

"Maybe I'll get lucky too," he said, thinking that Brenda might just have warmed enough to him to make it possible. He grabbed the car keys off the hook and headed toward the shed. He had showered and trimmed the beard a little. He didn't want to make any drastic changes. After all, this was who he intended to be while here. Still, at the moment, he wished he'd picked a more attractive look. He hadn't been with a woman in...hell, he couldn't remember. His wife had given up on him years ago. Since then, he'd grabbed attention and closeness wherever he could get it. But only briefly. No relationships anymore. There was too much risk.

As he drove by the bar a couple of hours later, it pleased him to see the lights on. He had a goal in sight and he intended to pour on the charm. At least until he could reach Smitty and get things moving again on his next project. Typical to the laid-back nature of this area, the door was unlocked. He slipped in and let his eyes adjust to the darkness. The scent of spilled beer and grease was mingled with Clorox. He raised his head at the scraping sound of chairs being moved and glanced around. Brenda was wearing shorts and a T-shirt as she swathed the floor with a mop. Her ragged tennis shoes were a dusty gray, rather than the pristine white they had started out. She had her hair pulled back in a band and her face was fresh and clean.

Without makeup he could see that he'd overestimated her age. The bar work may have taken its toll. A broom leaned against the bar, poised for use. He grabbed it. Without talking, he started swishing it back and forth, sweeping and gathering the debris from the prior night's fun. She kept on mopping. Minutes passed into an hour before she had worked her way across to where he'd finished with the broom. He had retrieved a cup of coffee from behind the bar and sat on a stool admiring her movements. She had a nice ass. Not too hippy, but not overly thin either. Her legs were a little on the short side but she moved well. She knew he was summing her up. He thought she liked it. She leaned over several times, her backside to him, as if making sure he had a good look. *Bingo. Yeah, this might work out well.*

"You hungry?" she asked.

He tore his gaze from the bare legs. "Guess so. I haven't had breakfast if that's what you're asking."

"I'll cook something up in the back." She gestured toward the opening behind the door as she gathered up the mop and broom and carried it all to a closet by the bathrooms.

"That'd be real nice. Thanks." Eric was pleased.

"Don't get too excited. You haven't tasted it yet." She grinned and walked past the bar with Eric following behind.

"I'm not choosy," he admitted. Not choosy at all. Horny, yes. Choosy, no.

Approximately three hours later, he pulled out of the parking lot and headed toward the park to make his call. He had left her panting and smiling with her shorts lying on the floor along with those ugly gray shoes. They hadn't bothered to take off shirts, although he'd pulled hers up enough to get his hands on her generous tits. He'd never screwed anyone in a bar kitchen before. All the stainless steel counters were kind of fun, especially as he rammed into her, pinning her against them. Pots, pans, and a shelf filled with knives of every size rattled. He could have grabbed a knife and dragged it across her throat in a second as she greedily wrapped her legs around him. Brenda was surprisingly pliant and generous. She wanted to please him. Obviously, it had been a while for her, too. It had taken no time at all to bring her to climax. Just as it had taken him no time either.

He hoped he wouldn't have to kill her. She was nice. For now, he would spend what time he could hanging around and see what happened.

Smitty's impatient voice spoke through the cell. "'Bout time you called."

"'Bout time you answered," Eric returned.

"Look, you're gonna have to come here. I've got a tail. Not sure but I think it's the feds."

Eric found that humorous. "Then why the hell would I want to come there?" Smitty's suggestion was idiotic.

"Because they're watching me. If you come to me, and by chance I can't lose them, they'd never know where you came from...or if you mattered at all." Okay, that made sense. Sort of.

"No, I think it might be better if I just wait a while." Eric never took chances, unless he had to. There was no point risking exposure now.

"Fine, but we're running out of time. This next job has to happen within three to four weeks."

"Then just give me the details over the phone."

"Can't. You know that. No phones."

"Whatever. Look, I'm going to Seattle for a few days. I have something to take care of. If you want to catch up with me there, great. If not, we'll just see how it goes." Eric would make Emily's play while he waited. Smitty's voice barely hid his agitation. The man was jumpy. But then, he'd always been a bit on the paranoid side. Too easy to ruffle. That was one thing Eric didn't like about the guy, along with a few others.

In this business, if you couldn't control your emotions, you were dead. It amazed him that Smitty still managed to control the links between Eric and the clients. He would have thought the clients had grown tired of his ups and downs by now. Still, it worked to his advantage. He never had to meet them directly and by not doing so, they likely didn't know who Eric was. They only knew Smitty.

Eric ended the call and grunted. At least he could go by the bar tonight and maybe see Brenda again. His thoughts kept going back to the stainless steel sex and he was getting a little worked up. The bad thing about getting laid after a long hiatus was that once the floodgate was open, one didn't want it to close any time soon. Wait, he reminded himself, what's bad about that?

"Come on Gypsy, let's go for a walk." He stepped out the back door and headed toward a path in the woods. His gear was locked in the shed at the back of the property. He'd hidden it below the dirt floor. It took him a week to dig through the frozen ground and shore it up well enough to store everything. A week that was well worth the calloused and bleeding knuckles. Any observer walking in would see an old barn with dirt floors worn down from animals tracking around. They'd never know that the pile of junk in the corner covered a plethora of underground weapons and surveillance equipment. Close observance would identify the satellite dish that sat higher up the mountain, but to a passerby nothing looked out of place.

With the latch opened, he pulled out the manila envelopes of contracts and closed everything back up. It had occurred to him that a phrase in the contract for this job might be problematic. They would not entrap him into going after anyone but the woman this time. He had learned to be meticulously specific when the objective was defined. They'd duped him on that—he'd once had to kidnap a man's entire family to get what they wanted. When one of the children, a small infant, accidentally died, he'd agonized over it. He was *not* a child killer. Yes, this was war, so to speak, but he still had some limits. The only reassurance he had, came from learning the child had been diagnosed with some respiratory problem weeks before. It wasn't his fault, he rationalized. Just an accident. Still, that one incident made him very careful with new contracts like the one he was assessing now.

He spent the remainder of the day reviewing what little information he had on the next job. He had a location, a profile of the person, but no name or address. He also had the objective. It had been revised twice. At first, they wanted him to go after the woman's family. He refused. When they explained that the woman was the controlling vote in a legislative decision that would literally shut down the borders between Mexico and Canada, he understood.

This wasn't necessarily political. It was driven by greed, drug-funded greed. People had tried to shut down the borders many times before without success. This would be no different. There was too much money behind it, the cartels, the gangs, the organized crime rings in the cities—even a few pocketed politicians. Unfortunately, this woman had made it her platform on election to put an end to the drug wars.

Her vocal attacks and her control over the legislature were vise-like. She was more likely than any of her predecessors to move legislation that would finally do something. They wanted her stopped.

Still, he refused to go after the family. She had twin daughters the same age as Emily. When he saw them, something in him snapped. They had no involvement in their mother's decisions or politics; their only concerns were likely surrounding what to wear to school, which boy to text "Hey" to, and who to sit with at lunch.

He made a couple of marks on the contract and left it on the counter as he went to pour himself a scotch. A quick glance at the clock above the bar cabinet elicited a curse. Ten p.m. He could never get used to the sun staying up so late. Brenda's bar would be in full swing right now and he wanted to get there in time to stay for closing. On a night like tonight, without the bands, that could be anywhere from eleven to two in the morning. She usually kept the doors open as long as she had paying customers.

"Keep an eye on things for me, boy," he said to Gypsy as he yanked the keys from the hook and headed to the car.

Chapter Sixteen

"Last day and lots to do," Sean said as people meandered into the lodge and gathered at the table. Kathryn had rushed back from the trees so she could enter before everyone arrived. By 1 p.m., she had packed and was pretty much ready to go.

Her cell gave the familiar ding that signaled a text message. She looked down to see the Dallas number. She had intentionally not added it to her address book and assigned his name to it. That would imply permanence. She knew better than to think there was anything permanent about this.

Ready?

Yes

Where do you need to return your car to?

Rental Shop in Anchorage

Too far, call and see if we can return it here.

She made the call to no avail. There weren't any rental car businesses in Kenai. She sent him a text. *No luck*

Okay. Anchorage then. I'll follow.

Leaving now

Kathryn loaded up her car and left without talking to him. Her phone rang ten minutes after she turned onto the highway.

"Everything okay?" Thomas sounded miffed.

"Yeah, fine. Why?" she asked.

"You rushed out of there like there was a fire. Is something wrong?"

"No, I just didn't want anyone to see us together."

"Oh." Silence. "Kathryn, pull over."

"Why? Is there a problem?"

"Yes. Pull the damn car over. Right now." His tone was menacing.

She eased to the side of the highway, pulling as far onto the shoulder as possible and rolled to a stop. Two cars passed, then his Jeep veered in behind her. Thomas' tall frame stepped out of the vehicle and stomped toward her car. He reached on the roof and heaved with one arm. She heard a scrape as he dragged down her carry-on bag.

There was a sharp rap on the passenger window. "Unlock the door, Kathryn." She hit the button, her face flushed with embarrassment. He opened the door and threw her case in next to her, then leaned in and spoke. "So, which is worse? Driving down the road with your suitcase on the top of your car and losing it—or being seen with me?" He gritted his teeth and stared hard into her eyes.

"I guess I was in t-too much of a hurry," she stuttered, feeling like an idiot.

"Yeah, guess so. Look. I'm not going to chase you. If you want to go on by yourself, get after it. If it's going to be a problem, let's just forget this." He slammed the door and walked back toward his Jeep.

"Hey!" She opened the driver's door and stood up. He stopped, squared his shoulders, and turned back toward her. "Come here."

His stride was slow and seemed filled with reservations. When he stood in front of her in the open car door, she waved her hand at the bag.

"Would you help me get this stuff into the Jeep? We'll just leave the car here and I'll call them to get it."

She thought a wave of relief crossed his face, she wasn't sure. The anger seemed to subside. His hair whipped out of his face. "Sure about that?"

"Not really, so hurry up before I chicken out." She smiled weakly up at him.

They rode in silence until a brief rain spattered across the windshield. Thomas reached for the windshield wipers and spoke, "You know, that was kind of an ego killer. I've never had a woman embarrassed to be seen with me before."

"I'm not embarrassed. It's just that I don't want people gossiping at work. I don't want to be known as the girl you did at the Team Building thing."

"Why would anyone say that?"

"Remember Helen Jorgan?"

"What about her?"

"She's the girl you did at the junior prom."

"What? Who said that?"

"Sam. And some girl that you met in college is now known as the girl from the toga party."

"You're joking." He looked sideways at her before shifting his gaze back to the road.

"No. I'm not. And there's also the girl with the flower tattoo on her ankle. And a slew of others."

"Okay. I get the picture." His knuckles turned white on the steering wheel. "Your brother's kind of an ass, you know. I can't believe he told you those things."

"He made a point of it. Almost like he wanted me to know who you really were. Or maybe he was jealous."

"Or maybe he had other reasons...and he didn't know what the hell he was talking about." He spoke quietly.

The rain grew steadily heavier. Loud plunks against the windshield and roof made it impossible to speak softly. "What does that mean?"

"Kathryn, think about it. He told me things too."

"Like what?"

"In high school, he told me you thought I was gross. I remember one time he said that you told him I stunk *bad* when I was at your house. I took two showers a day after that. In college, you were seriously involved with someone. Always. After that, for the past few years, you were still engaged. Even though you say it's been over for some time."

"Sam wouldn't do that. Why would he care?"

"You're his sister. He wanted the best for you. And—I was a problem then." He snorted. His fingers lunged out to increase the volume on the radio. It quickly drowned out the rain.

"I never told him you smelled bad."

She hesitated to ask more. The look on his face made it clear he wasn't interested in talking.

Kathryn weighed the information. Sam had no reason to lie about Thomas, did he? There wasn't anything to gain from it. Thomas barely spoke to her over the years, other than to tease and harass her on the few occasions they were together. Until this week, she doubted he'd even looked twice at her.

"I think you're over-analyzing ancient history. I seriously doubt Sam would flat-out lie like that. There's no reason to. It's not like we were—" Kathryn shook her head. "It doesn't matter anyway, it doesn't change anything, so let's just forget it. You obviously remember things a lot differently than I do."

He sighed, then smiled and looked at her. "Consider it forgotten."

"Good. And when the weekend's over, let's just forget this too, and go our separate ways from there."

He frowned. "If that's what you want." Ten minutes of silence followed. "Here we are." He nodded at the exit for the boat trip to view the glaciers. They maneuvered the winding road until it opened into a parking lot. Once parked, they walked to the ticket counter only to find they'd missed the last scheduled trip for the day. The final trip out started at three p.m., nearly thirty minutes before they arrived.

Chapter Seventeen

"Feel like a shot of something new?" Brenda taunted Eric. Her voice was lilting and suggestive as she turned her back to him and mixed something up in a shot glass. When she rotated back, she pushed a golden liquid toward him.

"What is it?" he asked.

"Just try it. You'll like it. It's sweet as hell, and really smooth."

He lifted the glass and tipped it back, letting the liquid flow down his throat. Wow. She was right. Sweet, like crème and smooth. They drank several before she offered to drive him home.

"I don't need a driver, I'm fine," he insisted.

"Sorry," she responded. Apparently, he'd been a little too harsh. He measured her for a moment, then decided to make a suggestion.

"Why don't I drive *you* home? To my place." He had lifted a toothpick from the bar, speared a cherry and rolled it around on his tongue. He watched her through veiled eyelids. It was probably not a smart thing to do but hell, the floodgate was open, and he liked the way she felt. Besides, he had to leave in the morning for Seattle, so there wasn't a lot of time to waste. He had rationalized that he'd only be gone for a couple of days. But to a man who'd been sex-starved for as long as he had, that seemed like an eternity.

It was surprisingly easy to talk her into staying the night, especially since it was early morning when they reached the cabin. He had spied the papers on the island in the kitchen when he unlocked the door, and after inviting her to sit on the couch, he snatched them up. Eric stuffed the contents back in the envelope, looked around for a place to stash them—and opted for the fridge.

Out of sight, out of mind, he thought. He carried two tumblers of scotch into the living room and within thirty minutes, they had drank and wrestled their way into his bed.

Eric rolled over in bed the following morning. His movement was restricted by the sheets tangled around him. He pulled on the cloth but it didn't give. It was anchored by Brenda's hip. He eased himself onto his side and watched her sleep. She was nothing special really, but there was a way about her that he liked. Something that drew him toward a warmth he hadn't felt in years.

Now, lying in the bed with sheets wrapped around them, he realized the mistake. He should not have brought her here. No one should be here. He walked his fingers up her arm and tapped her on the shoulder. When she opened an eye, he laughed at the expression. It was almost—normal.

"You need to leave," he stated. "I have to work this morning."

"Oh," she answered, surprised. "I guess I thought..."

"That I didn't have a job, right?"

"Well, I wasn't sure. You've been around at odd times. Like maybe you were just visiting or something. You never talked about work so I thought—I don't know what I thought."

"I work remotely. Insurance stuff. I have to go out of town for a few days, headed out this afternoon. There's some stuff I need to get done before I go. So, get dressed and I'll take you back down."

He had enjoyed Brenda. She seemed decent. Too bad he wasn't. Still, for now he'd let her think so. Having someone to romp with periodically might make the time go faster. After pulling on his clothes, he went to the kitchen, grabbed a glass and filled it with milk. He glanced at the envelope when he put the jug back and realized he needed to return it to the shed. Perhaps he could do so while she dressed.

A quick glance toward the bedroom killed that idea. She had her clothes on and was headed his way. Within minutes, they were in the car and he barreled toward town, quite happy with himself.

He had entertained a woman for three days and not given away a thing. And she still liked him. More importantly, he kind of liked her. With his bags in the trunk, he figured he'd just drop her off at the bar and head to Anchorage to catch his flight to Seattle.

"You in a hurry?" Brenda asked.

He probably should stop looking at his watch. He noticed a slight sting in her voice, probably should have offered her a cup of coffee or maybe even breakfast. Stupid.

"A little," he admitted.

"Just drop me off at the bottom, I'll catch a ride into town on the bus."

It startled him that she would be so accommodating. It sounded good for a minute, but he shrugged the thought out of mind. Maybe he could try to be at least *a little* decent. "Nope. I'm not in that much of a hurry."

Chapter Eighteen

Thomas let Katy's words simmer as they stood looking at the ticket booth. There would be no glaciers for them today. They were suddenly left with hours and hours of daylight and no plan. He could think of a lot of ways to spend it. All of them involved fewer clothes than they currently wore.

"Why don't we take that road we passed earlier up into the mountains and see where it goes?" he suggested. "It's something to do. Then we'll head down and see if we can find a place to stay. If not, we'll go into Anchorage. We can come back here in the morning and take the first trip out at nine. Does that sound good?"

He turned just as the wind grabbed her hair and pelted him in the face with it. With a grin, he gathered it all together and stuffed it down her shirt. "Can you keep that stuff contained, Katy? I'd hate to have to break out a pair of scissors."

"You were just looking for another excuse to get in my shirt," she stated with annoyance. "You know you wouldn't dare cut my hair."

"Am I that transparent?" he asked as he rested his arm on her shoulder and nudged her back toward the Jeep.

"One track mind. I think you were born with it."

"All men are. It's programmed into us in the womb." He followed her to the passenger door and opened it for her to step in. The smell of her shampoo lingered in his mind. He closed the door and got in next to her. The engine roared to life, he hit the gas, propelling them up the mountain.

The paved road turned to gravel after about ten more miles

and they bounced along, windows down, enjoying the smell of the trees. They rounded a corner sharply and Kathryn squealed, "Look at that!" Water cascaded down the side of the mountain less than fifty yards from them, descending like silver ribbons into a pool below. It crashed thunderously, sending foam sprays high into the air. Thomas slowed the vehicle and pulled to the side of the road.

"Let's go check it out." He opened the door and pushed his legs to the ground. He could smell the mixture of pine and water inviting them to explore.

"What about bears?" Kathryn looked around cautiously.

"There's a marked path there." He pointed to a small wooden sign that stated 'scenic view this way.' "I doubt the bears frequent a place that gets a lot of foot traffic. And they probably don't read signs either."

"Smartass."

"Yep." He grinned and grabbed her hand. "I'll lead the way just in case. If Smoky comes out of the trees, he can eat me first." Her fingers were thin between his. Who would have thought they could be so strong and aggressive when he kissed her. He held her hand up to look at them. No polish. Short nails. She wasn't exceptionally big on vanity yet somehow it accentuated her femininity.

"What are you looking at?" she asked.

"I was trying to figure out how someone with these tiny fingers and no fingernails, could leave huge red welts on my chest."

She turned her face away toward the waterfall so that he couldn't see her expression. "That wasn't me," she murmured.

"The hell it wasn't." He squeezed her hand and stopped as the path ended at the pool below the falls. Water gurgled and foamed, lapping against the edges. The only sound was the roar of it falling from above. The spray soaked them within seconds.

"It's beautiful," Kathryn said with reverence.

"Agreed." He was suddenly in awe that he was standing here with her, holding her hand, looking at this fantastic feat of nature. He pulled his iPhone from his pocket. "Let me take your picture." Before she could answer, he raised it and snapped two shots.

They stood a few minutes longer, then returned to the Jeep and continued up the gravel road.

"I was just kidding," he said without warning.

She looked at him, startled. "About what?"

"The welts." He grinned and hopped back into the Jeep. Thomas continued to careen the vehicle up the mountain road. The temperature had dropped considerably. As they made turns, shadows from the mountain darkened their way, then opened up again when they turned back toward the sun. The air was still heavy with the scent of pine and water but much cooler as the elevation increased. The gravel road became soggier and soggier. The Jeep careened over it as they moved.

"Maybe we should go back down," Kathryn suggested. "I think we've run out of road."

"It's still here, it's just under the mud. I'll turn around up there in that clearing." Thomas pointed to an area where the trees opened up next to the road. When he reached it, he tried to do a three-point turn but caught the back tires in the thick mud. The tires spun without resistance, humming loudly. He changed gears and tried to back out. No go. He'd been stuck before many times and knew to rock the car back and forth between gears to try to get traction. He tried that but the tires just dug in deeper.

"Shit," he grumbled and stepped out to take a look, sinking deep into the mush below the tires.

Kathryn opened her door to look.

"Don't get out!" he shouted. "It's complete marsh underneath." He leaned back in the door and looked at her. The sun cast a white sheet of light through the trees behind her, framing her face.

"Can you steer and I'll push?"

"Sure." She climbed into the driver's seat and held the wheel while he tromped through the muck to the back of the Jeep.

"When I say go, give it the gas," he called.

Thomas hunched down and anchored his feet before putting both hands under the bumper. He leaned into the vehicle and yelled, "Go!"

Kathryn hit the gas. The tires spun with a loud whir but no forward movement. They tried over and over again until Thomas was covered in sweat, his face red, and his chest heaving.

"I'm sorry Katy. It's not gonna work. We're stuck. We need a tow." He leaned in the door to get his iPhone from the console where he'd dropped it earlier. He held it up and frowned. "I can't get a signal. Can you try?"

She pulled out her phone. "I have no signal either."

"Great." He tugged off his shirt and wiped the mud from his hands. "Can you reach in my bag back there and get me another shirt?" Thomas pointed at the navy bag on the seat behind her and waited while she opened it. She tossed him a shirt and he slipped it over his head and shoulders then yanked it down to cover his chest. He looked up to catch her staring at him. "Katy, what are you looking at?"

"You." She grinned and looked over the dashboard.

"What's wrong?" He smirked as he caught the way she sized him up.

"I was looking for welts. Not checking you out."

"Really?" He quirked a brow.

"Yeah. Faker." She grinned as she crossed her arms over her chest.

"Well, when we get out of here, I'll be happy to give you the chance to make some," he teased.

She ignored him. "There was a drive about a quarter of a mile back down there." Kathryn pointed down the mountain. "We could walk down and see if there's a house or something, and see if we can get a cell signal."

"Okay. I'm already muddy. I'll do that—you stay here," Thomas ordered.

"No way. I'm not staying here by myself." She looked into the trees with fear.

"You're right. We both go, but don't get out. Let me lift you over to the road so you won't get muddy." He motioned for her to climb to him, then he lifted her in a fireman's hold and planted her firmly in the dry road. He considered clutching her firmly on the ass as he carried her but thought better of it. She'd probably get pissed—especially at the muddy handprint. "Anything you want to take with you?" he asked, glancing back at the bags in the vehicle.

"We're coming right back, aren't we?"

"It depends whether we can get help or not."

An hour later, they had worked their way to the drive and followed it up to a cabin. The cabin was deep in the trees with a single lane road leading in. Peacefully quiet and dark. No visible signs of life. They climbed two steps to a porch and knocked on the door. No answer. Thomas walked the perimeter and glanced in the windows of the outbuildings too. The place was empty. Probably a vacation home.

"No one's here."

Kathryn had disappeared from the porch when he came around the corner. The door was open; he wondered if he had missed the person answering the door. He peeked inside.

"I found the key under the pot in the corner of the porch," she said smugly.

"Well, aren't you resourceful. Did you happen to see a truck key too? There's a white Ford pickup in the shed. We could use it to pull the Jeep out."

"As a matter of fact, there's some keys hanging right there on that hook by the door." She pointed at the wall next to him. Sure enough. There they were.

"I guess they don't care too much about security up here, do they?"

"Doesn't appear that way." She was looking around the cabin, peeking into doors, opening the fridge. "Whoever this belongs to has food in here. Doesn't look like they're gonna be gone long."

He watched her snooping around like a kid looking for treasure—or a bag of potato chips. "Hey, nosey. It's almost nine. It'll be dark in a couple of hours—or at least as dark as it gets up here. If we don't get the truck out soon, it's going to have to stay there till morning. And I am not going to be out in those bear-infested trees in the dark. Right now's not really the best time either since they're normally searching for food about this time of day. Let's get this over with." He yanked the keys from the hook and headed toward the shed, not waiting to see if she was following.

The truck started reluctantly, spitting out a couple of clouds of exhaust before grinding into a steady rumble. Kathryn climbed in and pulled the door shut on the passenger side while Thomas grabbed some chains off a hook on the wall and threw them in the back. They headed up the mountain and were able to drag the Jeep out of the ditch backward using the chains and truck. Once out, Kathryn drove it back down behind Thomas to the cabin.

Thomas grabbed their bags and clumped up to the door, then dropped them inside. He stood on the porch and removed his jeans, shoes, and socks before entering the cabin in his briefs.

"I don't want to track mud everywhere," he explained as he left them on the porch, grabbed his bag, and went in search of a shower. He found it, along with what appeared to be the only bedroom behind the kitchen. One bedroom, one bed. Convenient, he mused. The shower felt like bliss after all the mud that had been seeping into his shoes and slathered on his hands and legs. He leaned into the hot water and let it flow over his head and back. He stepped out of the shower moments later feeling refreshed. He wrapped a towel around his waist and walked into the kitchen.

"Okay, it's decision time." He strode up behind her.

She was sitting on a bar stool looking out the window. She jumped and whirled around. She opened her mouth but said nothing. She looked at the towel, then his chest, then his face. He grinned warmly. "Checking for welts again, Kathryn?"

"Something like that." Her face reddened. "What about decision time?"

"We can leave now and see if we can find a hotel on the way back down. It's tourist season so that might be dicey. Or we can stay here, get a little sleep, and head back to the glacier tour in the morning."

"Oh." She looked disappointed.

"Katy?" He put his hand on her arm. "What did you think I was going to say?"

"Uh, I didn't really know." Her face instantly clouded over and she looked up, exasperated. "Would you get some clothes on?"

"I've got a better idea." He watched her for a minute, letting the seconds tick away, not sure whether to say it. He knew he would. He'd thought about this all week. A week's worth of pent up lust goaded him on. He grabbed her wrist and placed her palm on his chest. "Let's make welts. Not the painful kind. The slow, wet, sexy, fun kind." That wasn't exactly how he meant to say it. It sounded a little stupid, but good enough. He circled his arms around her and pulled her against him. She felt warm against his bare chest. He planted his mouth on hers and tasted something sweet. Caramel. She'd found some candy somewhere and it tasted great on her. He licked the seam of her lips and they parted for him, welcoming him in.

"What happened to casual?" she whispered against him.

"You said not casual."

"I didn't mean it."

"Okay, but I'm not moving." He looked down. "You're overdressed." He leaned back against the kitchen counter and pulled her with him. "What's it gonna be, Katy? Your decision. Tell me what you want." He waited, glancing briefly at her clothes. Then as he stood there and let the silence grow, she pulled away. Extricated herself from his hold.

She walked out of the room and left him standing with his bare back against the cold counter. His mouth dropped as she left. He stood staring at the door for endless minutes.

"That's it then," he whispered under his breath, trying to contain his frustration. He turned and put his hands on the counter and looked down at them, wondering what to do next. God, how awkward. He thought over his words and wished he'd said it differently. No teasing. He'd always teased her and she got mad. He didn't mean to but it was his way of dealing with the desire. He'd done it for so long it was second nature. Hard to stop.

"How was the shower?" she asked from behind.

He turned slowly and sucked in his breath. She stood in the door, a towel wrapped around her. It covered her breasts and flowed down to barely cover her ass. Long, flawless legs stretched out below it like a Barbie doll's. Her slender, bare feet rested one on the other, showing bright red nail polish. She had one arm braced loosely against the door jam, the other was draped across her waist.

"Huh?" Was all he could think to say. He had always thought Kathryn incredibly thin and almost figureless. He remembered her that way. The woman in front of him had a towel resting on her breasts and there was no mistaking the amount of curvature based on the cleavage showing above it, and the curves underneath. She wasn't tom boyishly thin, she was definitely all grown up—and built. Unbelievably built. He'd felt it under her shirt but now that he could see it too, the visual was an incredible turn-on. He needed to touch her. The towel gaped on the side and the flesh of her hip showed from the opening. He blinked and swallowed painfully before speaking.

"Are you planning to take a shower?" he said hoarsely.

"I can if you want me to." She tiptoed those lean, perfect legs toward him until she was within inches of touching him. He clenched his hands tightly to the counter to steady himself and watched her. She trailed fingers up his abdomen, tugging gently on the hairs above the towel.

"Kathryn." He groaned. She moved fingers up his chest and grasped into him like she'd done before. That was it. That was when he knew he was out of his league. She was toying with him and he was powerless to stop her.

"Tommy. Let me ask you something. What do *you* want?" she asked.

She leaned her entire body against him, searing into him with the warmth of her flesh. All he could think to say was, "You."

Chapter Nineteen

"Kathryn, what the—" Thomas said softly in her ear. His hands cupped her backside and squeezed hard. She pulled back sharply.

"What's wrong?" She searched his face.

"You pierced your belly button."

She smiled. The towel around him had slipped down and the loop through her skin had caught in the hair below his navel and tugged, tying them to each other. She thought he'd already seen it, or at least felt it. Guess not. "Yeah, years ago. Sorry."

"No. Don't say that. I just never would have imagined it." One hand moved around her waist to fondle the spot where the loop was attached. "Shit, that's—hot." He played with it using his thumb, sending sparks through her.

She tried to conceal the smile. "I also have a tattoo," she whispered.

"Really? Where?" He grasped her arms and eased her away. She was still clutching the towel behind her. Her last vestige of modesty hit the floor with a *swish*. She moved her hand to her hip. "Here." She slid her fingers self-consciously along a hipbone. She watched his fingers trail across the tiny line of curling letters, then raised her eyes to his.

"What does it say?" he asked. His feather-light touch tickled.

"It's Latin for seize the—"

"Day?"

"Moment."

"Seize the moment," he reflected, then bent his head to her waist and trailed his lips across the tattoo. He moved to her navel and licked the metal there, then moved up her stomach, trailing kisses all the way to her collarbone. He laughed softly.

"What?" she asked.

"It's just that—you're so unexpectedly crazy sexy. No one would know about those, they're so understated. It's like you have this subtle wild side you don't want people to see. You don't want it to show but you have to have it."

"You like that?"

"Hell, yes. I like it a lot." He stood and hugged her to him, then buried his face in her neck. "What man wouldn't like it?"

She didn't answer. David had hated the piercing. She already had the tattoo when she met him, but had she waited, he probably would have talked her out of that too. To him it was sloppy. Trailer trash, he called it. His reaction to the piercing had surprised her. It was a major argument. A totally unexpected display of his controlling personality.

She smiled at Thomas. Not just because it didn't bother him—but it pleased her that he understood it. That he found it attractive.

"What about you, Thomas?" She peeked around his back. "Where's your wild side?"

He raised his palms above his head. "No tattoos or piercings. I earned my marks the old-fashioned way. Drunken brawls and too much partying in college."

"As I remember it, you were pretty partial to that even before college."

"Yeah. Until I nearly killed myself running my car off the road."

"Really?" she said. "I never heard about that."

"It was kept pretty quiet. I realized that type of thrill-seeking wasn't going to make me a better person."

"I didn't know you cared about being a better person."

He reared his head back and peered down at her through half-opened eyes. "Good point. Maybe you do know me pretty well. Even after all these years."

"No. I know what Sam's told me. And who you used to be."

His expression was impossible to read. A sad smile, maybe. He spoke softly, "It's funny but this week made me realize just how much I haven't changed. How much of that person I used to be still exists."

"Is that good or bad?"

He wandered a glance slowly down her silhouette, taking in every inch of skin. He stopped at the white wisp of cotton covering her crotch, the tiny remnant that was her only remaining adornment. He smiled as if amused that she would show him everything else. Yet, she was still self-conscious standing in front of him ninety-nine percent naked.

"A little of both." He hesitated. "Kathryn, no regrets right?"

"Sure. Perfectly casual."

"No, that's not what I meant." He took her face in his hands and bore into her eyes. "You're not going to regret this, are you?"

Kathryn shook her head and kissed him, then wrapped her right leg around his and raised it slowly up until her thigh was rubbing under his towel against the top of his knee. The towel around his waist loosened and she pressed into him, her stomach warmed from his skin. He muttered something low and sexy but she didn't understand. He moved his hands down to clamp over her butt and pull her up. He slid both hands under her thighs, lifted her and turned her around, setting her down on the counter.

"Oh," she blurted, surprised. "This counter."

He smiled. "It's cold."

He followed her glance toward the couch in the living room. His arms shifted to scoop her up and within seconds, he was lowering her onto the sofa cushions. He leaned down, shoving his thigh between her legs. He braced his body with both arms around her, holding his weight off. The towel that had been tied around his hips lay in a roll on the floor, totally forgotten. His shoulders rippled with tension. She ran her fingers over them, clutching into the hardness. This was the thing she discovered about Tommy—

he had muscles that flinched and rippled every time he moved. She wanted to touch all of them. Run her hand over them and feel them tighten around her. He didn't have them as a kid. If he did, she never noticed. She marveled at the feel.

Then he pressed against her, shifting to get comfortable, and heat jolted from her eyes to her toes. She slipped her arms further around him and pulled him to her, clinging as she reached her lips up to him. He came down to her, his mouth hungry on hers, his tongue plunging inside to grope the roof of her mouth and her tongue. She felt him shaking.

"You okay?" she murmured against his lips. He laughed softly, a raspy tickle in her ear.

"Yeah. You?" She nodded, then reached behind her. The couch was too narrow for them both. She yanked the cushion from behind her back and tossed it on the floor. He grabbed the other two and tossed them after it. She scooted backward to give him room. The cushions under them gave as he lowered down by her side and entwined his legs with hers.

"Much better," he whispered, kissing her again. He trailed his big hands along her shoulder, brushed against the outline of her breast, then descended to her hip and thigh. Kathryn was delirious, shivering with anticipation. When he slipped a hand from the outside of her thigh down to the small triangle of cotton, she let out an uncontrolled moan.

He hooked a finger under the elastic around her hip and pulled. "Off," he muttered.

"Huh...what?"

"Take it off, Katy. Help me."

She lifted her hip as he wiggled the fabric down the length of her legs. She watched the back of his head, his face shielded by the thick strands of hair that covered his expression. Then he slid fingers up her leg to her hip. He trailed tiny wet kisses along the way inching his lips along next to his hand. His fingertips flickered over the tattoo and delved straight to the part of her that had been hidden only seconds earlier under the cotton. He stroked her, sending a shiver through every inch of her body. She sucked in her breath with a hiss.

"Still cold?" he asked.

She tilted her head and arched toward him, enjoying the feel of him against her, pressing into her, rubbing.

"No. Hot." She panted. "Blazing. Hot." She watched as he moved his mouth up her rib cage, flicking more little kisses along her body until he reached her breast. She moaned as he sucked her skin into his mouth, instantly causing her to stiffen.

"Mmmm. You taste good," he murmured.

She ran her hand along his back, down the indention of his spine and further. Then she glazed her fingers across the exquisite length of his torso and down. He sucked in sharply and grabbed her wrist. He lay still.

"Give me a minute," he mumbled. He rolled off the couch and walked to the door.

"Where are you going?"

His back glistened as he leaned out the door, shuffled through his clothes on the porch, and reached for something. He held up a small foil packet briefly before returning. Oh. Of course.

"Where was I?" he whispered and wound his arms around her. He pulled her mouth to his as if he wanted to make sure she was comfortable.

"You were here. Right here." She smiled. Her fingers drug through his hair, tightening as she felt him pull away briefly.

"Yes, that's right."

Kathryn dragged him back to her and kissed his collar bone, then nipped at his ear. He captured her lips to his hungrily then grasped her hips tightly, holding her against him, and with a single slow movement pushed into her, filling her with heat. She sucked in air and let out a small involuntary cry. The sound startled him and he reared back, searching her eyes.

"No." She clutched him against her and hooked her toes around his thighs. "It's okay. Don't stop."

She dug fingers into his flesh and he brushed the hair from her face. Kate could see his need but he stayed still. So she ground her hips against him, watching his eyes close as he rocked forward. She heard his breath catch and raggedly exhale. She moved again and he moved with her. His heart pounded against her breasts. Or maybe that was hers pounding. They rocked together building a rhythm that increased quickly like water flooding a dam. Her legs started trembling and then as she fought to hold it off, her entire body racked with the heat of their friction. Tommy shouted her name through clenched teeth as he planted his head against her shoulder and lunged a final time before collapsing next to her. She clung to him, gasping for air, the pulse below his jaw pounded against her temple.

When the tenseness in his neck subsided, he buried his face in her hair, his breath hot and steaming against her neck. Kathryn's own pulse was exploding as she held him tightly, clutching into his skin. She let her hands relax and lightened the stroke of her fingers as she soaked in the reality of what just happened.

She just had sex with Thomas Ryan. Really great, fast, super-hot sex. And while it should have just been casual and something she would leave behind, she knew it wasn't. His touch had branded her permanently. The more he continued to stroke her skin, the deeper she felt it. She had to be careful. She needed to temper the reality with heavy doses of common sense. It was just casual. No strings attached. They lay still for long minutes before he propped himself up on an elbow.

"Kathryn, be honest." He spoke softly when his breathing had slowed. He surveyed her face for reaction. "Did I hurt you?"

"What? No! I just..." *Wasn't expecting the rush of emotion that went with it.*

"Just?"

"I don't know. I was expecting things to go a little slower," she admitted, not registering the hurt in his eyes.

"Slower," he repeated. "Jesus. I've known you since you were twelve. How much slower can it get?"

She frowned. He hadn't even looked at her until this week. All those years that went before were non-existent to him. This was just a few days. A few days where he actually knew she was there and noticed her. She wanted to wallow in the feeling—having him notice her and want her.

"High school doesn't count. You were too busy chasing the cheerleaders to know I was alive."

"No I wasn't. I noticed you—don't think I didn't. How the hell could I have not? Look at you," he muttered as he rubbed his big hand down her back, sending spirals of heat through her shoulders and down her spine.

"Sure you did."

"Kathryn. Why do you think Sam told you all those stories?"

"What stories?"

"The ones about me. The ones about toga parties and tattoos. The ones where he made sure you knew what a sorry guy I was."

"He didn't say that. He thought you were great. He wanted to be you."

"You don't get it. I didn't either...until now. He wanted me to stop wanting you," he said calmly. Out of the blue.

"You never even knew I existed then."

"Yeah. I was trying to behave myself...and you were a brat."

"I was not."

"Kathryn. I think we need to talk..."

She didn't let him finish. She held up her hand to silence him, touching her fingers to his lips. "*I* think we need to try again," she said softly. "Maybe a little slower."

She didn't care about the distant past. She wanted to go back to the recent place where the stroking stopped and he took control. She wanted to start there and be able to keep her brain functional while they melded together.

Silence. "I don't know that I can go slow anymore," he admitted.

"No?"

"Kathryn, I'm twenty-eight years old. We've known each other for sixteen years. If I had known we were like...that, I wouldn't have—Are you telling me that not once during all this time you never thought about this?"

"You mean sex with you?" For a second, she thought he was talking about something else. She shook that thought out of her head. She stroked his chest nervously, concentrating on the spot her fingers touched. *Sure, I thought about it. Several times. But you were always chasing someone else.*

He clutched her shoulder. "What else would I mean?" He smelled of soap and she mashed her nose against him, inhaling the clean scent. She could smell this again and again and never grow tired of it. Without hesitation, she lightly kissed his throat. He put a finger under her chin and tipped her face to meet his, boring into her eyes. "How slow? You're gonna have to show me."

Kathryn pressed her lips to his and eased her hips over him. She proceeded to show him what he'd wanted to know and to her surprise—it was even better, more passionate than before. The ecstasy was overwhelming and brought tears to her eyes. She clenched her eyes to quell them from flowing down her cheeks. Afterward, they laid on the couch until the room darkened completely, legs and arms wrapped around each other loosely.

A reverent silence grew between them. Thomas eventually rubbed his eyes solemnly. His heartbeat thudded against Kathryn's ear as his chest rose and fell. He pushed against her with his shoulder. "Hey?" he breathed into her hair.

"Yeah?"

"I like slow. A lot," he whispered.

A smile crossed her lips as she nodded off to sleep encased in the blanket of his arms.

Chapter Twenty

Eric touched down in Seattle just after the noon hour. He had time to kill before Emily's performance so he decided to do a little shopping. His life was finally turning around. Maybe it could be normal after all. A quick text message to Smitty recommended a couple of spots to meet up, just in case. He wouldn't wait long though. He could sit for hours watching someone but when there was a meeting that needed to happen, he limited his wait time to around fifteen to thirty minutes, at most. If someone didn't show in that time, they probably weren't intending to at all. Waiting was exposure. He didn't like being exposed.

He picked up his rental car, a nondescript, small tan sedan. It was amusing that they call something like that a mid-size car. A few years ago, it was deemed compact. His ass barely fit in the seat and he wasn't really a big guy. Still, it was a ride and he only needed it for a couple days.

He drove through the tourist area and past the wharf. On a whim, he whipped the car in. He'd pick up gifts somewhere along here. One for Emily. One for Brenda. Eric smiled. Yeah, a gift for Brenda—she'd like that. He couldn't remember when he had purchased a gift anywhere but in an airport. The last gift he'd bought for a woman was his ex-wife.

A gift for Brenda. Yes. The thought was exciting. Emily was easy—a pre-teen of her age liked almost everything. Within minutes, he'd managed to get and gift wrap a nice vest and scarf. The kind he'd seen some of her friends wear—and all the models wore in pictures.

Brenda was more challenging. What do you buy someone who owned a bar, had a pretty healthy sexual appetite—and—

well, that was all he knew. Wait, she had a good sense of humor, too. That would be notable. Maybe something simply nice and humorous? His concentration was on ideas for gifts as he walked down the street, hands in pockets. He cast periodic glances at the pedestrians. The streets were almost empty with only a casual tourist or shopper every few blocks. A family of four filled the sidewalk ahead of him. Two women across the street, obviously out for a girl's day...and a couple checking out the jewelry stores behind him. No shocker what they were looking for by the way they groped each other. He lifted his lips briefly, remembering that time with his ex. The time before, when he thought he might be able to make a career change. His expression dropped as his thoughts came back to Brenda. There was no permanency with her, he knew that. Just sex, but that was enough for now. Still, she was nice and deserved a gift. If his guess was accurate, she probably didn't get many.

The window of the store next to him glittered with a myriad of crystal and color. A household décor type place would surely have something that would work nicely. Something pretty but not too personal. Maybe a little personal—how do you say "intimate but not permanent" in a gift? A woman dressed smartly in a brown top and tan slacks approached, smiling. She placed a vase filled with sparkling balls of glass and mirror tiles on a table. "May I help you?"

"I'm trying to find a gift for a friend." He darted a glance around the store, then wandered in the opposite direction of the brown-clad lady.

"I'm sure we have something that will work." The woman was persistent. "Tell me about the person and I can give you some ideas."

He was a little startled at the request. He had intended to just shrug her off, but he found her tactic interesting. Rather than asking what he looked for, she asked about the recipient of the gift. So, he described Brenda as best he could and let the woman lead him through the store. She pointed at various pieces that might interest him. He found her voice and smile pleasant. After a trek completely around, he traipsed back to a table and selected a nice crystal box. Elegant but simple and she could use it to hold jewelry—or whatever else she chose. Perfect.

The door jangled as he opened it to step back into the street, a pleasant tinkle that celebrated a successful endeavor. He glanced at his watch. Perfect timing. He slipped into the bookstore on the corner, went to the back and selected the appropriate book, then proceeded to find a nice chair to plop into while he waited.

"That's a good read," Smitty's voice stated. "My son recommended it to me a while back. The ending was a little less than I hoped but still kept you involved right to the finish."

"I haven't read very far so I will have to see," he answered.

"You might take a look at this one also." Smitty passed a hard cover edition to him. "Similar style but the author is relatively new so not many have heard of her yet."

"Thanks. I'll do that." Eric set the book in his lap and glanced lazily around. There were several people in the store around them. None of whom seemed the least interested in the two men discussing books. A woman passed, heading toward the craft section. She smiled as she passed but clearly wasn't interested in their conversation.

"I believe you'll find what you like there." Smitty started around the aisle of books as he gave a nod and wave. "Nice talking to you."

"Wait." Eric looked at him puzzled. Wasn't the guy going to sit down and discuss the project? Why was he so evasive? Then Eric saw the craft book woman circle the aisle behind him, appearing deeply interested in the books on the other side of the shelf. Smitty did not so much as shake his head, but the gesture wasn't necessary.

Eric stood. "I seem to have dropped my pen out of my pocket. Do you see one anywhere on the floor there?" He pointed at the carpet.

"No, sorry."

Eric frowned and headed to the front of the store with the two books. At the counter, while he dug for his wallet, he glanced around again. No one. Yet, Smitty was definitely shadowed by at least one person. He waited outside briefly, then stepped into a building across the street and watched the woman leave with a young man attached to her arm. Smitty preceded them by only seconds. It was two. Definitely two. He glanced at his watch once more. He was going to be late for the play.

Two hours later, he sat in the very last seat by the door as Emily made her entrance onto the stage. She was glittering. Literally. They had poured makeup and glitter all over her and the lights over the stage made it sparkle like crystal. He remembered when she was little how much she liked to dress up as a princess and dance around the living room in her socked feet. They had given her one of the Disney costumes for Christmas; it came with a makeup kit. The glitter got everywhere. He left for a job once and realized he had a streak of glitter down his cheek and across his neck. Remnants of a good-bye hug to Daddy. He missed those times. He hoped he'd get a chance to hug the glitter off her cheek after the performance. That would assume he'd get the chance to talk with her.

She knew her lines well—didn't miss a cue. She bobbled a step once as she crossed the stage to pat one of the other kids on the head, but quickly righted herself and continued. He had made the curtain call for the play but just by seconds. The lights had already gone down and the curtain lifted on the first act as he sat. Yet, she knew he was there. She couldn't see him, but he'd never missed a performance—and had no intention of doing so. Once in a while, her eyes searched blindly in the audience and he hoped it was for a glimpse of him. He waved just in case, but she just kept going. No acknowledgment.

His wife was on the third row, center stage, surrounded by other parents. He narrowed his eyes and surveyed the man sitting next to her. A new face. Almost as soon as the curtains went up, it seemed they were going down again to signal the break. He stood and stretched his legs.

"Glad you made it, Eric." His ex's eyes were cold as she reached out a hand. "Emily will be so happy you're here." *But you're not happy, are you, Laura?* he thought as he took her hand and gave her a quick peck on the cheek.

"You know I wouldn't miss it," he chided and let her hand drop. The man with Laura shuffled and cleared his throat.

"This is my friend, Robert." Laura hooked a hand into the man's arm and drew him forward as she held out the other hand in a gesture toward Eric. "Eric." She introduced.

"A pleasure," the man said. "I've heard so much about you."

"I'll bet," Eric said wryly.

The three stood trying to think up something to say, before Laura finally saw a face outside the doors and spoke, "Oh, there's Aubrey's parents. Let's go say hi." She drew Robert away from the awkward silence.

Eric sighed and dropped back in his seat until the lights dimmed, signaling the second act. In no time, the play ended and he waited outside in the lobby with the intention of stealing a few minutes with his daughter before she was whisked away by her friends. As she exited the back stage door and headed down a side hallway toward him, he noticed how much taller she had grown since he last saw her. Sadness engulfed him as he realized that he had missed so much. The growth spurts. The friendships gained and lost. The last-minute studying for tests. The gossip and drama. Still, when she saw him, her face lit up—even more so with the mounds of glitter still caked on her eyes and cheeks. She smiled broadly and squealed as she ran to his open arms. "Daddy!"

He beamed. "You were fantastic, honey." He pulled her up and held her off the ground as he hugged her tightly against him.

"Oh, did you see me mess up? I nearly tripped." She laughed slightly. Perspiration dotted her forehead, then seeped into glittering rolls of water down her temples. He dotted them with his thumb and smiled.

"No one noticed. And you didn't miss a line. It was perfect."

"Thanks so much! I'm so glad you're here." She dropped to her feet, beaming at him. "I want you to meet my friends."

With that, she pulled his hand and threaded through the crowd. He followed behind, thankful for the moment. She introduced her friends and he chatted with them happily until everyone dispersed to go home or out to eat. The time went so quickly. Within minutes, she was waving and laughing as she ran off to join her group for pizza. And he strode out the door toward his rental car, his hands shoved calmly in his pockets. He looked down at his glitter-covered shirt with a sad smile on his face. Another normal moment had passed. Slipped right through his fingertips.

Forty-odd minutes later, he sat in his car under a streetlight, glancing at the small memory card he'd cut from the binding of the book he'd purchased. He leaned back and pulled his laptop from his backpack and slipped the card in to read it. It took a few seconds to type in the decryption codes, then he went through the information. He committed it to memory, then as he passed over a small bridge a few minutes later, he tossed the card into the water. Things would be busy now.

The sound of his phone going off pulled him to attention. He looked at the number and frowned. It wasn't Smitty and no one else had the number. He let it go to voicemail. It had to be a mistake. No one ever called; he didn't give out the number. When he'd finished a shower at the hotel later, he checked the message. He stubbed his toe on the dresser when he heard Brenda's voice.

Chapter Twenty-One

Thomas woke at seven in the morning. The muscle in his arm pulsated and tingled under Kathryn's weight. He considered waking her and going for another round. Her chest was mashed against his rib; he could feel the soft, steady rhythm of her breathing. He slowly eased off the couch, then covered her with a throw they had shoved off with the cushions. Lustful amusement crossed over him as he glanced around at the cushions scattered on the carpet. Slow. Fast. Everything in between. It really didn't matter—whatever she wanted had excited him. It was all good. Better than good. Fantastic. He pattered to the bathroom and put on his briefs. Moments later, he heard a soft splat, splat, splat of footsteps near the door and looked up to see her watching him.

"Good morning." He smiled at her. His towel from the floor was draped around the curves that he'd recently kissed his way over. "We'd better get moving if we're going to make the tour at nine," he reminded.

"In a hurry, Thomas?" she asked. Lines of a frown surfaced on her face.

"No, but we had a plan. I thought you wanted to see the glaciers. Besides, wouldn't it be awkward if the homeowner showed up right now?"

"Yeah." She hesitated. "I'll shower and get dressed." She pranced away to gather her things then disappeared into the bathroom.

Something about the way she moved made him want to follow. It was stupid, he knew. He remembered the urge as a kid and he thought it was a crazy, hormonal thing. At the time, he had expected to grow out of it with age. Obviously not. He wanted to follow her then—and now. He hadn't really grown up much.

He shrugged it off and opened the fridge. He glanced around to see what they might do for breakfast. A container of eggs. Good. He reached for it. A carton of milk against the wall propped up a brown paper envelope. What kind of an idiot puts a manila folder in the fridge? The person leaves the place easily accessible, keys everywhere. Obviously a bit on the demented side if he's leaving paperwork in places like this.

Thomas slid the folder out from beside the carton of milk and opened it. Lots of papers inside along with a number of USB drives, each with labels containing numbers. He eased the papers from their encasement and realized they were copies of legal documents. Contracts. With numbers that corresponded to the USB drives. With names and large dollar amounts. Big names, some of which he recognized. Words that made it evident the contracts were for actions these people did not want known. Yet it was documented.

Oh shit. Thomas panicked. First Rule of Law according to Thomas: if it looks wrong, it probably *IS* wrong. A folder in the fridge doesn't belong. Leave it in the fridge. Unless it's yours, of course.

They needed to leave. Fast. Whatever this was about, these faces and names weren't meant to be seen by anyone. They were insurance for whoever put them there. The kind of insurance that keeps someone alive. Or dead. Knowing what was on these decreased their chances of leaving safely by half, *if* the owner came back.

Thomas rushed to the bathroom, leaned in and blurted, "We're leaving in ten minutes. Get dressed. Don't waste any time."

"What! Why? What's the rush?" Her voice kicked up a notch and came out shrill.

"We need to go. I have a phone call to make ASAP and I can't get a signal," he lied. No need to tell her. Then he thought about it and realized the best way to protect them really *WAS* to make sure he knew what he was dealing with. If the person thought he'd seen them, they were at risk. If the person knew they'd seen them and had copies, they'd have insurance too. Insurance was critical.

"Okay, you have twenty minutes. Move it."

He went to his bag for clean clothes and dressed in seconds. He stuffed everything he had, even the muddies, into his bag and dropped it by the door. Then, went back to the kitchen. He pulled out each of the eight documents and set them on the counter, then used his phone camera to photograph the pages, working quickly, not checking to make sure they were readable. No time to delay. When the docs were copied, he shoved them back into the envelope and headed for the door. Grabbing his bag on the way out, he threw it in the Jeep and grabbed his backpack. He yanked his laptop out and ran inside, nearly running over Katy as she came out of the bathroom.

"Oops!" He smiled. "I just need to write up something while you dress, so I can send it as soon as we get in where there's a signal."

Kathryn frowned and looked at his computer. "So, that's the rush? Big legal deal going on and you can't wait to get back to work? I didn't mean to keep you tied up."

"It's not that. I just need to take care of this before noon." Another lie. Can't tell her—she'll freak. Besides the less she knows, the safer it is for her. He spat over his shoulder, "You're not one of those women that takes hours to get ready to go, are you?" He had his laptop on the counter and plugged in the first USB and started a copy to a folder.

"I'll be ready when I'm ready, Tommy." She was pissed. The edgy sarcasm gave it away.

He continued to copy each drive to his laptop, then dropped them back in the envelope and returned the package to its home in the fridge. It took him about fifteen minutes to get them all. He walked the cabin to make sure they'd picked up everything and returned the space back to its original state. All good. Ready to go.

"Katy?" He looked for her. She wasn't in any of the spaces he checked. He walked out to the porch and called her.

"Here!" She leaned her hand out of the Jeep and waved. So much for waiting on her.

He walked to the car and jumped in, then a thought came to him. "Did you return the key to where you found it?"

"Oh, no—I forgot. I'll get it." She jumped out and went inside. He waited for what seemed like forever, before she returned. She moved across the porch, returned the key, then came back to him and they were off. Thank God.

As Thomas descended the mountain, he thought about the data. He had glanced briefly at the USB copies. They were pictures with copies of some emails and other documents. When he put a safe distance between them and the cabin, he'd try to send them off. He knew who to call. Always good to have a contact in the FBI. He hadn't talked to him in a few years, but the man would know what to do. He'd turn it all over to his friend, Trevan.

Thomas looked at his watch when they finally hit pavement again. Excellent. They could still make the glacier tour if she wanted. His common sense told him it wasn't a good idea, but he ignored it. They hadn't left anything behind. Once he'd sent everything to Trevan, there was nothing more to do and they could relax. Still, there was something about the fact that they had been in that house in a most intimate way that scared him. Not because he'd been with Katy. Shit, that was great. Memorable. But that he'd been in the home of someone that was very obviously linked to some pretty heinous crimes.

Katy was fuming next to him, silently pouting as if he'd hit her.

"What's up, Katy?"

"Nothing," she grunted. She leaned back in her seat and closed the crystal blue eyes that had startled him on Monday.

"You're lying."

"Am I now. Why would you think that?" Her lips moved but the rest of her remained motionless.

"Because you've barely spoken to me since we left. Actually, you've barely spoken to me since we put our clothes on. What's wrong?"

"Wrong? What kind of a question is that?" She shifted up and turned toward him. "There's not a thing wrong with me, Thomas. And you know it."

"Then, why are you being so quiet?"

"Because I—" she started, then stopped. She watched him for a second and he turned to see why she hesitated. Her eyes were wet. She was damn near crying.

He slammed on the brakes and stopped the car, pulling only slightly to the side of the road so they wouldn't repeat the mistake of the night before. He turned the key in the ignition to quell the engine and moved in his seat to face her. The sound of birds above them filled the silence along with the rustling of leaves in the wind.

"Because you what? Katy, I can't read your mind."

She waved him off. "It's fine. I just want to leave. I'm ready to get back home. This has been a long week and I guess I just need a semblance of normalcy again. You think you could just drop me at the airport? I'll see if I can get an earlier flight."

"What? Why? You're joking right?" He panicked. He wasn't ready to let her go yet.

"No, I'm not joking. Seriously, it's been great. Really. I just want to get home."

"So, that's it then? We just spent a few hours together naked and you're ready to ditch me and get back to your real life. Is that it? Wow. You *have* changed. I would never have thought you to be that kind of person. I thought you'd at least stay through breakfast. And you talked about me."

He leaned a hand out and thrust his fingers into her hair but she yanked her head back as soon as he tried to pull her toward him.

He swore her lip quivered as she spoke. "Let's don't pretend this is anything more than it is, Thomas." Still, the water puddled in her lower lids and he watched her bite her lip then turn away.

"What the hell is that supposed to mean? You can spend the night with someone like that and then just bail out without even thinking twice?" He was pissed. She couldn't wait to get away. She was done with him. He had no idea why that would make her cry. Maybe she felt guilty about it, who knows. But she wanted away—far away. And for the life of him, he couldn't understand why it bothered him so much. Normally, he was just as anxious to leave himself.

"It's not like that."

"Then what the hell is it like?"

"Let's don't draw it out, okay? You aren't interested in sticking around. And neither am I, really. Your home is five hours away from mine. The distance alone makes the possibility of continuing to see each other low. It's just easier to go ahead and get that part over with, so it's not awkward. You're quite comfortable with short relationships so that shouldn't be a problem. I know you, remember?"

"No, Kathryn. You don't know shit about me. And I, obviously, know a lot less than I thought I did about you," he snapped, then twisted the key in the ignition and jolted the car back onto the road, slamming on the gas. He wanted to punch his fist into the dashboard but he squared his shoulders and clamped his teeth together. She wasn't getting off that easy. She could dump him when he was ready for it. But not that fast. "As I told you earlier, I have something I have to do for work—and I'm going to do it as soon as we get down to the tour. If I can get a signal. Then we're doing the glacier tour like we planned. If that bothers you, you can just sit in the damn Jeep for all I care."

"Why are you acting like that? I'm trying to make this easy for you."

"Is that right? Maybe I don't want it easy." Thomas spoke with sarcasm. *And I'm not going to make it that easy for you.*

He slid the vehicle into the lot at the glacier tour office and cut the engine. "I need about fifteen minutes to take care of this." He pulled his laptop from the backpack that he had wedged behind her seat and set it in his lap, then lifted a hip and reached in his back pocket. "If you want to take the tour, here's my wallet— would you mind getting us tickets?" He forced a smile.

"You really want to?" She looked surprised.

"Yes." He tried to control his tone, not to show his frustration. "It was my idea to begin with. But if you're really in that big of a hurry to get home, we can skip it. Wait. No, sorry. I probably won't ever get the chance again. You're just gonna have to humor me on this. Go get the tickets. Please." He tossed his wallet in her lap and stepped out of the Jeep with his laptop. Once he'd set it on the hood and opened it, he tried to get a connection with his wireless card. The signal was weak but there. He slid his finger across the screen of his phone, and dialed Trevan. He hadn't spoken to him in two years so he wasn't sure if the number was still good. He looked at the sky for a second and snapped his legs back and forth nervously waiting for the call to go through. When the voice on the other side answered, he couldn't help but let out a sigh, "Thank God. I thought you'd never pick up."

"Thomas?"

"That's me. How's it going, man?" He watched Kathryn walk into the office, then turned away.

"I'm doing great. I haven't talked to you in forever. I'm glad you called! What's up?"

Thomas didn't waste time because he didn't know if he'd lose the signal or not. "I need your help. I'm going to send you something. I need you to look at it and tell me what to do. I found it in a cabin Katy and I spent the night at last night."

"Who's Katy?"

"This isn't about her, man. This stuff I'm going to send you scared the shit out of me. I think we stumbled onto something pretty serious. Tell me what you think."

"Okay. No problem. Send it on. Zip and encrypt it though. It won't get through if you don't."

"Hey, I heard you were getting married. Tell me it isn't true," he teased.

The voice on the other end laughed. "Yeah. It's true. You'll have to meet her. We'll send you an invite if you give me your address."

"Sounds good. Look, I'm sending this right now. I'm in Alaska and getting ready to go on a glacier cruise so I've gotta go. Can you call me back in about two hours if there's anything we need to do?"

"Sure."

"Great. Talk to you later. Sorry I have to cut it short but the signal here is crap and I want to make sure I get this sent before we lose it."

"No problem. We'll talk later. Bye, Thomas."

"Bye, Trev."

He zipped, compressed, and encrypted the files then attached them to the email and hit the send button. He watched the screen patiently as the bar trailed across.

Chapter Twenty-Two

The counter had a line of five people. She eased forward as the next person in line received tickets and moved away. Kathryn opened the wallet he had pitched at her and pulled out a couple of bills to pay for the tickets. The leather of the wallet was worn and smooth on the edges. There were credit cards in the sleeves on the side and a few business cards. She tried not to snoop but her curiosity got the best of her. Worn edges of pictures hung out of the side where the bills had come from. They'd been in his pocket long enough to get completely frayed and tattered...until they felt more like a piece of cotton than a photo. She slipped out the top one, just far enough to get a peek—his parents. They looked older in the photo but she recognized them. She raised the photo with one finger and glanced at the one behind it. The top corner showed light glittering on water—she slipped it out further. The top of two heads showed. She realized the photo was folded in half and pulled it completely out of the wallet.

Kathryn stepped forward in the line as another person successfully completed the purchase, then glanced around for Thomas. She saw him through the window, standing over his laptop on the hood of the Jeep, his concentration on the work in front of him. She lifted the photo and stopped; her feet were cemented to the floor. She was holding a picture of Tommy and a girl in a blue and pink bikini with a T-shirt over it. He had his shirt off and was tanned—a teenager that had summered at the lake. His arm was resting on the girl's shoulder and he was laughing at the camera. Kathryn was the girl in the T-shirt. The girl with her arm on his waist, laughing back at him—smiling at him—not the camera. Her other arm was extended in the opposite direction. The crease in the photo cut off the rest. Kathryn unfolded the photo and saw Sam standing next to her holding a fishing pole in his other hand and smiling.

The photograph had to be more than ten years old. Why had he kept it all this time? She frowned down at the picture in her hand.

"Miss, are you ready?" A pleasant voice summoned her and she looked up to see the gray-haired lady behind the counter motioning her forward.

"Oh yes. Sorry!" She stuffed the picture back into the wallet and supplied the cash. Tickets in hand, she headed back out the door, her thoughts clouded over in confusion.

"Two tickets for the nine a.m. tour." She slapped the wallet and tickets on the hood next to his laptop.

"Great!" He flashed a grin at her. "Thanks! I just finished sending it off so I think we're all set to go now. We have about twenty minutes. What's inside to see?"

"I don't know. I didn't look around," she admitted.

"Well then, let's go look." He slid the laptop into his backpack, dropped it behind the seat, closed up the Jeep, and grabbed her hand. He led her toward the ticket office. He didn't even give her a chance to respond. He adjusted shoulders with determination as he strode in front of her. His fingers were pressing so tightly against hers that she couldn't pull them back. The sadness she had felt earlier returned as she recognized that within the day, he'd be gone and this would be over. She would return to Houston and her normal life. He'd be back in Dallas and their week would be just another memory.

How do you give up something you didn't really get a chance to hold on to? She watched him move and knew she'd done a lot of that over the week. It was hard not to. Tommy had always been nice looking. The picture he'd kept reminded her of times he'd been around Sam. He had teased her mercilessly—even more than Sam did. She thought him a terror when she was sixteen. The summer of that year had changed things, though. He had talked to her more, and teased less. He had often dropped by the house to see Sam and then spent hours in the kitchen talking to Kathryn and her friends. Her friends all had crushes on the skinny blond hunk. As she remembered, it angered her that he spent so much time flirting with them, rather than hanging out with Sam.

Then, after his senior year started, he was once again involved in school and she didn't see him much. He stopped in for a few minutes once in a while, but he didn't talk with her. He wasn't interested.

She'd seen him only a few times since she graduated. Each time, he was pleasant—charming. The last time was before her parents' party.

"Thomas, why did you come to the training this week?" she blurted.

He held the door for her to enter, his fingers still entwined with hers. His steely glance darted to her face. "My boss signed me up for it a few weeks ago. Why do you ask?"

"It just seems odd they'd send an attorney. You probably know the law of management backward and forward—and that's the most important part, isn't it? Who *is* your boss, anyway?" She tried to match his gaze but couldn't. It made her uncomfortable to stare into those eyes, knowing that they'd been so intently focused on every inch of her less than twenty-four hours ago. She looked down at her shoes.

"I wondered that myself at first. It didn't make sense." He flashed one of his sexy smiles. "But now, I'm fairly sure my dad insisted on it."

"Why?"

He was right. That didn't make sense. His dad was a serious man. Always intently focused on business. He had little patience for the "touchy, feely aspect" of this type of training. She had overheard him at one of the board meetings as he espoused his view of the money wasted on such expenses. He felt that management was common sense and good managers have it. If they didn't, they shouldn't manage. You couldn't train them to be the right kind of leader.

Thomas laughed. "You'll have to figure that out on your own, Katy. I can't explain it. Who knows why he does what he does, but my dad always had a weird way of making things right." He leaned his head down against her ear. "God, you smell good."

Thirty minutes later, Kathryn remained in a dreamy fog as she let him guide her onto the tour boat and subsequently followed him around as they listened to the guided tour and surveyed the scenery. Just before they boarded, Thomas had left her briefly to purchase two hot cocoas. As Kathryn stood on the upper deck of the cruise boat with her fingers grasping the warm cocoa, she realized she wanted desperately to hold onto this week. Every second of it. Store it away in her mind so that when they went back home, she'd have it permanently.

"Would you mind taking a picture for us?" An elderly lady with a purple felt cap stretched out a camera toward her with questioning eyes.

"Of course!" She smiled.

The woman returned to her husband and they wrapped their arms around each other and smiled toward the lens. Kathryn zoomed in a little to get their faces along with the beautiful background of the glacier-draped mountain, then pressed the button. "There you go."

"Thanks so much! Would you like us to take one of you two also?" The lady offered. "What a handsome couple you are."

"She's the prettiest girl on the boat." Thomas grinned as he pushed a disposable camera he'd purchased in the gift shop toward them. "I'm just the lucky guy that happens to be with her."

The woman laughed. "Well, give us a big smile, lucky guy."

"You bet." Tommy pulled Kathryn in front of him and wrapped both arms firmly around her, holding her against his chest. He then leaned his head down and rubbed his cheek against hers, and smiled.

Kathryn started to pull her face away, but he tugged gently and begged, "Come on, Katy—smile for the camera." So she did. She put her hands on the arms that had her captured against him and let the warmth show.

"Perfect." The lady handed the camera back to him. "I can see you guys are very happy together. Maybe someday, you'll make it to thirty-five, just like us." She motioned to her husband and left before they could respond.

"Boy, did she have the wrong impression," Kathryn pronounced.

"Did she? I don't know about you but I'm a pretty happy guy. I just had hot sex with the prettiest girl on the boat. If they only knew, they'd all be jealous."

She jabbed a bony elbow back into his gut, and he loosened his grip on her as she growled, "Stop gloating. It wasn't that hot."

"It wasn't? Shit, Katy—you looked pretty damned happy yourself at the time, so don't try to ruin my mood." He had his forehead against hers, looking into her eyes somberly.

"Okay. It was."

"Was what?" he prodded.

Was he really going to make her say it? Right here, in the middle of a crowd, on a boat tour? Yes, apparently he was. She sighed heavily.

"It was great, okay. It was awesome. Fantastic. Best sex I've had in years. There, is that what you wanted to hear, Mr. Ego?" Someone behind her tittered and she realized she had said it louder than intended. Loud enough for a few of the people around them to hear. She dropped her head in embarrassment.

Tommy pulled her against his chest, his hand forcing her head into his shirt, and hugged her tightly. "Yes. That's exactly what I wanted to hear. But I didn't really care if they heard it too," he teased. "My ego isn't that big." He leaned down and whispered into her ear, "So, why are you in such a hurry to ditch me?"

Chapter Twenty-Three

"Okay, first of all, I'm not trying to ditch you. I just want to get home. Second, let's be realistic. We don't even live in the same city. Third, I'm not so stupid as to believe this is going anywhere. And there's a fourth."

"Really? I thought great prophesies only came in threes." He smirked as he let her pull away from him. "Come on, Katy, enlighten me. What's the fourth thing I need to know about that's wrong with us—or with me?"

"When you're done, you run. And unless, I'm mistaken, we're done now. Which would explain your rush to go earlier." She leaned toward him and whispered it into the air, apparently not wanting another announcement.

"Is that right? Done with what? And exactly where am I going to run to?" he asked, amused. So, she really thought he wanted away. Maybe he did, he didn't know. He'd never really thought about it. Sure that would be easy. Only problem was, they were in Alaska, on a boat. And there was a slight possibility they might be in danger. Did he want to run? No, that wasn't it. He wanted his hands under her shirt again and his mouth on her body. He wished they were still at that damn cabin, even if it was dangerous.

Thomas let out a groan, threaded his hands into his hair and pulled hard. "You drive me nuts, Katy," he spat, then turned and walked to the other side of the deck.

The air in Alaska was crisp. He imagined that it remained so regardless of the season. That was one of the things that was noticeable right away. The sun might be shining and the temperature fairly high, but the air still had a chill to it that was a subtle reminder of the winter harshness waiting in the future. He pushed his hands into his pockets and hunched his shoulders while listening to the guide orate about the glacier in front of them. The sun shone on the ice, making the blue center even more arresting. The history and science the man explained was definitely captivating. He hadn't paid much attention to it when he was with Kathryn. No surprise there. His focus always gravitated her way when she was around. She pretty much had done that to him for years. Thinking back, he realized that in some ways it pissed him off.

If he'd been smart, he would have ignored everyone's insistence and just asked her out then. Maybe they'd have dated a while then one of them would have lost interest and moved on. He wouldn't be standing here over a decade later wondering what might have happened. He wouldn't be trying to squash the most ridiculous desire-driven need to constantly touch. He'd ruined it now. He should have left her alone. They'd never be able to talk to each other normally again.

A casual glance at the old couple gave him a slight change in perspective. The man had his arm around the woman and was talking softly to her. She was pointing at the ice and commenting, then she turned and smiled. There was warmth there. A laugh. The old man answered with another laugh. The boat hit a rough spot and spray flashed up and splattered them, rousing up more laughter. Thomas smiled. That's how it should be. Sharing adventures, life, and laughing it off when you get splattered in the face.

"They look happy, don't they?" He heard Kathryn's voice next to him.

"Yeah, it's kind of cute, don't you think?" he admitted. "I bet they fight like cats and dogs too, but I like it that they can laugh together and spend time out like this. A lot of couples grow apart when they get older and barely do anything together. Those guys look like they still really enjoy each other, still feel 'the spark'. Your mom and dad are kind of like that, aren't they? Good sense of humor. Still like each other. You know what I mean?"

"I always thought yours were too."

"No. Not like that. They used to be. Then Dad became so serious about work that it was hard to get him to even see my mother—or any of us for that matter. They never did anything together. That's why I was always at your house. They were fighting most of the time I was in high school."

"And now? How are they now?" Her eyes were fixated on the mountains, searching the trees.

"They're fine. Actually, I'd say pretty good. He takes her out for an occasional dinner date, they go on trips. Dad smiles once in a while. I've always wondered what happened back then that made them so angry all the time. I thought maybe it was me."

"That's ridiculous. How could you be responsible?"

"I got in a lot of trouble. A lot more than you know. My dad was angry at me for a long time. We could hardly speak without fighting. It wasn't until I was about ready to graduate from college that he got over it."

"Look at everything you've achieved since then. You're a lawyer. He has to be proud of that. You and your parents are okay now, right? You guys talk?" She slid her gaze from the mountains to him. He could feel her staring at him.

"To Mom, yes—every weekend. To Dad—not that much. I've never really forgiven some of the things he's said—or done."

"You never seemed like the type to hold a grudge, Tommy."

He shrugged and turned to her. "And you never seemed like the type for a one-night stand." He watched as her mouth dropped open and her eyes flashed with anger. "I'm just kidding!" He held up his hands as she balled her fingers into fists and started to lunge at him.

"Tommy Ryan, I can't believe you said that! That's just ugly. I've never—" He couldn't help but laugh as she sputtered angrily.

"Never what? Never had a fling?"

"Never wanted to punch someone as much as I do right now."

"Would that make you feel better? Make it easier to run away as soon as you can? Come on, Katy. You know I'm just joking around."

"Are you? Look, Tommy. I liked it better when we could talk without it automatically turning to something about sex. This entire week, every minute we're around each other it steers that way. Now that it's out of the way, can we just drop it. We're done. Okay?"

His hands tightened on the rail. When did she get so callous? It was annoying. So annoying that it was time to dispel the idea. "I don't want to drop it." He leaned over and brushed his lips against hers, tasting the faint chocolate of the cocoa. "In fact, I'm pretty sure you don't either. You can say it all you want to if it makes you feel better, but you're not convincing anyone."

"Stop teasing me."

He grinned and kissed her again. "I'm not so sure I like the shallow guy you think me to be. Our conversations have veered in a direction they should have years ago as far as I'm concerned. So, the word 'done' may fit this situation to you, but I'd like to think of it more as—progressing. I'm just getting started, Kathryn. Just getting started."

"That sounds a little threatening, don't you think?" she whispered as she leaned into him.

"It should," he whispered back as he tasted her lips again. "You want to know something really scary? The only place I feel like running to is that damn cabin again. We're not even close to done, girl."

Her jaw clenched as he watched her swallow and look away. He put his hand under her chin and pulled it back to face him. He brushed his thumb across her lips. God, she was beautiful. The freckles killed him. He loved the way they dusted her face lightly like brown sugar sprinkles.

Chapter Twenty-Four

The blaring sound of a car horn was out of place on the tour boat. Apparently, it took a moment for it to register with Thomas. Everyone turned at the sound as he yanked his phone out of his pocket and sheepishly apologized for the distraction. "I have to take this." He smiled at Kathryn. "It's about the data I sent earlier." He glanced briefly at the lips he'd just left and turned away.

"Thomas Ryan," he blurted into the device. He listened.

Kathryn watched his facial expression turn from the smile he'd given her to a strangled, almost fearful one in seconds. Whatever news he'd received, it had rendered him speechless and agitated. He looked at her, then moved a few feet away to the railing of the deck.

"Are you sure?" The wind brought the sound of his voice back to her even though he tried not to be heard. "It doesn't make sense. The place was wide open." More silence as he listened to the person on the other side. "Okay. Okay." His voice became agitated. "Yes, I'm positive. He never saw either of us." More silence. "No, we left it clean—he won't know we were there."

Kathryn watched as he stood, moving his legs back and forth nervously, swaying at the hips. She didn't know for sure, but she thought it was something about the cabin.

He reached up and rubbed the back of his neck with his free hand as he turned around. His eyes met hers and narrowed almost to pinpoints. "I will," he muttered before ending the call.

"Everything okay?" she asked, bewildered.

"Not really." He didn't expand. Just stood watching as the tour boat eased into the docking bay and the passengers began to leave.

He grabbed her hand and squeezed, "Katy, I probably should tell you something."

"Okay. What is it?"

They had worked their way off the boat with the other passengers and were now walking toward the Jeep. He still clung to her hand, looking around, taking stock of the people around them.

"I think you're right. We should probably get back as soon as possible."

They got in the car. So, now he was ready to leave. The phone call had changed it? Now he wanted to get away?

"What's wrong? What's this about?" She watched his fingers as he started up the Jeep and put it into gear.

"Honestly, I just need to get home. I've screwed something up and I need to fix it." He pounded his fist against the steering wheel. "Damn it. I, we should have left yesterday."

"So, that's it then? You're ready to go because you need to patch it up at home?" She wondered who was waiting on him. What he needed to fix.

"I'm sorry, Katy." He squeezed her hand on the console. She drew it away as quickly as he touched her.

"Go to hell, Tommy. Let's just go. You need to get back to your life and I need to get back to mine. You could have told me that there was someone waiting for you—someone that required 'patching things up with.'" She bit her lip and looked out the window. She was an idiot.

"What? No! That's not it—there isn't. I wouldn't do that. Not to you. Jesus, not to anyone. Look, I can't really explain everything right now but I will. As soon as I can, I will." He leaned over and whispered toward her, "I don't really want to go back. I want to stay here. Right here with you, but we can't."

His profile was strong, his jaw angular and serious. The hair was always a little out of control but it made her want to touch it, to push it back from his face. He turned abruptly and bore into her with his eyes until she felt that burning sensation in the pit of her stomach. "I mean it, Katy."

"Okay."

"No regrets?"

"No regrets," she answered half-heartedly. Sure, she didn't regret anything, not a second of it. But she'd miss him the minute he was gone. The smell of his skin, the feel of it, would haunt her for months. The taste of him on her mouth wouldn't be easily forgotten. It angered her and saddened her that she had, in essence, become just like all those silly girls that had chased him before. In truth, though, it was not something she'd ever regret.

They rode in silence to the airport. As they approached the entrance, he broke the silence. "What airline are you returning on?"

"United."

"Oh, well—we're on Alaska-Air now."

"We?"

"Yeah, our flights were changed—we're flying together."

"Why? We're not going to the same places. You're going to Dallas. I'm going to Houston."

"Not anymore."

"Why not? Of course we are. You can't just hijack me."

"I'm not, but the FBI is. We're going together. They haven't told me where but we're on the same plane. That's why we had to leave." He pulled the car in and stopped. As the engine rattled into silence, Kathryn's door was yanked open and a hand extended to her. She batted her eyes, instantly blinded by the sun that streamed through the open door. A silhouette of a man stood over her.

"Ms. Delroy? Agent Bernard."

She shook with him and stepped out of the Jeep. The man greeting her was about two inches taller. A strong, but not stocky build. He could have been anywhere from her age to ten years older, with a smile that seemed forced.

"Nice to meet you. What's going on?" She turned to look at Thomas in confusion as he came around the back of the car and tossed the keys to Agent Bernard.

Secrets always ticked her off. She was not the sort to hold things back. In her mind, it was a curse, more than a blessing. Sometimes, every detail of a problem would be exposed for world-review—at work, that was one thing she had trouble with. Telling too much versus telling only the needed. Right now, though, it would have at least been helpful to know why the FBI wanted to talk with them and why it was necessary to change their itinerary completely. She gathered the cabin was involved—did it belong to a federal employee? Had they trespassed on government property?

"Mr. Ryan." Agent Bernard nodded. "Thanks for the information."

"Of course. You need to pick up her car too. It's on the side of the highway just outside Kenai. We ditched it yesterday. As far as the information—just doing what anyone else would, given the situation."

Bernard's hand extended toward the revolving door close to them. "You'd be surprised how not true that is. Let's get started. Can you come this way please?"

"Sure." Thomas reached for Kathryn's hand. She shook her head. "It's okay, Katy. You're safe but we have to do this. You'll understand everything in a bit."

Kathryn glanced through the airport at the fluorescent restaurant signs and felt the gnawing emptiness that had settled in her stomach. "Is there any way you might let us eat something, Agent Bernard?" she blurted, ignoring Thomas. "By my watch, it's been about eighteen hours since we've eaten. All this fresh air and exercise has left me starving." She glared at Thomas as she hesitated on the word exercise.

Bernard nodded and raised an eyebrow as he glanced at Thomas. "She doesn't know?"

"No, she didn't see it. I did. She was there with me, but doesn't know anything," Thomas confirmed.

"Doesn't know what, Thomas? Didn't see what? What's going on?" she demanded. "Why do you have to be so damn secretive! Would one of you tell me what's going on?"

Bernard looked past her, ignoring the tirade. "Then maybe we should talk to you separately?"

"No!" Katy denied. "I don't know what's going on but I'm guessing it has something to do with a cabin up above Glacier Park. Whatever you guys have to talk about, I want to hear it too. I was there."

"You're not going to want to hear this, Katy. The less you know, the safer you are." Thomas used his pet name for her and it pissed her off.

"That's something I can decide for myself, *Tommy*." She glared at him as she passed, following Agent Bernard through a door just inside the revolving entrance. A long hallway opened up before them. Their footsteps were the only sounds as they clipped along to an office halfway down on the right.

"Inside here for a few minutes while we get some details, then you'll be on your way." The office was warm and accommodating in contrast to the cold, stark hallway. A small round conference table sat at one end of the room, alongside floor to ceiling glass windows. The dark mahogany furniture was polished to a gleam and invited fingers to glide over its smooth surfaces. Pictures graced the walls, all random scenes of Alaskan landmarks. Bernard barked an order down the hall and a young man with a Glock on his hip came into view.

"Get these two some food." He turned to Kathryn. "You want salad or steak?"

"Steak would be great," she answered. The young man disappeared.

"Does that mean I get steak too? Not salad?" Thomas commented with attempted humor. Bernard offered a raised eyebrow in response.

Patience is difficult to find when the FBI escorts you into a room for questioning about something that is completely a blank page. All Kathryn's senses raced around in chaos, trying to determine the appropriate reaction. Her eyes darted back and forth between the two men flanking her. One doodled notes on a large white tablet, the other clasped hands nervously in his lap.

A tall, regal woman with short, gray-streaked hair rushed into the room and dropped into the remaining empty chair. "Are we ready to start?" she asked. Her voice was breathless as if she'd run around the airport and down the hall before meeting them.

"Yes, This is Trevan's friend, Thomas Ryan." Bernard gestured a slight wave above the table.

"Special Agent-In-Charge Barbara Foster, Mr. Ryan. Thanks for the information. We've been looking for this guy a long time. Never thought he'd be up here. Strange place for a terrorist-type." She smiled, then added, "It's smart, but strange."

"Terrorist!" Thomas and Kathryn said in unison.

"Well, sort of. Not really." Bernard frowned at Foster.

Kathryn and Thomas would soon figure out that Barbara Foster loved to phrase things for impact. The more dramatic the better. She never embellished to a point of untruth though. Just liked to use words that over-emphasized, rather than played down the seriousness. Amazingly, the young man with the Glock appeared in the doorway with a hotel wheeled cart full of trays. He rolled it up to their table, muttered quietly, "Let me know if you need anything else," and disappeared.

Satisfied with their reaction to her announcement, Foster waited for them to move their food and water glasses to the table before she continued, "The man refers to himself as an 'insurance agent.' He's funded by certain well-known political and terrorist-cell groups that are suspected to be responsible for recent bomb threats in Europe. They've also been linked or suspected in a couple of political murders." She tapped on the USB device in front of her, "This man has handled much of the work. He's also instigated a few kidnappings that were done to influence political decisions or military movements that his funders required."

"Why does he prefer the 'Insurance Agent' title?" Kathryn asked. "Does it look bad to put 'terrorist and hired killer' on a business card?" She slipped her napkin into her lap.

The water Thomas had just swallowed started to return as he coughed back a laugh. A quick glance made sure he knew she saw no humor with the situation they currently faced. Foster patted Thomas on the back, a little too strongly, then changed the last pat to a friendly shoulder rub. A little too friendly.

"You okay?" Foster asked. For pity's sake—even the feds flirted with him.

He held up a hand to wave her away and cleared his throat. "Yeah, fine. Thanks."

"The man likes to think of himself as providing the client with insurance that their objective is met to their requirements. Sort of a contractual guarantee," Bernard supplied.

"He doesn't take payment until the stated objective is achieved. This makes him very popular," Foster added. "And very dangerous."

Kathryn didn't ask but it was still incredibly unclear what "objectives" they were talking about.

Bernard cleared his throat and leaned over the table toward Thomas, lacing his fingers together. "We need you to tell us how you came across this information." He pointed to the USB drive on the table in front of them. Foster, mimicking Bernard's movement, entwined her hands and leaned into them with her elbows supporting her.

"We missed the last glacier tour for the day, so we took a drive up the mountain instead," Thomas started after swallowing a bite of food. He then proceeded, with Kathryn's assistance, to explain the Jeep snafu as well as their trek down to the cabin looking for help. As they devoured the food, they told how they had dislodged the Jeep with the truck and returned it as well as stayed the night for lack of better accommodations. Kathryn appreciated that some of the other, more personal details were left out.

Lastly, Thomas added, "While Kathryn showered, I raided the fridge. There was a manila envelope stuffed in next to a carton of milk. I thought the guy was on the forgetful side and just placed it there by mistake. I slipped it out and, being a little nosy, I peeked. Should have known better."

"We're glad you didn't," Foster interjected, then waited for him to continue. "You've just found the first really solid lead in months."

"Well, I'm not glad." He glanced sideways at Kathryn. "I could tell by the names and the small amount of information I saw that this was big, so I called Trev."

"You mean Special Agent Trevan Prater, right?"

Thomas laughed. "I mean my college buddy Trevan Prater, who just happened to make it into the FBI about six or seven years ago. He graduated two years ahead of me. It's strange to think of him as Special Agent Prater." He lowered his voice deeply as he repeated the title. "He was just another guy like me trying to get through school then. Smart but quiet. Kind of stand-offish too. But once you got to know him, he could be pretty fun."

"Fun? Somehow I doubt that," Bernard scoffed, causing Foster to glare at him before commenting.

"Trevan's a good agent and has been pretty successful in several fraud investigations in the South. That's more his forté, so to speak. This type of thing normally doesn't get his attention. That's why he passed it on to Washington. And they called us. It was too short-notice to get the people investigating this guy up here, so you're talking to us." Foster glanced at Kathryn, cautiously quiet through the last few words. "Do you want to add anything, Ms. Delroy?"

Kathryn gulped the water in her glass. Suddenly the food in her stomach was gurgling, threatening to return.

Before she could speak, Thomas interrupted, "She didn't see the data or the documents. She doesn't know anything about it, so she doesn't really need to be here."

"Okay, that's good." Foster sighed. "We'll need to get you on the plane now." She gestured toward Kathryn, "She can go home but you'll need to go to our Houston office and meet with the agents on this case."

"I left a note," Kathryn said quietly.

"What?" Bernard leaned toward her.

"I left a thank-you note. I felt bad for being there and using his things without asking. For basically breaking and entering. So, I left a thank-you note." Their mouths dropped in unison. They looked like one of those 'toss the bean bag' games that kids play at school carnivals.

"Shit, Katy." The worry in Thomas' voice rang through.

How could she have known the guy was hiding up there for a reason—a very dangerous *I may come kill you* reason?

"What did the note say?"

"I don't remember exactly. Something about 'We got stuck up the mountain and borrowed your truck to get out. Hope you don't mind us helping ourselves to it and a night's stay in your very nice place. If we can ever repay the favor, don't hesitate to call.'"

"Did you leave a name and number?" Foster asked.

"Yes, mine and my cell."

"Well, *that* certainly changes things a little. You're both going to need to talk to the guys in Houston." Foster exchanged glances with Bernard and they both stood up together. "We need to make a quick phone call. If you need anything, the gentleman outside the door can get it for you—food, drink, anything. We'll be back in just a bit."

Kathryn waited until they left the room before she hurled questions at Thomas. "Why didn't you *tell* me? If I'd known what was going on—understood why you were in such a hurry, I would have never left that stupid note. I would have been out of there in seconds and wouldn't have been all bent out of shape about it."

"The fact that I saw it was bad enough. I didn't want to get you involved. Besides, I thought if we just got the hell out and left the place the way we found it, no one would know we'd even been there." He shrugged and reached to touch her fingers. "I was trying to keep you out of it."

"And then I left that note." She stared at his fingers stroking hers. He grinned and gave a pat before moving back.

"Yeah, I didn't really anticipate that. But then, knowing you— it makes sense. I'd never leave a note, wouldn't care. I figure if he left the place that easy to get into, he didn't really mind if anyone did. But Katy always thinks of the other person first. Right?"

"I thought it was the right thing to do. Maybe I need to change that?" she grinned back.

"You can't—it's who you are. Just like not thinking of it is who I am. You have a nice streak in you."

"You make that sound like a bad thing."

"Don't put words in my mouth. I didn't say that." He frowned. "In this particular case, a little less niceness would have been better for both of us. But it's too late now. Besides—I trust Trevan. So, I trust these guys too. They'll take care of it and we'll be home in no time."

"Tommy, you may think it's not true, but there's a nice streak in you too. You just use it selectively. You know that 'no regrets' agreement we had?" she said with sincerity.

"Yeah, I guess you've changed your mind about that, haven't you? I wouldn't blame you if you had. Although, avoiding a terrorist wasn't really the kind of regret I meant at the time."

The door flung open. "The great thing about working for the government," said Foster as she entered the room alone, "is that they can turn on a dime if required. You both have flight plans to go to Houston later this afternoon. However, before you go—Agent Bernard is going to need you to accompany him on a little helicopter ride. We're sending a team into the cabin right now and sealing it off for the investigative group that will arrive later tonight. We need you to go and confirm the location for them. It should be quick—and safe. You're not touching down, just a quick fly-over. You point and tell. The ground crew does the rest." She slapped her hands on the table loudly, "Okay? Okay! Let's get moving. We want to make sure the owner doesn't get there before we do."

Chapter Twenty-Five

The message on his phone had made Eric nervous. Brenda had been at his house.

"Hey there. I went up to check on your dog and put out some food. What a sweetie. I brought him back to the bar with me. I hope you don't mind. You can come get him when you get back. See ya."

Eric had managed an earlier flight than expected and was in his car by ten a.m. and headed back to the cabin. As he pulled into the drive, the absence of the loyal mutt made him lonely. He eased around the cabin and got out of the car.

When he let himself into the house, it felt wrong. Nothing seemed out of place but it was. He could smell it. The hair on the back of his neck prickled. He eased the gun from his ankle and trod lightly through the spaces. All was empty.

He started to sigh a huff of relief when he spotted the white paper laid out on the kitchen counter. It's stark brightness glared against the cold, dark countertop. He peeked around the corner, then worked his way toward the paper. Standing over it, his mouth dropped. *You fucking idiot. You left the key out when you took Brenda home.*

He slammed his fist on the counter. And yanked the fridge door open. *Thank God it's still there.* The envelope appeared undisturbed. He freed it from the milk carton that pinned it against the wall and the contents spilled on the floor.

The tab was open. The fucking tab was open.

He gathered the contents, the notes, his bag from the closet, and rushed to the car. He pulled the car back to the shed and considered loading up his supplies. If by chance the police stopped him—it would be pretty suspicious to have an arsenal in the trunk. No, he would have to leave it.

As he started to drive away, he realized he needed to be sure. Brenda left the voice message. This Kathryn person left the note. Who had looked in the envelope? Brenda had the dog, did she go inside too? Did she snoop around? Somehow, the thought sickened him. He didn't want it to be her. He didn't want to have to make that decision. The one that would end his relationship with her. And end her life.

The next thirty minutes were a frantic drive down the mountain to her bar. Thoughts tumbled various scenarios around in his head.

He strode into the bar and grabbed the broom. He quelled the panic in his mind. She was in the back somewhere clanking around, but he thought he'd just wait and see how things went. It was always wise to wait and watch until you knew for sure. So, he started sweeping just as he had a few days before. He covered about a twenty-foot square section before he heard the squeak of the door opening, and then the pattering sound of animal footprints as Gypsy preceded her through.

"Oh!" She gasped at the sight of him. The dog leapt toward him, his tongue hanging out. "You're back already. That was quick."

"Yeah, it normally is." He watched her warily. "Hey, Gypsy." He reached down and scratched his ears. The dog looked too damned comfortable here.

"I hope you don't mind but I realized he was going unfed so I went up there, thinking I'd drop some food out for him, but you didn't have any outside so..." she hesitated, tapping her fingers on the bar, "I just brought him down here and fed him out back." She nodded toward the back door. "I keep my dog food in the shed behind my house so I never thought about you not having any outside."

"It's in a big can on the stoop by the kitchen," he answered. So, she hadn't gone inside. He didn't need to force the smile that came next.

"You want to get some lunch?" It was stupid to ask. He should be high-tailing it after the other girl. Still…the warmth of relief made him momentarily soft. The floodgates were open and he'd been gone for a bit. Besides, he hadn't given her the gift.

The other girl had left a phone number; it would be easy enough to find her. From the note, she was half a continent away—so an hour or two wouldn't make a lot of difference. It would still require travel.

After lunch, he dropped the package on the table in the nice, crisp paper from the gift shop. She slowly and meticulously undid the ribbon and folded back the paper. Her eyes fogged and teared up a bit when she saw it, but the look quickly changed and all she did was give a simple, "Thank you." She liked it.

After Brenda opened the box, she had talked him into taking her home to put it "in a proper spot" before she opened the bar.

"I'd hate for one of my customers to get drunk and break it," she said as she returned it neatly to the paper. When he dropped her at the bar an hour later, relief flooded through his veins. He watched her go inside, then took the knife out of his pocket and turned it over in his hand. He had gathered it from the kitchen before they left for lunch—one of the ones he'd seen on the counter the first time he was there. The coldness of his original intentions passed. He shoved the knife into the glove compartment, glad he didn't need to use it. Brenda had not disappointed him.

With Gypsy on the seat next to him, he started back toward her house. The dog would have to stay behind; that was the best place for him. He needed to catch a flight.

Chapter Twenty-Six

The full magnitude of their predicament hit Thomas like a block of ice when they were escorted down the hallway to a door, then whisked to a military helicopter by four armed agents. All were covered in protective gear with multiple firearms and were careful to ensure they weren't obstructed from getting their passengers safely to the chopper. The first wave of panic had subsided and now, a heavier, more threatening emotion channeled its way icily through Thomas' veins. He had not bargained for a full military escort, nor had he expected to be under full guard. Judging by the size of the detail, he seriously doubted they would be home by tomorrow. And they certainly wouldn't be back at work on Monday.

Agent Bernard stood under the flapping blades, motioning them inside. He helped Katy up after Thomas and climbed in behind her. The pilot handed headphones back to each of them, and motioned for them to cover their ears and speak into the microphone as needed. "You'll need those," he shouted. Four of the armed men perched on the edges of each seat, securing coverage of the cargo inside.

Thomas recognized that fear was basically a foreign emotion to him. He'd not had any situations where he was ever truly concerned for his safety or anyone else's—other than the bear. He'd never served in the military. Never fought for his life or country. Never had any major brawls. His only real physical battles were on sports fields or a couple of times in a bar. There were rules in sports. Rules that one had to follow or you didn't participate. He frowned as the asphalt of the tarmac dropped away from them, showing the speed with which they ascended into the air. Every person sat still and quiet. The men on the outside were visibly watching the motion around them. The others appeared to be mesmerized by the ground. He didn't know the rules in this match. There was nothing to signal what the right thing or wrong thing was. No indication that the person you should fear, wasn't the one sitting across from you...or one of the armed men around them.

He wondered if he should have left the package alone, told Kathryn, and the two of them high-tailed it back to Texas. Would the man in the cabin have come after them? Would he have sent someone else? Or would he have never even known they were there and they could have just got back to normal life.

Normal life. He didn't even know what that would be now. Without all the drama associated with his findings at the cabin, would he and Katy have just gone home and parted ways? She seemed all too eager to ditch him as quickly as she could. He glanced at her profile as she watched out the window. He could still smell her. He had not showered since they left the cabin and her shampoo still tickled his nose. The feel of her skin was still fresh on his.

Years ago, he had imagined what it would be like to be with her. He had soothed his curiosity with other girls, telling himself that they were basically the same. Too young to know otherwise. He hadn't expected the reality. Katy had never really been like most girls anyway. It was stupid to think that sex with her would be unremarkable.

It wasn't the same. She wasn't the same. The realization made him lonely and he wished he had left it as it was. Knowing her now was going to make him miserable when he went back home, a curse that he'd not survive easily, nor quell with distractions. Not this time.

The helicopter had reached the road that led to the glacier cruise and the pilot turned above it, following its path. He looked over his shoulder and pointed at the earphones as he spoke into the microphone, "You're going to have to tell me from here. I see a fork ahead of us."

"Stay to the right. The main road goes left, we veered off. When you get about five more miles up, there's another fork. Take the smaller road there too. When it runs out, you'll probably see the tracks where we pulled the Jeep out. The drive to the cabin is about three quarters of a mile below that. It goes back a good four hundred yards to the house and barn." Thomas tried to point over the pilot's shoulder but the dashboard in front obstructed a clear view and he wasn't comfortable standing up.

"I see it. We're going to go down and circle over until our guys get there, then we'll head out. The place looks abandoned."

"It was empty when we got there, but whoever was there hadn't been gone long. There was food in the fridge and the milk was fresh."

The helicopter carved a wide loop above the property, giving everyone a chance to survey it more thoroughly. Other than the barn where the truck was snugly hidden away—there was another building farther up the mountain another hundred or so feet. The roof was barely visible through the trees. Those three structures were all they could see; the entire property was engulfed with forestation so thick it was impossible to view anything else below it. Even the drive to the house was barely visible from the air. A heavy winter snow would render it inaccessible by any vehicle other than possibly a snow machine. Even that might be tough. The nearest property was at least eight to ten miles back down the mountain on the main road.

Thomas raised his eyes in a silent thank you for whatever stroke of luck ensured the man was not at the cabin when they walked up to it.

They continued to hover over the place until the four dark vehicles sped up the tree-covered road, lurching to a stop in front of the cabin. Several people rushed to the door and checked for inhabitants. It was empty. They helped themselves to the key that Kathryn pointed them toward, and then gave the "all clear" within a few seconds. Thomas looked down to see Special-Agent Foster waving them off just before the helicopter banked steeply left and sped back to the airport.

An hour later, he and Kathryn were on a plane headed to Texas, flanked by two federal agents. Thomas felt like he was opening a new chapter in his life, one that had a very uncertain outcome. He had always liked a good mess—God knows he had sure made a few. In typical form, he squared his shoulders, furrowed his brows and muttered, "bring it on."

Chapter Twenty-Seven

"I beg your pardon?" Katy turned to him, not sure she'd heard it right. "What did you say?" His face clouded over instantly.

"Nothing. I was talking to myself." Thomas' face had been almost ashen since they entered the FBI office. He'd spoken only a few words to her and those words were warm, comforting, and innocuous. She didn't know what was going on in his head, but he was obviously wrestling with the whole situation.

"You okay? You've barely said a word."

"What do you want me to say? We're guarded by two feds, and headed who-knows-where because we ended up in the wrong guy's cabin."

"Where else were we supposed to go?" She turned the latch on her fold-down table and let it drop as the attendant brought the drinks they'd ordered earlier. It banged solidly on his knee, which was bent into her foot space. He growled and rubbed it as he readjusted in his seat.

"Thanks, Katy," he snarled. "I hate these little airplanes. Never enough foot room for someone that's tall. I usually book an aisle seat just for that reason." He frowned angrily at the two body guards; he knew they'd secured their seats at his expense.

"Well, you'll just have to make do," she matched his anger, "and I don't remember you having a problem with that cabin when you were naked on the couch, trying to get my—" She suddenly noticed the pitch of her voice and shut it down.

"Trying to what, honey?" he grinned. "Come on, you're on a roll. Tell everyone. These guys have already heard the first part." He motioned to the agents flanking them, "You might as well tell them the rest. Trying to what? Take off those sexy little white panties of yours?" Neither agent looked at them.

The man next to Thomas continued to flip blindly through the airline magazine he'd grabbed from the slot in front of them. The other one just stared forward, not flinching, but he heard. She knew he did. She punched Tommy solidly in the leg that he'd just finished rubbing.

Thomas' lips twitched in that sexy gesture he made when trying not to smile. She should have been mad but Kathryn found the lip thing irresistible. Don't focus on his mouth, she told herself. There was a crisis going on around them and all she could think about was—that mouth. Ridiculous. The stress was getting to her.

"Katy, honey," he whispered in her ear, "you're going to have to stop looking at me like that or it's going to be a really long flight."

It was impossible not to rise to the challenge. She leaned toward him, resting her forehead against his and stared into his eyes as she slipped her hand under the table and up his leg. When she reached the top of his thigh, she squeezed into the fabric and flesh and whispered back, "Like what?" His Adam's apple plummeted in his throat as he averted his gaze out the window and pushed her hand away.

A few seconds later, he leaned back and answered, "You're playing with fire, Katy. Don't make me embarrass you."

"Not possible, Thomas. You couldn't embarrass me if you tried." She was baiting him, but she couldn't stop. It was too tempting. Besides, she liked getting under his skin. Get real. She liked getting against his skin too. The agent on the other side cleared his throat and crossed his legs into the aisle as if to stifle her.

"Okay." Thomas stretched the word into three syllables before he matched her threat by drawing his hand to her cheek and descending down to take her lips. He didn't wait for an invitation. His lips were hot, wet, and emotionally draining. Common sense told her this was the wrong place. The wrong time. Still, Kathryn's hand moved from his leg to his shirt; her fingers twisted into the cloth pulling him into the kiss, deepening it. Wait. She was on an airplane. People surrounding them.

Then his hand started slowly moving down her cheek, down her neck, and—down the inside crease of her neckline. He rubbed her skin lightly with his finger and the surge of desire flamed up. Have some reserve girl!

She grabbed his fingers just as they reached the top button, her lips were still completely lost. She wrestled herself back to the present and pushed against him. "Okay, you made your point."

He broke away, grinning into her eyes as he lowered his hand. "So you're not embarrassed? I like your—lack of embarrassment," he said softly. "It goes a long way toward improving my mood."

Her pulse had made it all the way into her throat. *All right, Thomas. I give up. You win. You're clearly way out of my league; way beyond my concept of sexy. Way too good at this game for me. I haven't got a clue how to handle you—or how to stay away from you.*

She inhaled a deep breath, leaned back into the seat and closed her eyes, then waited for her nerves to calm and her pulse to slow. She opened one eye. "I don't get you, Tommy."

"Come again? What's there to get?" he responded as he pulled a magazine from the bin in front of him and began flipping through it.

She sighed. "I wouldn't expect you to be too comfortable with the PDA thing. I would think that might cramp your style, so to speak. Someone watching might get the wrong impression." She had noticed the pretty redhead eyeing him when they boarded. She'd also seen his return smile.

"And what impression do you think they'd get?" He raised an eyebrow, glanced her way, then continued to look at the pages in front of him.

"Well, that you were actually interested, not just a casual friend. At least that's probably what I'd think as an outsider looking in.

I'm not saying that you are—just saying how I'd see it." She turned back and closed her eyes.

The agent on her right side, peered over at Thomas with one eye cocked half-way open, a purely investigative move. His low, grumbling voice surprised her. "Miss, I don't mean to butt in—but I kind of doubt there's anything casual about that lip-lock he just placed on you. Or the fact that you were shacked up in a cabin on the mountains with this guy. If you're looking for something easier, I'd suggest you look elsewhere. You just happen to be sitting with three single guys...and that one," he pointed at Thomas, "is likely the least casual one in the group. *IF* that's what you're looking for, you just let me know." He spoke out of the side of his mouth, not looking at her.

Kathryn kept her eyes shut and didn't respond. Clearly, the man didn't know much about them. "Excuse me, what was your name again?" she responded.

"Greg." He smiled briefly. "Greg Dierden."

"That would be Agent Dierden then?" She watched his face sober and heard a slight snicker from Thomas.

"Agent Dierden." She stopped herself. A sharp scolding would do nothing to improve the situation. This man was here to protect them, after all. Alienating him wouldn't be wise. Besides, what would it hurt to flirt a little? "Tell me about yourself, Greg." She curved her lips into a smile and turned his way.

The remaining few hours on the plane were fun for Kathryn. She listened to Agent Dierden talk about his hometown in Kansas. She forgot the name of the place, but it sounded nice. He'd been a lot of places and spoke intelligently about the cultural differences of each. He had perfected the ability to talk about locations without divulging his reason for being there or the work he did. By the time they exited the plane, he had Kathryn laughing until it hurt.

"Time to get back to work, ma'am." Dierden stood and pulled her bags out of the overhead compartment. "I'll lead the way. You two just follow me. Agent Kirth will be right behind you. There's a car waiting outside."

"Is it really necessary to guard us so closely, Greg?" Kathryn asked. There had been no unexpected interest from a passenger on the plane. Not a glance. The smile he'd given earlier disappeared. Agent Dierden frowned.

"Yes, most definitely. These people that you stumbled onto are serious. Really bad guys. You may not see them coming and they'd kill you without a thought, then go home to their family. This is a business to them and they do it well." He tilted his large frame slightly and led the way off the plane, giving the group in front of them a large lead. Nervously, Kathryn glanced back at Thomas, briefly meeting his eyes. She found no comfort there.

The four moved quickly off the plane and through the airport. When Kathryn and Thomas headed toward baggage claim, the agents nudged them straight to the exterior doors and into the waiting car.

"Your luggage will be delivered later," Agent Kirth said as he slid in behind Thomas. Pressing her legs together to conserve space, Kathryn sighed at the irony of their situation. If the idea was to be well-hidden or low-profile, it made no sense to pop into a huge, black, obviously government-issue vehicle and whiz away. It also seemed rather obvious that two additional armed agents were waiting for them at the curb, standing next to the black Suburban. Their profiles were reflected in the window glass, which was so dark it was impossible to see the interior.

"What time is it?" Kathryn asked suddenly. She glanced at her watch, not waiting for the answer.

"Just after three. Why?" Thomas responded, even though he saw her movement.

"Good. We have plenty of time. Gentlemen, I need to be at the Richmond Y at five p.m. Whatever you have planned for us, can it wait until after that?" She glanced around at the five men surrounding her, hesitating only a second before continuing. "You see, I signed up to coach a nine- and ten-year-old soccer team and we have practice at five. The kids and parents are depending on me to be there. It's our first practice and I really don't want to miss it." If she were a weaker personality, she would have wilted under the incredulous looks they all gave her. As it was, she just sat and smiled at them, waiting for a response. Ask for what you want, Thomas had encouraged.

"Ms. Delroy, do you remember what I told you about the seriousness of this situation earlier?" Greg asked. "You sure that's a good idea?"

"I don't see the harm. Even if the guy showed up at the cabin after we left, there's no way he could have gotten on a plane and arrived before us. In truth, he probably couldn't even get a reservation for at least another day or two. That's all depending on *if* he saw my note and got out of there before your guys showed up, which I seriously doubt he did. Besides, it would be impossible for him to know where I am right this moment, nor what I have scheduled at five." She rubbed her hands on her jeans and laced her fingers together in her lap.

Three of the agents turned to the man in the driver's seat for a response. His head faced forward, not at her. Dark sunglasses rendered his expression completely unreadable. He turned the keys in the ignition and eased the car away from the curb.

"Are you serious?" Thomas leaned over her shoulder. "Can't you get someone else to fill in for you?"

"No, I can't. I don't even know any of the parents yet so I can't call them, not to mention it's too late to cancel anyway. They're expecting me to be there and I want to be. When a person commits to something, they should follow through. I committed to coach. So, gentlemen—what's it going to be? Do I get to show up for these little girls' first soccer practice or not?"

"Then you'll just miss it," Thomas interjected. "You can explain later and apologize." It irritated Kathryn that Thomas spoke for the agents.

"No," the driver said firmly. "I think we can make it, but keep the practice short and no wandering away. I need to call it in, but I guess it'll be okay. I think they're still working on arrangements for where you'll be tonight anyway."

"Arrangements for where we'll stay? I thought I was going home. Are you saying that we're under lock and key right now?"

"Sorry, Ms. Delroy—and you too, Mr. Ryan. We can't let either of you go home yet. Not until we have a few things taken care of. Mr. Ryan, you're not going to get back to Dallas tonight either. It shouldn't take long for us to set it up. I'm pretty sure we can get you back home tomorrow or Tuesday. It's too dangerous for you to go home yet."

"What about work? Are you going to let us go to work? Or at least me, Thomas works in Dallas so I would assume that if he can't get there, he won't get to work either."

Thomas shrugged. "I can work out of the Houston office with Katy if necessary. I just need my laptop back from you to do so."

"Good, then you'll both go to work tomorrow. The laptop's going to have to wait though—they're still going over the data on it. Maybe you can get a loaner. We'll figure out the details. Ms. Delroy, do you have a kid on the soccer team that needs picking up from somewhere?"

"Me? No! I don't have any kids. I just volunteered to coach. A friend of mine was talking about it when I was out jogging with her a while back. Her daughter's on the team and she mentioned how badly they need coaches at the Y. I made the mistake of admitting that I played soccer in high school and she wouldn't leave me alone after that. I didn't want to let her down."

Chapter Twenty-Eight

The Richmond Y was adjacent to a large park that cornered one of the busier intersections in the area. Parking was at a premium and maneuvering the black beast into the lot proved to be a challenge for the yet-to-be-named driver. Several teams were scattered across the four fields, kicking and chasing balls. More chasing than kicking, it appeared.

Thomas smiled at the organized chaos, remembering his many efforts at childhood sports. A group of kids milled close to the goal on the second field, their parents chatting comfortably with each other. Kathryn strolled toward them, breaking into her normal beautiful smile. Agents Kirth and Dierden followed close behind. The other agents remained in the vehicle with Thomas.

Kathryn faced the parents, her hands moving energetically as she spoke. She was apparently introducing herself and then asking the children to identify themselves as she read down a list of names. Hair bows bounced over peppy ponytails as the girls moved nervously around her, tapping their soccer balls back and forth between their feet. An excited energy bubbled amongst them. Every time a name was called, a hand went up and a girl responded with a smile.

The variety of talent levels was amusing. Thomas could see that Kathryn had a couple of good dribblers on the team, but most had more potential than talent. There were twelve kids all together. The size range was broad. As well as the personalities. He felt himself smiling as he watched the interactions between coach and team members.

He didn't want to sit in the Suburban and watch through

darkened windows. He'd been cooped up almost all day. Suddenly, fresh air and giggling kids and families sounded enticing. Without asking, he popped the door open, stepped out, and meandered to the side of the field. He felt the presence of the agents following, but paid little attention. The aluminum bleachers had baked in the sun all day and were sizzling hot. The heat seeped through the denim of his jeans, instantly causing perspiration to form behind his knees and under his thighs.

"Which one is yours?" The voice startled him. He turned to see a petite blonde with short-cropped hair smiling at him.

"Oh, none of them. I don't have any children," he answered.

She shot him an odd look, engulfing Thomas with an almost accusatory feeling. He thought it best to explain somehow, rather than give the impression that he was stalking little girls at the soccer field. "I'm with the coach."

"Oh! Are you helping her? I love it when couples coach together. The girls get the best of both worlds. Plus it keeps them in better control. You'd be surprised how hard it is to keep up with twelve nine-year-olds full of energy."

"No, uh. I'm just a friend. I'm visiting from Dallas." That seemed to appease her so he turned back toward the soccer field.

A small girl ran up to within inches of him, then stopped and leaned over to put her hands on her thighs. The girl spoke between stilted breaths, "Mom, where's my water?" She pulled up a sock that was slouching to expose the top portion of a shin pad underneath. It's elastic had obviously worn out from use. The needed water was tossed softly and caught mid-air. The budding soccer player whirled and rushed back to the players grouped around the coach.

"So, did she play soccer?" The woman pointed briefly at Kathryn.

"Yes, in high school. She played midfield. She was pretty good. She also ran track."

"Midfield. Tough position. Where did she play?"

"Cypress."

"Wait, what's her name?" He smiled. It clicked then. Anyone who followed local sports over the years would have seen the pictures in the paper. She was all over the news when she breezed through the state finals. Kathryn was a recruiter's dream—a good athlete with good grades and a good attitude. The Aggies and the Longhorns fought over her along with several out-of-state schools. And then, for some reason, television stations took an interest. Hell, he knew why.

"Kathryn Delroy."

"Oh! Of course. I recognize her now. Wow, that's great. She's a local celebrity. I heard she tore up the track in college."

Thomas laughed. "Yeah, that's her. She pretty much tears up everything she sets her mind on. Quite a determined girl."

The short-cropped hair swayed sharply as the lady slapped her hands to her thighs and gave him a closer look. "Yes, and she keeps similar company, doesn't she?" He wasn't sure what that meant. "You're Thomas Ryan, aren't you?"

"Yeah, that's me." He nodded. A lot of people had heard of Kathryn; it surprised him that anyone would know him. He wasn't a local athlete star. He'd played football and ran track. While he'd been pretty successful in high school, he didn't have the size to play in college. He bulked up later than most.

"Your mom is my doctor. She has your picture all over her office. Really proud of you."

The twelve girls were lined up across the soccer field, each with a ball at their feet. Kathryn clapped her hands and shouted, "go!" and the girls started dribbling the balls toward the other end. At the center of the field, they put a foot on the ball to stop. A short pause. Then they covered the remainder of the field, stopping at the other end.

"That works both ways. I'm pretty proud of Mom, too."

Kathryn instructed the girls to go again down the field. All twelve bobbing ponytails dribbled and chased their balls to the midway mark, paused, then continued to the goal line. When they stopped, the majority of their faces were red splotched, and sweaty. Hair had loosened and was falling out of the pretty colored ties that their mothers had put on them. They didn't seem to notice or care about the bows anymore.

He didn't want to be rude to the mom, but the soccer practice was getting more interesting. He excused himself, stood up, and moved toward the end of the field where he could hear the coaching instructions more clearly. He glared at the agents briefly so they wouldn't hover. Kathryn looked like she was really enjoying herself.

A surge of warmth crept through him as he watched her answer questions and talk playfully with the girls. They wanted to know all about her and she didn't mind—not one bit. He still couldn't hear what she told them. The wind carried her voice away rather than toward the side of the field. A girl with a blonde braid pointed toward Thomas. His ears pricked. Kathryn gave him a friendly smile as she answered a question, causing the girls to laugh loudly.

She clapped her hands and waved them all together where they stacked hands on top of hands. A brief chant signaled the end of practice and all twenty-four soccer-clad legs raced back to their parents.

The agents had joined Thomas at the corner of the field, waiting as she approached, a satisfied smile on her face. It reminded him of earlier years. He'd seen that look before as she came off the soccer and track field. It was a look of enjoyment and expectation. Pride in what she'd done gave way to a need for feedback; a desire for confirmation of a job well done. Her eyes had been on her parents' faces then as she sought approval. Now, those eyes were on him. Seeking a response.

The desire to pull her into his arms was overwhelming. He

quelled it and shoved his hands into his pockets until she stood across from him, her face flushed, small spots of dampness darkening her shirt.

"Well, what did you think?" she asked.

"They have potential. A couple of good ball handlers with fairly decent foot skills. I don't know anything at all about girls' soccer so I can't really say how they'll do." He handed her a bottle of water that he'd grabbed out of a cooler. One of the parents had generously supplied drinks for the team. A disappointed look crossed her face.

It didn't occur to him that she was asking what he thought of her coaching. Surely she didn't need confirmation on that? He'd never really cared what others thought himself. Besides, nothing Kathryn did ever fell short of expectations.

"They're cute. Lots of energy," she said as she took the bottle from his hand, twisted the cap off, and lifted it to her lips. Several parents offered a passing thank you and ushered their children to the parking lot. She waved and smiled in response. Another sip of water. The sun glinted through the bottle as she raised it to her mouth, sending a rainbow of colors across her neck and the portion of skin showing on her shoulder. He couldn't take his eyes off her. He stood there, grinning like an idiot.

This was how he remembered her. A sudden pain in his chest made him look away. A familiar tightness from years past that he'd forgotten. Knowing the feel of her skin didn't make the tightness lessen. He thought it would. It was worse now. Stronger.

With one hand, he smoothed her hair back from the flushed face. "You look like you need a shower," he blurted, wanting to catch the sweat that was trailing down her neck, lick it off, taste it.

"Gee. Thanks, Thomas." She smirked, running a wrist across her forehead to swab the drips. "You always know exactly what to say." With a huff, she whirled and strode toward the black Suburban, trailed closely by Dierden. The agent's smug smile indicated he was keeping score and the odds had just bent in his favor.

"You're good with kids, Miss Delroy," Dierden muttered, his bulky frame disappearing into the vehicle behind her.

*

"I like the girl with the braid," Thomas said as the vehicle rumbled back toward Houston. "She's quick and tough. Good ball skills too. The other girl, with the blue bow, she's not bad either."

"Abby." Kathryn put a name with the bow for him. "The one with the braid is Maddie."

"Thanks. I liked the way you handled them too. When Maddie was going down the field, I noticed a little competition between those two. They must have played together before—or maybe against each other." He leaned toward her, his elbows resting on his knees. "When they collided and hit the dirt, Abby got up rubbing her knees like she was going to cry. Maddie was up and charging for the ball like nothing happened. Reminded me of someone I know. She's scrappy. You didn't acknowledge or sympathize, just clapped and encouraged. I liked that." He smiled.

That's what she needed to hear. What she'd wanted from him. Something to tell her it was handled right. She was an addict for praise. It had been difficult to come by with brothers. "Girls need to know that it's okay to be competitive and fierce on the field. They also need to turn the collisions around quickly and get back in the game. So many parents baby their daughters and that only teaches them to be weak."

"You think so?" He was close to teasing now.

"You're laughing at me," she said.

"No. Not at you, Katy. It's just that I thought it was cute the way the girls showed up in bows and pretty colors. Their hair was perfectly combed and their faces clean and sweet. I can't remember ever caring what I looked like when I went to practice. Girls are different I guess, but some of it's the parents too. The ones that spend more time worrying about how their girls look on the field, rather than what they do, have missed the point. Don't you think?"

Kathryn nodded. "To some extent, yes. But I think society as a whole places more emphasis on looks than we acknowledge. Especially in girls' sports. If you don't believe that, get on the internet and search for 'female athletes.' One of the first links you'll see points to a site that lists the hottest female athletes for the year."

Thomas laughed. "They do the same thing for male athletes—or haven't you looked?"

"No, not really," she admitted.

She didn't have time to surf the internet looking for hot athletes. The only reason she knew about the females was because at one point, a picture of her in running gear had made it onto the list. She was furious at the time. What gave them the right to post photos of her like that, and make some of the comments they did? In the picture, she was in her track uniform in college: spandex pants that were no more than a bikini bottom, and a tank that because of her height bared some of her stomach. She had bent over to tie her shoes and the picture was taken as she stood back up. One leg was stretched taught behind her, showing her hip and the muscle in her calf and thigh. Her abs were pretty ripped at the time. More so than now. Rather than athletic, she looked—sultry.

"You're still mad about the picture, aren't you?" He must have read her mind. "Sam told me you were pissed. He was bragging about it. Wanted everyone to know that was his sister. He hadn't even seen it until you called him, all ticked off. Why does that bother you?"

"You saw it?" Of course he did. Almost everyone she knew had seen it. She had been sick of the comments.

"Yeah, but I have to say—knowing what I know now, they didn't do you justice. You were only twenty-four on the list. Of course, that was a few years ago." Dierden's eyebrows perked up as he listened, his eyes focused out the window. "You didn't have the tattoo then, did you? That would have been a big hit. So would the piercing. Could have bumped you up to twenty at least." Dierden shot a glance her way, a startled but interested look.

"Stop it. How did we go from talking about little girls playing soccer to the sexy athletes list on the internet?"

"Hey, you're the one that brought it up. Not me." He raised his hands in defense. "Besides you should be proud of it. Only fifty women in the country make that list every year. The other millions want to be one of them. You shouldn't be mad about being beautiful AND talented."

It was incredible how Tommy could make a back-handed compliment seem almost accusatory. He'd called her beautiful at the same time he chastised her for not wanting to be on the list. Didn't he understand how demeaning it was for people to see you every day and look down at your legs or hips? It made her shiver sometimes the way some strangers had almost ogled her. She knew instantly they'd seen the picture. It was creepy.

"I just think the accomplishment in the sport is more important. That takes work. No one has control over their genetics. The looks are given to them, the athleticism is made by the individual."

"There's a little genetics in that too," he corrected.

He obviously didn't get it. She rolled her eyes, sighed, and closed her mouth. Leaning back in her seat, she crossed her arms and ceased talking until the car pulled into a parking garage. Thomas looked confused. The agents exchanged amused glances.

Chapter Twenty-Nine

A car horn blared at them as they exited the Suburban and walked toward the covered passageway to the building next to the garage. Thomas looked around to see who was complaining. No vehicle. The horn blared again. All eyes were on him. Oh yeah, his phone.

He pulled it out of his pocket and gave a one word answer. "Ryan."

The voice on the other end was warm and energetic, "Well, hello there! You must be back in Dallas." His mom was checking up on him. Even after all these years, she couldn't resist once in a while. More so now that he was closer to home.

"Hey, Mom. No, in Houston. I had a detour. We've had a little work emergency that needed attention." He looked at the agent walking next to him, who gave him a frown and shook his head as if to say "don't tell."

"Does that work emergency have anything to do with one Kathryn Delroy?" Apparently, she'd found out that Katy was at the training, and called out of curiosity. He laughed. She wasn't really interested in his well-being—her nose was out of joint. He stopped walking into the building and moved toward the edge of the garage. He held up a hand for them to either wait or continue without him. They moved away, but waited.

"As a matter of fact, it does." He didn't expand on the details. Let her think what she wanted.

"How is Katy, honey?"

"Fine, just fine. Look, Mom, I can't really talk right now. We're going into a meeting." That always seemed to work when he needed to avoid questions.

"It's Sunday, Tommy. No one has meetings on Sundays."

Unless of course, you're being escorted by the FBI because you unearthed a wanted fugitive. He grinned. If she knew, she'd flip. "I have to go, Mom. I'm sorry."

"She's with you right now?"

"Yes."

"Oh! Okay. Well, let me know how it goes then." She paused for him to hang up, but suddenly a thought came into his head.

"Mom? You knew about her, didn't you?" He didn't have to tell her what he meant. She'd always been able to read him. He hated that because sometimes she read the ugly parts; the ones no one wants their mom to see. Parts like how he'd drowned himself with alcohol and sex to try to forget or substitute for other things. She had recognized it for what it was, a coping mechanism. For years, she'd said nothing—then, when he quit coming home—she tore him up. Let him know exactly what an ass he had become, a drunken, whoring, stupid ass, and that he'd better clean it up and fast. Somehow, the message got through.

"Of course I did. I raised you, remember? You always wanted the best. And if you didn't get it, you tried even harder. That was the only time you didn't try." She hesitated a second. "I never understood why. Then you went a little nuts and I thought maybe you didn't think you deserved it. Or maybe I was wrong."

"You could have enlightened me too, you know. I just now figured it out."

"You wouldn't have listened. Besides, you both had other mountains to climb then. Your dad had big plans for you, and so did hers. It worked out better this way. You'd better get to your— meeting, honey. Tell Katy I said hello." She hung up as a smile crept across his lips. He turned back to the group and walked briskly into the building.

The security in the office was top-notch. He'd never seen anything like it. The four FBI agents motioned toward a metal detector, one said, "Ladies first." The agents went through another entrance that required them to place their weapons into a shelf of some sort, then pass their hand through a detection device. Once their identity was confirmed, they were allowed entry and stood on the other side waiting for Kathryn and Thomas.

A red light and loud buzz sounded as Kathryn passed through the detector. The heavy-set female guard sent her back, stating flatly, "Place any change in the bowl before entering. Your watch too. If you have metal heels in your shoes, take them off."

Kathryn removed her shoes and dropped her watch in the bowl. Again the red light and buzz denied her entry. The big lady surveyed her with distaste, "Maybe the earrings, ma'am. Check your pockets."

She slipped her hands into her pockets and came up empty. Pulled the earrings out and dropped them into the bowl, then tried again. No go. The guard shifted impatiently in her chair. Thomas didn't know why she had an attitude, there was no one behind them. No one waiting.

"Kathryn," he said calmly, "lift your shirt."

"Shut up, Thomas," she snapped.

"Damn it, Katy." He grabbed the hem of her shirt and flicked it up just enough to display the ring laced through her skin with a small sparkling charm attached. "See," he said to the guard. "That's what's setting it off. Not a weapon. Just a damn piercing."

He dropped the shirt and glared at Kathryn. "Quit being so damn modest. Lots of people have them. Nobody cares."

"Well, it never sets them off at the airport, so I didn't think it mattered."

"Anything else you *don't* want to show me?" the woman asked.

"No," Kathryn spoke softly.

Dierden and Kirth stood with hands together waiting. Dierden's face contained a noticeable smirk while Kirth's skin flushed red. Katy's face clouded angrily as the woman passed a hand wand over her and finally was satisfied enough to let her by. Thomas removed his watch, wallet, change, and shoes and sailed through without a problem.

They were greeted a few minutes later by a tall, lanky form that he recognized. "Trev! How's it going, man?" Thomas smiled and reached out a hand. Trevan took it then gave him a small hug. "I didn't expect to see you here."

"Since I was your first contact and I know you, they had me drive over." Other than a little facial hair, Trevan Prater hadn't changed much. "Cut your hair a little." Trevan said as he tussled his fingers on Thomas' head teasingly. "You still look like a hippie."

"Yeah, a hippie lawyer. How about that?" he boasted.

"Well, glad to see you finally finished, Tito. I was beginning to wonder if you intended to be a permanent resident on campus."

"Hey, law school takes time."

"So I hear. Someone told me you passed the bar the first try, made one of the highest scores they'd seen in some time. Is that true?"

"What can I say—I have a photographic memory. I'm good with details. I guess that got us in trouble this time. I should have just left everything as it was and disappeared."

"No man, we'll take care of you. Both of you. Besides, this is huge. History in the making. Don't you want to be part of it? You did a good thing. Probably the only thing you could have." Trevan turned slightly, put his arm around the woman behind him and edged her forward. "I want you to meet Sophie. Sophie, this is Thomas Ryan. I already told her about you, so don't start making a move or anything stupid like that. I'd hate to have to shoot you."

She extended a slender hand and smiled a greeting, then looked at Kathryn and began to introduce herself. "Sorry, this is Kathryn Delroy," Thomas said. "She and I work for Dad's company."

"We've known each other since we were kids." Kathryn shook hands with Trevan and Sophie and exchanged greetings before they moved along. She hooked her fingers through Trevan's arm and escorted him down the hall, "So tell me about this nickname you have for Tommy."

Trev laughed nervously and slid his arm from her grasp, looking back with panic. "I don't really know that story. I wasn't there. I think his friend, Sam, can tell you more than I could. Something about a girl wearing a bikini and how bad it looked on her. He'd seen it on—wait." Confusion crossed his face just before he looked at Thomas with widened eyes. He exhaled a curse, and then moved his gaze to Kathryn.

Thomas grinned and nodded. "Come on, Katy. Give the poor guy a chance to know you before you start asking him for the dirt on me. No friend is going to spill the beans to someone he doesn't even know. Look. You scared the crap out of him."

Trevan reached for Sophie's hand, an apparent move of desperation to escape Katy's interrogation. "Sophie, babe, can you wait for me in here?" He urged her into a room furnished much like a doctor's waiting room and closed the door behind them.

Having been deserted, Thomas and Katy followed the remaining group down the hall until they reached another door. They passed through to a conference room, joined a bit later by Trevan. Thomas smiled when he entered. The guy looked absolutely blissful. He'd always been a bit on the silent, perhaps even grumpy side. Stuck to himself mostly, but he was a good guy. He adored Sophie. You could see it in the way he touched her. Who could blame him? The hair, the almost Grecian goddess looks, she was certainly pretty.

Chapter Thirty

Nearly four hours after soccer practice ended, Kathryn finally put the key in her door for the first time in eight days. In truth, it felt like months—so much had happened in that short time.

She entered the apartment flanked by Dierden and Kirth. She was glad she had been successful in convincing them to let her go home. She rationalized that it was unlikely their man could travel that fast without special clearance or private planes, nor that he would move that quickly or haphazardly. All would change tomorrow but for now, she'd sleep in her own bed and the thought was comforting.

Their meeting with the FBI had been a repeat of the one in Anchorage. Just a different set of ears. She was now able to recite word for word everything that Thomas knew. She felt like she was with him as he discovered the envelope in the fridge. The severity and concern had escalated significantly when the agents provided further details on the man they were following. They were ecstatic over Thomas' find.

It was the first really strong lead they'd had in weeks. The impact this would have on her life was yet to be determined, but the danger was huge. What on earth possessed her to leave that stupid note? In doing so, she'd given the man her identity. She might as well have painted a large red target on her chest. Her intentions were good, the result might be deadly.

As soon as they were in the door, the agents brushed her aside and walked the entire apartment. They peeked in closets and cabinets, then glanced under the beds in the two bedrooms. The apartment was exactly as she left it, nothing disturbed.

When Dierden gave the all clear, they excused themselves and left her. "We'll be right outside if you need us, ma'am." She'd already been given a cell number to call in emergency. They were listening in on her phones so the FBI would know if anyone called. She'd also been informed that they'd likely wire the apartment for video surveillance in the morning. Since she'd given the suspect her contact information, they expected him to come after her.

One of the things Kathryn had missed while in Alaska was a bathtub. Showers are functional and fast. Baths are heaven. Good for the soul, and her soul needed one right now. She turned on the water, set the temperature, added bubbles and turned on some soothing music. When the tub was full, she slipped out of her clothes and eased into the water's warmth. Ahhh. Nice.

She wondered where Thomas was right now. They must have put him in a hotel. Somewhere close to the office probably. As she ran the soap over her torso, she remembered his fingers stroking there. A knot of excitement formed in the pit of her stomach. She remembered watching him slide the white cotton down her legs.

"Geeze." Kathryn shook her head. *Clear that thought right out of your mind girl. It's over now. Move on.*

Move on to what? He'd ruined any chance of that and probably didn't give it a second thought. Besides it wasn't as if there were a line of guys waiting at her door. And it wasn't like she would ever forget anything that happened between them.

The loud chanting music of her cell interrupted that thought. She jolted up, sloshing water everywhere. Splashing out of the bathroom to her purse, she pulled it out and answered. The number was Dallas. Him.

"Hello, this is Kathryn," she answered.

"Hey. What are you doing?" he asked.

"I'm standing in my room, dripping wet talking on the phone. What are you doing? Did you get settled into a hotel somewhere?"

He didn't seem too interested in her questions. "I'm sending you a picture. It appears they've attached a face to our Alaskan friend. He looks familiar but I'm not sure. I'll text it to you right now. Call me back when you get it and let me know what you think. Okay?"

"Sure." *After I towel off and get dressed.*

"Katy? Just curious, why are you dripping wet?" Of course he would ask. He just couldn't let that one go.

"Why do you think?" she said with a touch of sarcasm.

"Hmmm. I'm trying hard not to think about that at the moment. Call me back when you get the photos okay?"

"Okay."

She tossed the phone on the bed and went back into the bathroom to dry off and put on her nightclothes. After dressing and combing her hair back into a neat ponytail, she picked up the phone and checked her messages. There were two—no words, just the pictures.

It's an eerie feeling to look at a picture and know that you stood within five feet of a person that could have killed you in a heartbeat. A person that would do so without any hesitation or remorse. The first picture she received of a man with short brown hair and a short-cropped moustache could have been anyone. The second picture, however, was a man with a bushy beard. The kind that easily collected food—or beer foam. The kind that was on a man sitting in Hooksetter's Bar when she was there. The man that walked past her as she and Thomas were lip-locked in the parking lot. A coldness rushed over her as she recognized the face and realized how closely they had brushed with disaster.

She lifted the phone off the bed with a shaking hand and hit the button to dial Thomas.

Chapter Thirty-One

"I just figured it out too," he blurted as soon as he picked up the phone. "Hooksetters, behind the bus."

"Yes." He heard her suck in a deep breath. "So, what should we do next?"

"We need to let them know. Katy, I'm sorry about all this."

"It's not your fault. There's nothing to apologize for. I shouldn't have left that note. Without that, maybe it wouldn't be such a big deal."

"Yes, it would have. The note doesn't change much. I just didn't mean to—cause trouble again."

"Again? What does that mean?" He couldn't go into it. There was no way he was talking about Sam, the promise he'd made, the trouble he'd gotten into then. That was over. And it was trivial compared to this. He had thought he wasn't going to deal with any more big issues in his life. His confidence that he'd finally rounded the corner was premature. When his Dad signed him up for this management workshop, he was excited about it. He was also apprehensive. He'd come a long way over the years in rebuilding the bridges he'd burned. This one with Katy had never even been built, so burning it was impossible. Yet, for some reason he felt like there was a redemption needed of some sort. A clearing of the air. Or maybe it was a new start?

"I don't know. Not sure why I said that." He hesitated. "Look, since we'll both be working out of the Houston office for a while, would you be interested in going to lunch with me tomorrow?" She was quiet. "It's just lunch, and we'll have our escorts along. You'll be safe."

"I wasn't really worried about safety, Tommy. I just don't think it's good for either of us to spend too much time together right now. Especially since we both know that when they catch this guy and things are normal again, you'll go home to Dallas and I'll be here. I don't want to mislead you."

"Mislead me? Into what? Maybe another lunch after tomorrow? Or perhaps you might entice me into dinner too? God, that would be awful. Hell, if you really worked hard at it, you might even get me to go to some kids' soccer game or something with you." He paused, grinning. "Wait—you already did that, didn't you. Listen, you have to eat. So do I. If we go together, they only have to put two agents on us instead of four. So, if you think about it, I'm being considerate of these guys who are watching us. I'll come by your office around 11:30 tomorrow. Decide where you want to go, okay? I don't know my way around this city and I'll eat pretty much anything." He hung up without waiting for a response.

The Houston office was lit up like a Christmas tree by 6:30 a.m. That was in stark contrast to the Dallas office, which kept a more low-key, lazy schedule. Most of his office didn't start moving until right at 8:00. On Mondays, it was often closer to 9:00. Houston's pace was faster, which made it a little harder to get concentration time first thing in the morning.

He and his entourage were in the legal department, set up in an empty office and working within fifteen minutes. He'd called his dad the previous night before talking to Katy and advised him of the situation, without specifics. Calls were made and an empty office was waiting for him, one adjacent to a conference room in case it was needed. By 7:30, he'd answered emails, learned about a couple of new human resources issues he needed to address, and received some new contract drafts that required his revisions.

It was habit to do most of his work standing. He found it good for thought development, plus he had no desire to become chained to a desk all day. Not ever. As he paced back and forth in front of the window, he saw her exit the parking garage across the street and walk to the light. The realization came that he'd been pacing hoping for that and relief came strong, followed closely by amazement.

He'd only seen her dressed up once that he could remember, for her parents' anniversary party. Today, she was in a black dress and strappy black heels. As the light changed and she entered the building below him, he wished he'd asked her to meet him for breakfast instead.

*

Kathryn's cell chanted at her and she dug it out of her purse as she swiped her ID badge to enter the office building. She paused to hold the door for the two men with her. The doors opened at eight and card entry was mandatory any time before or after normal business hours. As she looked at the number on the phone, she smiled. "Good morning. Did you miss me or did you just forget something?"

"As a matter of fact, I saw you come in the building. I have a nice office that looks over the street. Great view." Thomas' voice was always pleasant—kind of calming. "Are we still on for lunch?"

"You never gave me a chance to answer," she chastised.

"Maybe I should rephrase that. Where do you want to go for lunch? Have you made up your mind?" He wasn't letting her back out. "I'll pick something, but don't complain if you don't like it."

"Have I ever done that?"

"I don't know. I've never taken you to lunch. Or anywhere else, for that matter."

"Other than a couch in the middle of nowhere." She wanted to bite her tongue after she said it, but it was too late for that.

"Yeah, but that was one hell of a couch. Still, I guess that wasn't real romantic, was it? I'll make it up to you next time."

"Next time? We're just going to lunch, Tommy."

"Yeah, I know. I'll see you then. You look beautiful in that dress by the way." He hung up.

*

At exactly 11:30, he strode into her office and closed the door behind him, jolting the guys following him to a stop. The men at her door had no option but to wait outside. She stood and reached for her bag. "Ready to go?"

He returned the smile and strode around her desk to stop within inches of her. He pulled the purse from between them, dropped it on the desk, and slid his hand around her waist over the slinky black material. His palm laid flat against her as his fingers spread across her back and eased her forward, closing the distance between them. Her hand was on his chest and he took it in his other hand before leaning down to taste her lips slowly, then deepening it until he stirred the response he had hoped for.

"Thanks. I needed that," he said softly when he finally drew back. "Yes, now I'm ready." He drew her hand into his and pulled her with him to the door.

He had no intention of getting a table for six at the restaurant. It was a cozy Italian place his dad had recommended. Upon entering with the agents in tow, he promptly asked for a table for two before Kathryn could speak. A frown crossed her face, but he ignored it. He understood the agents were here for their safety, but that didn't mean they had to be in his business completely.

A hostess walked them to a private booth toward the back of the restaurant. The booths were large wooden structures with walls that went up almost to the ceiling. Large, deep burgundy curtains swagged across the top of the opening above the booth and draped gracefully down to tiebacks at each side. If one wanted, the ties could be released and the curtains closed for more privacy. As much as he wanted to close them, doing so would probably cause panic on the part of their security posse, so Thomas left them alone.

He stood back and let her slip into the booth first, then slid in opposite. The meal was superb. She talked about her job extensively and he listened with interest. The guards sat at a table just outside the booth and seemed immersed in their own conversations. They skillfully checked out the surroundings on a regular basis but, with such a small space, it was easy to manage.

The lunch flew by and they returned to the office on time. "Want to come check out my temporary digs?" he asked, not wanting her to leave yet.

"Sure, but I have a meeting at 1:30 so I can't stay long." She entered the elevator before him. He'd held it open for the six of them. As much as he realized the importance of the FBI, it was rather awkward to have this many people trailing along with them everywhere. Especially when they insisted on entering spaces first, checking everything thoroughly, and constantly surveying the terrain wherever they went. And it definitely made it difficult to have a decent conversation with Kathryn.

The office was on the sixth floor. The mirrored glass on the windows ran from floor to ceiling, providing a clear view of the street yet ensuring complete privacy. Kathryn walked into the office and went straight to the window. The building allowed a perfect view out to the world, and none whatsoever into the offices. She stood with one hand on her hip in the black dress, surveying the street. He couldn't help admiring the muscles in her calves, and the polish on her toenails that peeked out from the black heels. The dress hit mid-thigh showing the perfect curve of her runner's legs. God, she was beautiful. She wore makeup today. She'd worn very little last week, but today the colors only served to accentuate the wideness of her eyes, the dimples, and the angular lines of her cheeks. The freckles had all but disappeared.

"Nice view," she remarked.

He came up behind her and watched the business below as people hustled along the street on foot, or in vehicles. "Yes, I was a little surprised. I didn't expect this. I thought I'd have a cubicle in a corner somewhere. If they're not careful, I may get used to this. I may never leave." He stood behind her, close enough to smell her shampoo. Close enough to want to get even closer.

"Sure you will, Thomas. That's what you do best." The sarcasm wasn't missed.

"You haven't seen what I do best yet," he answered blandly. He leaned over her shoulder and pointed to the street corner below them. "See that couple there at the light? Watch them. He dropped her off there this morning. Must be new romance or newlyweds. They're cute."

The couple held hands as they crossed the street to the opposite side, then the young man kissed her goodbye. He started to leave but she pulled him back. The young man's hands were in the girl's hair as he kissed her again, a long, sensual kiss. They let go and parted, each walking away to their jobs. A few seconds later, the young man turned and watched the girl prancing along. She tossed him a kiss, and disappeared into the stark office building across the street. The young man jammed his hands into his pockets and walked on.

"They did that this morning too?" she asked with a smile.

"Yep, I'm kind of looking forward to the next few days just to see if they keep it up. I wish I knew their story. It makes me smile every time I see them."

She stood quietly. How odd that he would notice this couple as well as the old people on the boat.

A tap on the door interrupted their silent reverence.

"Yes?" Thomas asked as he turned.

Dierden stood in the doorway, hesitant. "We have news." He ushered Kathryn and Thomas into the conference room adjoining the office where the other agents were waiting.

"The agents in Anchorage have concluded their investigation of the cabin," Dierden began. "They wanted to give us a brief update. If you have time, I'll give them a call. They're waiting."

Kathryn looked from Dierden to Thomas, then back. "I'm supposed to be in a meeting in a few minutes," she said.

"You might want to go a little late. I think you better hear this." Dierden pulled out a leather-backed roller chair, and sat. He rolled up to the table, placed his elbows on the glass top, and leaned forward to dial the number into the conference phone. Kathryn sent a short text to one of her staff to attend the meeting on her behalf, then focused on the present conference call. The conversation lasted less than twenty minutes.

According to Foster and the team in Alaska, the cabin was empty. The envelope was missing. The man was gone. Some of his clothes remained behind but he must have returned shortly after Kathryn and Thomas left. There was no note, so the agents assumed he'd kept it. From the forensics, they'd lifted his DNA as well as that of two other men and a woman.

They discussed some of the evidence. Based on the conversation, Thomas knew he himself would be the owner of one set of DNA. It hadn't occurred to him to cover his tracks. Why should it? He'd been too intensely involved in the time with Kathryn. His thoughts had only been on her. He volunteered that information.

"Some of your evidence will tie back to us." He glanced nervously at Katy. "We were there through the night and left early the next morning. We slept on the couch so anything found in that area would likely identify one or both of us." He motioned between Katy and himself. She didn't react. The agents showed no surprise. They'd already evaluated everything and knew the situation. There was something pretty intrusive about knowing that the people around them had found the stash of condoms he'd stuffed in the trash bin.

She kept her hands on the table, clasped together and didn't make eye contact. He wasn't sure that she'd put it all together yet. Her lack of reaction could either indicate that she hadn't, or that she wanted to ignore it. Or she was terrified.

"So that leads us to where we are today," Agent Foster said. "With the information we had, our staff were able to do a facial profile on one of the suspects. His DNA matched one set. By checking the facial recognition software against our data, criminal records, DMV records, and passport data—we were able to come up with five aliases."

Dierden motioned to a woman standing to the side of the room. She moved closer and pressed a button on a remote in her hand. A video presentation began on the wall, showing faces, along with background information associated to each. The first profile Thomas recognized. He glanced at Kathryn, she gave a brief nod. The others were the same man with various changes in hair, facial hair, dress, or other distinguishing characteristics. None were familiar. Thomas made a point to implant each face permanently in memory. From this point forward, every person they faced would be analyzed against those images. Not just by him, mostly by the agents that were their constant companions. The comparison had already begun. The FBI agents at the airport had run the facial recognition software against all cameras at the airport, attempting to see if their suspect had boarded any flights in the past few days. They had staff on site daily that continued to search for suspects.

The facial recognition would take a photo of each person entering the airport, then try to find at least five matching points of reference. They found eight possible matches in their database. Only one that mattered. Based on the information they'd accumulated, they were confident that the subject left Anchorage today. He flew on the 11 a.m. flight to Seattle. He did not change planes in Seattle, instead rented a car with a return date of the following Wednesday.

Thomas was relieved—that meant he wasn't here, with them, in Houston. "So we don't need to worry about him for a few days?"

"Maybe. Maybe not," the voice on the speakerphone answered. "There may be another person. We have someone in Seattle trying to locate and track him. If he drove, it would be a few days to get this far. That's unlikely. He wouldn't want to take the time or risk. It's possible he met with someone there. If so, there may be others involved. We aren't sure right now—we'll know more later today. The lab is checking the DNA samples and that, too, may identify a third party. A known or likely associate."

Kathryn looked up when the suggestion of another person involved was raised. She met Thomas' eyes without smiling or showing fear.

"Dierden," a voice on the phone said, "for now—we need to continue as we are. Everyone, be aware of the people around you. No large crowds or trips out alone for these two. Let's continue with this conference call for the next few days—same time, unless anyone disagrees. Things should change pretty soon. When it does, we'll need to move fast. Ms. Delroy, right now he only knows about you. That's who he'll come after. If he comes at all. You have to minimize your public time. Stay with your group there in the room. Vary your routine as much as possible. Do not tell anyone what's going on—not in person or on the phone. We should be able to flush him out soon."

"Understood," she confirmed. "What about my soccer team? We're supposed to have practice Thursday night. Should I cancel?"

"Let's wait until Wednesday to make the call. I don't know right now. It's hard to say what the situation will be then."

Dierden nodded and added, "We want to see if there's another person involved. If that's the case, it complicates this further. If not, we should be able to pick him up quickly. That's pretty much all for now. Anything else?" He darted looks at each person at the table, waiting for responses. Everyone shook their heads.

"Okay then. Thanks for the update, we'll talk again tomorrow." The voices on the other side offered goodbyes. He pressed the button on the conference phone to end the call.

Thomas and Kathryn were free to go back to work. Neither moved. The black loafers on his feet felt like they were cement-filled. The heaviness of the news glued them to their chairs. Thomas slid his hand sideways, covering hers with his fingers and tightening them. She tugged against him, trying to pull her hand back. He held tight.

Dierden glanced at the table, noticed the movement without acknowledging it. "Okay," he said rubbing his hands together, "if you need anything, you know where to find us. Right outside your door." He grinned and winked then ushered the others out of the room and closed the door.

Perceptive guy. If it weren't for his apparent interest in Kathryn, Thomas might like the man.

She missed the afternoon meeting. She could have made it, but instead she sat zombie-like in the conference room. Very little was said between them. Instead, with a shift of her chair toward the window, he understood she wanted silence and needed to digest what she'd heard. Overlooking the street, they watched the people below them hustling around, immersed in their daily routines.

After eons of silence, Kathryn inhaled deeply, lifted her shoulders and turned to him. "You know, Tommy." She paused for a moment, a glint creeping into her eyes. "I remember being around you was always a little bit exciting—never a dull moment, but you really took the prize with this one."

"I can't believe you can joke about it. Last week was pretty exciting, sure. This isn't so great. I'd kind of hoped things would continue—at least with you and me. I hadn't intended for us to be under lock and key, followed around by a bunch of bodyguards. It really cramps my style."

Kathryn laughed, "Yes, I imagine it's pretty hard for you to chase a skirt with someone else always tagging along. Or in this case, four someone elses."

Thomas turned his chair to face hers, levered his elbows on his knees and stroked his finger down her leg. She tensed.

"I want to tell you a story," he began. "We had a frat party for the pledges at the beginning of my junior year. It was one of those beach-themed things. There was a tiki hut for a bar, lots of Jamaican music, rum drinks in coconuts. You know, all the beach luau stuff. Everyone wore swim clothes. Lots of bikinis."

"I don't think I want to hear—"

He held up his palm to stop her. "Just listen. Okay? It's going to make sense in a while."

She closed her mouth. He clamped his hands around the arm of her chair and twisted it around. When she was facing him, he pulled the chair closer so that her long legs were against his slacks. Continuing to lean forward, he cupped his hands around her knees and started to speak again.

"There was this girl standing at the bar when I showed up at the party. I lived off campus then and only showed up when I had to. Anyway, I was wearing trunks. We all were. This girl at the bar had on a blue and pink striped bikini. She had brown hair tied up in a thing in back." He lifted his hand and twirled his fingers to emphasize the hair thing. "I knew the bikini. I'd seen it twenty or so times a couple years earlier on another girl. It reminded me of good times—of that girl. I thought it *was* her. I would have followed that damn suit anywhere. Two little pieces of material that were like a best friend to me, simply because of the girl in them."

"So, you were obsessed with the girl in the bikini?" she asked.

He laughed. "Maybe so, but I didn't know it at the time. I just thought of her as a good friend. When I saw that bikini at the party—it reminded me of home. Like I said, I would have followed it anywhere. So, thinking it was the same person, I walked up to the bar. I said, 'I never thought I'd see you here' to the girl in the bikini. When she turned, I realized it wasn't the right girl. It was the same suit, wrong girl. This one had huge boobs." He held his hands in front of him to emphasize the point. "It was all wrong. I jumped back and went 'Ohh!' when I saw them, uh...her. It was a completely involuntary reaction but the guys heard it, roared with laughter, and from then on, I was called Tito—for the girl with the big tits."

"I don't think that's the least bit funny. You made a joke out of this poor girl just because she was wearing the same suit some old girlfriend wore and because she was...big."

"Not some old girlfriend—and no, I didn't make fun of her. I felt terrible that they laughed at her. I talked to her the rest of the night just to be nice. I even walked her back to her sorority house. Everyone thought we did the—we didn't. She was nice, but it was all wrong. I wanted her to be the person that owned the suit that I remembered."

"So, what happened to your friend who you wanted it to be? Where is she now? Funny, I never knew you had a huge crush on anyone back then."

"That's the good part." He smiled. He rubbed his thumbs back and forth over her knee caps, gently. The feel of her legs stirred the same nervousness in his stomach he'd felt many times. "She's sitting right in front of me now in a black dress." He moved his eyes from the knees to her face to gauge a reaction.

"Me?"

"Yeah."

"Pink and blue striped bikini? I don't have—" Her frown cleared as she remembered. "Oh, yes. I guess I did. The lake water had changed the bright pink to more of a dusty rose color and I wore it all the time because it was comfortable and already ruined."

"Ruined. Good word. It definitely ruined me." He laughed softly.

"So, that's why they call you Tito?"

"Yes. All the guys thought it was because of my reaction to the girl with the boobs. Her name was Carline, by the way. It was really a reaction to wanting her to be—you. So, that's how I got the nickname."

"I still don't get why that old ratty suit was such a big deal. You never spoke to me at all then, other than to tease me. And you teased me brutally."

"Couldn't help it. It was the only way I knew to handle it."

"Handle what? I didn't need to be handled. I was a kid."

"My incessant lust. At the time, I didn't recognize it. I was too young and hadn't really—gotten familiar with all that. Now, I know exactly what it was. I wanted to be with you." He just said it, as if it was no big thing. It surprised him that he could calmly tell her after all these years.

"So, then, because you didn't sleep with me back then—you thought about it all this time? Is that what you're saying? And if you had—slept with me—maybe you wouldn't have thought about it and we wouldn't be here?" She could really over-think his words sometimes. He watched her face as she tried to digest what he'd said. He frowned.

"No, that's not what I meant. I just wanted you to know how I ended up with that stupid nickname. I didn't want you to get it from someone else like Trevan because it would sound—bad. Like it was all about a girl with big boobs. It was really about you."

"So, you ended up with that stupid nickname because of me and not the girl with the—Carline."

"That's right. Pretty much."

"Tommy, that's the stupidest thing I've ever heard." She leaned back in her chair and turned her head toward the window.

She was right. It was pretty stupid.

"So," she let out a breath, "in a roundabout way, you're trying to tell me that if we had been together in high school, we wouldn't be here right now? With four bodyguards on the other side of that door. In essence, this is my fault? If we'd had sex then, all would be fine."

"No. Where the hell did that come from?"

"Then why did you tell me the story?"

"I just wanted to lighten things up a little. To tell you how I-I don't know. I guess I hoped you'd like it."

"To tell me about yet another girl that you hooked up with? Or to tell me that I screwed up by not having sex with you years ago? That really sucks, Thomas. I don't care if you do want to try to pin it on me. You still got what you wanted—maybe a little later than expected, but it still happened. We can move on now. Or at least we could have if you'd left that stupid envelope alone. You just can't let anything be can you?"

"I always was a trouble-maker," he admitted. "And there is a small matter of a well-intentioned note from you."

Her face crinkled into a nervous smile and Thomas responded by taking her hands in his again, pulling her up against him and wrapping a big bear hug around her. He laughed into her hair, then placed his lips against her forehead. "Well, it can only get better from here, right?"

"Can I answer that in another week or two? That is, if I'm still alive?" she joked, but he knew it was masking a heavy dose of concern.

"That's not funny, Katy." He leaned back and looked down at her. "I promise I won't let anything happen to you. Neither will the guys standing outside that door." Without letting go, he nodded toward the entrance.

"Okay. But then what?" She asked. "When—or if—they catch this guy, what happens then? Do I get my life back? Or do I go into hiding for the rest of it? Will we spend the next twenty years looking over our shoulders for shadows?"

He wasn't sure how to answer that. Judging by the data he'd sent them, it could go either way. It all depended on how important it was to the people on those contracts. It all depended on the feds and how they intended to handle it. For the first time in as long as he could remember, his future resided on someone else's actions and successes. He hated the feeling, but he wasn't going to let her know.

"I don't know. But I'm curious—if we do have to go into hiding for the next twenty years, I just want to make sure you're ready."

"Ready?"

"Yeah. Do you still have that pink and blue bikini? I think we're gonna need it."

Chapter Thirty-Two

The agents moved Katy to the same hotel as Thomas. They planted a female agent at her place as a decoy and the decoy girl took on Katy's routine travel to and from work. While Katy was closer to him after hours, she hadn't seen Thomas other than the daily conference calls. He'd sat in on each one, listening to the updates. She felt his eyes boring into her daily, but he didn't come near. He hadn't touched her, or spoken to her on their escorted rides to the hotel. She ate her lunch in her office so didn't see him then. He had distanced himself. Not by linear distance, but emotionally.

As she rode the elevator down to their waiting car on Wednesday, it dawned on her that they were approaching a holiday weekend. "Gentlemen, do we have plans for the long weekend?"

"Long weekend?" Dierden asked. Obviously, he'd forgotten too.

"Yes, Fourth of July. We have Friday off."

"I had totally forgotten. Do you have plans for the Fourth, Ms. Delroy?"

"Yes. Or at least, I did. I need to call my parents and make sure. We always go to the lake. We've done that for years."

"I'm not sure that's going to work, ma'am." Dierden frowned. "Let me call it in this evening and we'll discuss it in tomorrow's meeting." He held the elevator for her to pass, then led her to the waiting car.

One nice advantage to having an FBI escort everywhere you go is not having to buy gas or pay toll roads. Kathryn managed a slight smile as they whizzed through the toll road gates on the beltway.

Thomas, Kathryn, and the agents rode in silence, staring out the window for fifteen minutes and her head was about to explode. Her phone interrupted the quiet. She looked at the name on the display. Sam. Good, a friendly voice. She remembered he'd left her a message to call last week.

"Hi there! Sorry I forgot to call you back," she started.

"What the hell is going on with you and Tom?" So much for a friendly voice. The muscles in the back of her neck tensed up and she raised a hand to rub them.

"Wow. Good to talk to you too, brother," she answered with sarcasm. Thomas obviously was paying attention now because he managed to finally look at her. She ignored him and continued staring through the glass.

"Sorry. I didn't mean to snap, but seriously—why didn't you tell me you were meeting him at some business camp? What's going on?"

Okay, that was it. She could handle Thomas' silence but she wasn't taking this crap from her own brother. Not right now.

"Maybe because I didn't know...and I wasn't *meeting* him. You can't meet someone if you don't know they're coming. My boss signed me up to go to a teamwork thing. It was in Alaska. Alaska, brother. Who wouldn't jump at a chance to go fishing and sightseeing there—even if you do have to do some business too? Oh, and by the way, *nothing* is going on. But even if it were, it's none of your business." She pulled her hand off her neck and flicked her hair back from her shoulder. The act sent it flying in Dierden's face, like the slap of a hand. He blinked.

"Oops. Sorry," she offered and held out a hand to touch his arm.

"No problem." His voice grumbled like thunder in the car.

"Who the hell is that?" Sam growled.

"What's wrong with you! Why are you all bent out of shape? Did you have a fight with a girlfriend or something?" She was almost spitting into the phone now. Thomas' eyebrow lifted as he watched. She shot a finger up at him. "Stop looking at me like that!"

"Katy!" Her brother's voice was impatient. "Who are you talking to? Would you do me a favor and let's just have one conversation at a time? If you can't talk, just say so and I'll call back later."

"Oh, sorry. I'm on my way home. I'm in a car full of people."

"Then I'll call back."

"No! No, it's okay. None of them are talking to me anyway. Why did you call?"

"You never called back. Listen, about Tom—" Okay, that was one conversation she had no intention of doing right at the moment. Not with him listening in on every word.

"We *are not* talking about him, Sam. That's off limits. Anything else is fine but not that."

"But I need to tell you something. It's important."

"No. You don't." She scowled. "There's nothing you can tell me that I haven't already figured out. Listen, are you going to the lake this weekend? I haven't talked to Mom since before I left. It's been crazy here and I didn't make any plans to be there."

"Of course. We always do. You're coming, aren't you?" His voice had lowered and was almost normal. "Who am I going to challenge to late-night pool games if you don't show up?"

"I'm not sure if I can yet. Let me check."

"Just curious, but who are you checking with?"

"No one. Well, my boss, I guess. I just might have to work. I'm not sure. I'll let you know tomorrow."

They said their goodbyes and she dropped her phone in her purse. She hated lying to Sam. He'd spotted it right away. He could always tell. She could fool her parents but never him. At this point, she didn't care—he'd meddled enough for a lifetime. Time to draw the line.

Thomas' phone sounded off and he answered. He looked at the display and swallowed a laugh. "What's up, man?" She couldn't hear the other side but she suspected Sam had just hung up from her and called him. "No," Thomas said. "Thanks for the invite but I'm in Houston right now so I can't." He paused, listening. He smoothed his slacks, adjusted his jacket, and gave her an almost braggart glance. "Yeah, it was good to see her. She looked—just as I remembered. You would have been proud, she really showed up a couple of the guys there on the exercises." Another pause. "Okay. I'll think about it. It sounds like fun." Pause. "Sure would. Okay, I'll call you tomorrow night." Pause. "Thanks, it was good talking to you too." He hung up.

Kathryn waited for him to say something—to confirm it was her brother. He didn't. "So that was Sam, wasn't it?" she snapped when he refused to offer it up. She turned and looked down her nose at him.

"You're listening in on my calls now, Katy? Since when did it become your business who I spoke to?"

"I didn't. It isn't," she stuttered and leaned back in her seat, placing her arms over her chest. "But it *was* him, right?"

"Why don't you just call back and find out?" He grinned, then turned to the window, dismissing her.

Kathryn let out a huffy growl as the car pulled into the hotel and dropped their entourage at the entrance. As soon as she'd made it out, she stomped into the building and headed straight to the stairs.

"Hold on, Ms. Delroy," Dierden tried to grab her arm, but she shook him off.

"I'm taking the stairs. If you don't like it, that's too bad. I'm sick of being cooped up—I need exercise." The two agents scurried after her to the stairs in a dead heat to keep up.

By the time she reached her floor, perspiration ran down her neck and threaded down her cheeks. Her breathing was stilted at best...she didn't care. The agents didn't even flinch. She slipped the hotel key into the door and pushed her way in, slamming it behind her. She didn't care if they checked her room first—she was sick of being watched. Sick of being followed.

And sick of Thomas. But God, he looked good in dress clothes. The gray fabric had hugged his legs lovingly today. It almost rippled when he moved. She hated him for looking like that. Absolutely like a damn movie star. The jerk. She pulled the hotel door open and stepped out.

"Look," she blasted at Dierden, raising a finger to his face. "I can't spend all my life cooped up in this damn room. I am an outside person, not an inside person. I like to run, fish, swim, wakeboard, ski—those are *outdoor* activities. Get it? Outdoors. My parents have a big family get-together every year on the Fourth and we all go home for it. I really want to go. Okay? I have to get outside. I will go crazy sitting around waiting for some creepo to come after me so you can do your hero thing. I'm leaving tomorrow after work. If you have a problem with that, take it up with whoever your boss is. Better yet, let *me* take it up with him." She swiped her sweaty hair from her face and glared at him.

"Well, Ms. Delroy, I suppose we can manage a trip to the great outdoors. We certainly don't want you to go crazy, ma'am." For the first time, the big oaf showed a grin. A nice grin that made his eyes crinkle up and it completely shut her down. He was teasing—making fun of her rampage.

"Good. And you're not showing up looking like a bunch of celebrity body guards, okay? My parents will freak out." She nodded her head once and turned into her room to change clothes. "One last thing." She was on a roll. "I'm eating out tonight so get ready."

"Yes, ma'am—but don't you have soccer practice first?" He smirked and she thought she saw him wink. So, they were going to let her do that. Good. She needed some fresh air badly. Needed some sunshine, those kids, and a little exercise.

Chapter Thirty-Three

Kathryn stepped out of the black SUV flanked by Thomas, Dierden, and Kirth. She breathed deeply the scent of lake water and pine trees. The distant tingle of the wind chime on the back porch tendered a smile. Her father had put one up years ago and though the neighbor to the east had complained about the "incessant, god-awful, jangling noise"—he replaced it every few years with another. She found it humorous that he would intentionally buy the noisiest one available just to prove his point—"No neighbor's going to tell me what to do on my own property."

Trudy, her parent's dog, greeted everyone with a low growl and single obligatory bark. Once she'd done her job of announcing their presence, she dropped her achy hips on the step and watched them approach. She was too old to run out to greet them, and seemed to consider it more of an effort than required. They'd just have to come to her. Kathryn was always amused at the way Trudy had taken reign over the lake house even though she saw it only three or four times a year. Her fourteen years were a marvel to everyone, considering her breed. Mastiffs usually didn't make it past ten. Still she chugged along with a tail that could clear a table in one swoop and an appetite that beat out any human. Then there was the drool, which she was affectionately allowing to drip down Agent Dierden's leg as he patted her on the step.

"Sorry about that, Greg, you probably want to stay clear of her tail and her chin. She drools badly, and her tail can swing as hard as a bat." Kathryn laughed as he swabbed the drool with his hand, looked for something to do with it, then finally wiped it back on his jeans leg.

The door flung open. Her mother swooped Kathryn into a hug, kissing her on the cheek. She then gasped at Thomas, "Good Lord, you're huge! In a good way, of course. Come here, Tommy, and give me a hug." She beckoned him in, and he obliged. "Sam said he'd invited you down along with some friends. I was so glad to hear that. We haven't seen you or your parents in such a long time—I think since the anniversary party, wasn't it, Kathryn?"

Kathryn nodded as Thomas turned to the agents and offered their names up. "This is Roy and Greg, Mrs. Delroy." He waved toward them. There were brief exchanges before she ushered them in. Kathryn had made everyone promise to keep their identities low key and not alarm her parents.

"This is a pretty big crowd for our little cabin, so you will have to double up," she said. "There are four bedrooms downstairs and a pullout couch in the den. Divvy it up however it works best for you. Kathryn, take them down and show them, will you? Sam's not here yet. He said he had to make a couple of stops first. He should be here soon. Hopefully before it gets too dark." She glanced out the window at the sun slowly receding behind the trees across the lake.

An hour later, everyone was settled into a space and had regrouped in the den around the pool table. Kathryn's parents were upstairs watching *CSI*.

"Want to play teams?" Roy pulled a pool stick from the rack on the wall.

"Okay with me." Thomas followed him. It would be rude not to oblige, so Kathryn grabbed a stick too and paired up with Dierden against Thomas and Roy.

They were on a second match when Sam's heavy footsteps descended down to meet them. He hugged Kathryn, then held her at arm's length for a second. His eyes squinted as he looked over her.

"What?" she asked. "Do I have something on my face?"

He laughed. "No, just checking to see if I needed to deck anyone." He shot a glance around the room, then grabbed Thomas' hand for a quick shake before pulling him into a hug too. "Good to see you, Ryan. Who're the two cops dressed like hippies?" he joked. Both the agent's mouths dropped open as they looked at each other. Kathryn giggled at their discomfort.

"They're not cops, idiot. Just friends of Thomas'. He said you told him they could come. I've just spent the car ride getting to know them since I was forced to hitch along."

"Why'd you have to hitch a ride? Something wrong with your car?"

"Yes, as a matter of fact, there is." She was getting pretty good at lying to Sam.

"So, who's winning?" Sam kicked off his shoes and went to the fridge to grab a beer. The others had already helped themselves.

"Right now, Roy and Tommy," Kathryn answered. "But it's getting ready to change."

"Don't bet on it, Katy," Tommy teased. "You haven't hit anything but the wall the last two times you were up."

"Is that a challenge, big boy? Because I'd hate to give you an old-fashioned ass whupping. Texas style, of course." She flipped her head to get her hair out of her face as she leaned down to take the next shot.

"You can whip my ass anytime you want to, Katy girl." He spoke in jest, but as soon as it came out, she turned three shades of red and missed her shot. "But you'll have to hit one of those balls on the table to start."

"Stop messing with me, Tommy. You keep talking when I'm supposed to hit. That's not fair. I never talk during your shots. You're still a cheater."

"I'm not cheating. You're easily distracted." He laughed.

"Oh, God." Sam exhaled. "It's the twilight zone—I feel like I've just been dropped back into high school. You two haven't changed a bit—still bickering like brats." He watched them warily.

"I'm no brat, brother—but your friend here doesn't play fair," Kathryn replied. She enjoyed the banter. It brought back memories. Memories of late-night games with Sam, Tommy, and a bevy of other family friends. Her eyes met Thomas' as the sparkle behind his gave way to a smile. That smile always seemed to tug a gut reaction that went all the way to her core. Then it was full of wonder and what-ifs. Now, she didn't know where the tug came from. Maybe just lack of sleep.

"She sure as hell doesn't look like a brat to me," Greg admitted in a low voice. Both Thomas and Sam turned to give him a glare before Thomas leaned over the table and took his shot. He sank two before missing. Greg then hit three to give them a lead. Kathryn thought he was amused. By the promise he'd made Kathryn, he now had liberty to act normal and drop the stiffness of his position. The boundaries blurred between professional decorum and fitting in. As she looked from Greg to Thomas, she realized that could pose some competitive interchanges. Interesting. She twitched her lip slightly at the thought.

The big surprise came when Roy, the silent onlooker, stepped up and cleared the pool table in one turn. He didn't say a word, just moved around like clockwork dropping one ball after another into the pockets. When finished, he picked up his beer from the edge of the table and sipped it. "Ready for another round?" he asked calmly.

All four mouths hung open, stunned. Greg was the first to speak. "You've been holding out on me, man. When did you learn to play like that? I could have made some money off you."

Roy shrugged. "Lots of late-night stake—bar hopping. I'm not much of a drinker and as you can see, not great with conversation. So, it was a way to keep busy and kill time."

"Shit! You're a hustler."

Roy laughed. "No, but I've won a little cash here and there. All legit."

Kathryn passed her cue stick to Sam. "Here brother. I'm done. You take over for me. I can't beat that." She pattered barefoot to the fridge, pulled out a beer and eased open the back door to walk down to the water.

Kathryn heard a clatter as Dierden dropped his stick and started after her but Sam stuck an arm in front of him. "Hold on there. I think you'd better stay right here, dude. Bratty or not, she's still my sister and I need a pool partner." Sam's voice held a hint of threat. Kathryn noticed the exchange briefly—their voices carried on the breeze. Greg wasn't going to like this—she knew she'd hear about it. Still, to be able to walk freely outside, even for just a few feet, was invigorating. She heard voices behind her laughing, then the screen door slammed. It came as no surprise that Tommy had walked up a few seconds later, the tenseness in her stomach gave it away.

"What's the matter, can't stay away from me?" she teased as she sat down on the dock and stretched her arms back to prop herself as she looked up at the stars.

"You want me to answer that honestly or make something up?"

"Honesty is always best."

"Well, then...no, I can't—I never was able to stay away. You're like a frickin' magnet."

"I'd hate to hear the lie," she responded wryly.

"You wanted honest—I gave it to you. If that scares you, tough shit." He shrugged and dropped beside her. "Guess you can't handle the truth."

"I can handle it when I hear it." She turned her head slightly so the breeze would stop brushing her hair into her face. Another deluge of laughter erupted behind them. She looked across the water at a lone boat sitting in the darkness. The moonlight cast a gleam over its bow that glittered and glinted with color. A lone night fisherman. There were a lot of dedicated old goats like that here. Fishermen that felt the late night fishing to be more productive and peaceful than daylight.

Thomas slipped his hand behind her neck and rubbed his fingers lightly against her hairline. "Katy, the truth is staring you right in the eyes. Just open them up and take a look." He pulled her to him and gently touched her mouth with his. She thought he'd draw away, but no. He geared up the kiss until she was reeling in it, grasping toward his chest again. She found it frustrating that he could do that so easily—turn her to melted butter. It wasn't fair.

He backed off suddenly, leaving her unbalanced. "Let's go inside before Dierden has a stroke—and before I try to get inside your clothes in your parents' backyard."

"What makes you think I'd let you? The fling's over, Tommy."

He laughed softly. "Yes, it is—isn't it?"

At least he had admitted it. Somehow, his response had made her feel almost melancholy. A part of her that she'd held onto for years had now broken off and disappeared. The part that had imagined what it was like to be wrapped up in those arms.

He lifted her and pushed her toward the door and the people inside. Resting his palm against her lower back as they moved, he reached his other out to tug the door open for her. She slid past him toward the group inside. Leaning down and pressing his nose against her ear, he whispered. "Sleep with me tonight, little magnet girl."

Chapter Thirty-Four

Eric's eyes were sweating from the pressure of the binoculars pressed against them. The summer heat in Texas was sweltering even in the pitch dark. He wanted this over with so he could go home. It would have been nice to at least have a small breeze as he sat in this boat, waiting for an opportunity. But no such luck. He watched her come out the door and sit, but the boat dock was between them. Then the guy came out and sat with her. He found it interesting that he had to come across the continent to silence someone that was within fifteen feet of him only days ago. And the man with her. Was he part of it too? Obviously, that was who she was with at his cabin. Who else could it be?

It had been pretty easy to track them down. She was a local legend apparently—everyone knew her and knew her routines. He was sick of all the running around though. He'd found her apartment easily enough but she wasn't there. The lady there looked like her but he knew instantly: a roommate. He had considered talking with her but decided not to. Something about the woman didn't feel right.

His cell, on vibrate only, nagged at him and he answered it with one hand while keeping the binoculars perched in front of his face. The wind had picked up and whistled against his ear.

"What are you doing?" Smitty's voice grumbled.

"Tracking down a problem."

"Problem? Something I should know about?"

"Right now, no. Just someone that may have seen too much."

"Seen too much? Too much of what?"

"My files."

"What?" Despite the wind, he could hear the man choking on a drink over the phone. "What the hell does that mean?"

"Probably nothing. I don't know—but I can't take a chance. I've been following her to find out."

"Her? It's a woman? What did you do, Eric? You screwed some bitch and now she's blackmailing you?"

"No! Shut the hell up. It's nothing like that." He tossed the binoculars onto the seat of the boat and transferred the phone to his other hand as the door closed behind Kathryn and her friend. "She broke into my cabin a few nights ago with some guy, looking for a place to shack up. She may have seen the files, not sure. She left a thank-you note, so I doubt it. If she'd seen anything, she probably wouldn't want me to know she'd been there."

"Then what are you doing? Why do you think there's a problem?"

"I don't know. My stuff was...disturbed. Moved. As if someone had opened it and looked."

"You're a dead man if she's seen any of it. I don't know why you insist on copies of everything. That just opens the door for something like this."

"Don't threaten me, asshole. I'm fixing it. And you know why I insist on the contracts and the copies. You can't guarantee something that you don't agree to in any detail. The detail is critical. Don't get all worked up. I followed her and I'll fix it."

"How? Exactly what do you intend to do?"

"Nothing unless I know for sure she's seen it. If so, then she'll have to be quiet, won't she?"

"God, you're getting messy, man. These people don't like messy—I don't like messy. Have you done anything at all with the project? We're running out of time."

"Yes, I've done a lot actually. I think you'll get the result you're looking for. I have to check back again in a couple of days but she seemed—with us."

"Are you going to explain that? Or is that all I get?"

"Look, sometimes it's better that you don't know all the little things. I'm not going to tell you everything I've done unless there's a problem. You've never bothered with that before. I will meet the obligations of the contract. Everything is under control."

"Of course it is," Smitty snapped. "It always is." The phone clicked and the conversation was over.

He pulled a beer from the cooler on the deck and sat down to cool off—and wait.

Chapter Thirty-Five

Little magnet girl? That was a line she hadn't heard before. Stepping through the door, she darted an angry scowl his way before smiling at the others. *He gives her the silent treatment for three days, then he says that? What gives?*

"So, who's winning?" she asked as she joined her brother and the agents.

"Who do you think?" Greg nodded his head at Roy. "He's stealing us blind. Everything okay out there?" He gestured lightly at the door.

"Of course. It's pitch dark except for the stars. Not a soul stirring. I would guess that everyone around the lake is already asleep—but us and the fishermen."

Greg eased to the window, lifted the curtain edge, and peeked outside.

Sam moved around the pool table and hung up his cue stick. "So, how's work going, sis? Any big projects or new gossip?" He walked toward her and dropped on the couch, lifting his legs to rest them on the small table in front.

"Nothing much, other than trying to catch up after the week away." She plopped down next to him. "You know Tommy's been working in Houston this week?"

He cast a curious glance toward his friend before responding, "He told me." Sam looked over his shoulder and called back to Thomas, "Hey, Ryan—bring us some beer so we don't have to get up."

"You lazy ass," Tommy answered, but he obliged. "Here you go." He handed a bottle to Sam, then opened the second and wedged himself between Sam and Kathryn before giving it to her. "Yeah, I have to be in Houston for at least another week or two. Then, back to Dallas."

"So, why'd you choose contract law, Tom? That seems so boring compared to—well, just about anything."

"You ask me that every time I see you. Get over it. It's a good career. Besides, it's what my dad wanted." He shrugged and lifted the beer to his lips.

"Since when did you ever do what your dad wanted you to? The guy I remember never really cared what anyone expected of him."

Tommy's thigh was against Kathryn. His shorts did nothing to stay the warmth of his skin next to her. He had slid his hand between them, his fingers didn't move but the feel of them against her knee was like a caress. "I've always cared what people expected," he answered Sam. "I just didn't necessarily let that decide my actions. Except law, of course. I thought it might make me a better person and I didn't really know what else to do. As it turned out, I did a lot of things the way Dad wanted."

Kathryn wondered if he really considered himself in need of betterment. It seemed out of character from the young man she remembered. She had thought his confidence unwavering. Just like his way with women. Sure. Masterful.

He turned to catch her eyes on him and raised a brow in curiosity. "So, Katy," he grinned, "where do your parents keep the sheets now?"

"What?" She blinked.

He patted the couch. "You're sitting on my bed. I'm getting a little tired."

"Oh. So, you drew the sofa, I guess. Lucky you."

"I volunteered. I slept here more times than I can remember as a kid. This old thing is a friend to me. It only seemed fair to let the new guys have beds and privacy. Since your room's the last one down the hallway, there will be plenty of big, burly men between you and the door. No chance for any old boyfriends to sneak in. The sheets used to be in that coffee table that was right here, but now that they have this new thing I don't know where to look." He pointed to the table under Sam's feet.

Greg and Roy were standing next to the pool table, talking quietly. She wondered what great espionage they were reminiscing about. It must be exciting to eavesdrop on their conversations. More so than hers, at least. They seemed to agree on something and put the pool sticks away, then excused themselves.

"I'll get your sheets and a pillow." Kathryn pushed herself up from the couch and went upstairs in search of linens. Returning minutes later, she found him standing with his beer in hand, staring at a picture on the wall. Sam had apparently retired also.

"Katy, when was this picture taken?" He pointed at the frame.

With a plunk, she dropped the linens on his pseudo bed, and moved to his side. The frame depicted the four faces of her family, smiling cheerfully with arms around each other.

"The anniversary party a few years ago. It's probably the only time I've ever seen Sam wear a suit. I was a little surprised that he did. He threatened to show up in jeans."

"It's a great picture." He glazed his free hand lightly up her back, sending fluttering sparks through her. "Everyone looks— happy. I can't remember the last time my family had a picture together. Or even were all in the same room at once." His voice sounded wistful. He leaned his head toward her as if to kiss her. Kathryn took his beer and lifted it to her lips quickly. Her eyes watched him over the neck of the bottle.

"Your linens are right there." She pointed. "Sleep tight." She handed the beer back to him and started to turn toward the hall to her room. His hand laced around hers, engulfing her grasp.

"Katy," he muttered, pulling her back.

"Don't, Tommy." She slid a toe back and forth on the floor as if to draw a line between them.

"Don't what?" He set the empty beer bottle down but kept his grasp on her hand. "Don't touch you?"

"Don't play with me. Not here. Not in my own house." She'd thought she could handle it but she was wrong. Casual with him just didn't work. Not for her. Maybe he could turn it on and off, but she couldn't.

"I'm not. I wouldn't do that. Not in your *parents'* house—or anywhere else." He looked past her. "This thing has always been here, Katy. Between us—it's always been here. Kissing you is like coming home. I wanted to do it fourteen years ago."

"Then why didn't you? It's not like I was hiding." She wanted to believe the words. They were good words. Even if he might have used them on someone else, she liked the way hearing them made her feel.

"Well, smarter heads prevailed. I made a promise not to." He had eased his hand up to rest at the nape of her neck and rubbed a thumb across her collarbone. It sent hot stabs of need along her shoulders. She leaned forward and dropped her head on his chest to give him better access.

She murmured against his shirt, "You made a promise not to kiss me."

"Well, to be accurate—I made a promise to stay away from you." He threaded his fingertips up and down her forearm.

"Then what are you doing now?"

"I decided last week there's a statute of limitations on promises like that. Doing the right thing all your life is highly overrated." He nibbled along her neck, sending flashes of heat throughout her body. She wasn't sure if she believed what he said or not—but she didn't care. The reality was clear. At least to her.

"Tommy." She raised her eyes to him. "I thought I could do this, but I can't. I'm just not that kind of person. See, I don't really do flings. I—can't really—sleep with someone, then pretend we're just friends."

"I know." He kissed her forehead. "I never thought you could."

"But you agreed to it. No regrets, you said."

He kissed the end of her nose and she frowned. "Katy," he whispered as he leaned down to pull her against him. "Look where your hands are, honey." She glanced down at her fingers—involuntarily stroking against his chest, tickling his torso. She forced them still against his skin. He laughed. "There's nothing casual about wanting someone. Not like this. And we're not just friends. There's no way in hell I want to be friends with you. Do I have regrets? Sure—but not about this." He touched his lips to hers lightly. "Just to clarify—you're the one that keeps saying casual—not me." He licked at her mouth, teasingly at first, then with more pressure. "Come on, Katy—kiss me. There's nothing wrong with this. Tell me you want it too."

"Shut up, Tommy," she mumbled. "You talk too much." She yanked him closer and threaded her fingers into his hair as she tangled her tongue with his. She liked that she had elicited a low groan in response. "Yes, I want it too." Her breathless words blew out against his lips between touches. She pulled him toward the couch, but he gently nudged her past.

"No more couches, honey. I'm not getting naked on the sofa in your parents' basement. I want a bed. One with you in it."

"Okay, but I hope you don't have a problem with bright pink and purple." She led him by the hand to her room. The same room she'd used since her parents bought the lake house when she was ten. There was a vaguely smug realization that Tommy had called her honey. Twice.

*

Thomas woke abruptly hours later. He thought he'd heard movement—either in the hall or the room. It was so damn dark, who could tell? Katy's hair was spread over his shoulder, his chin against her forehead. Her arm lay across him and her knee rested heavily on his thigh. The bed was small—too small for two adults. Yet, he'd slept hard for the last couple of hours. Even this small bed was better than the one in the hotel. He hadn't realized how tired he was. Or maybe it was just restless. Still, only two hours of sleep wasn't enough to clear the fog.

He brought his free hand up and rubbed his eyes, trying to peer into the darkness. The fragrant smell of wax from the candle they'd burned next to the bed was still in the air. His thoughts returned to the flickering of the rosy glow across her skin as she had moved against him. It made him want to wake her. He fumbled for the lighter to light the candle. Where was it? They'd dropped it right there next to the flame as they slid onto the bed. His fingers felt around until he came in contact. He turned it to get to the curl of the switch.

Another noise. This time he was sure it was in the other room. He didn't want her family to find him in here. As much as he wanted to be here, it wasn't fair that they found out like this. No, he needed to do this right. He eased himself from below her weight, lightly touching a kiss to her lips as he lifted himself from the bed. Another sound—like an intake of breath. He looked down at her—was she awake? It was too dark in this damn room to tell. He stayed motionless, listening to confirm her steady breathing. No, she was still very much asleep. She didn't snore—just a light, soothing huff as she breathed in and out. He twisted his lips up slightly before tiptoeing to the door.

He walked silently on the carpet as he worked down the hall to the sofa. A clank of glass and a whispered, "Damn it" caught his attention. He reached to the wall and flipped the light.

"Shit, Thomas," Sam hissed. "You scared the hell out of me.

What are you doing sneaking around down here like a damn cat?" Sam took in his dress—or lack of, then his eyes moved to the linens still sitting on the sofa—then the hallway behind him. He stood there quietly, as if trying to gather his thoughts. Thomas watched him warily. Sam's eyes narrowed to slivers. "You son of a bitch."

Thomas walked toward him in his boxers, his hand out to quiet him. "It's not like that, Sam."

Sam shook his head, and put a finger up to stop any explanation. "Don't tell me what it's like, you fucking asshole." He pointed to the hallway. "You couldn't just leave it alone, could you? Couldn't just let this one go. She's a good person. She doesn't need this crap. God, you're pathetic."

"Yeah, I am," Thomas admitted. "I'm pathetically in love with your sister. I've been in love with her since high school. You knew it. Don't pretend you didn't."

"You just wanted to get in her pants. Like every other girl you knew. I wasn't going to let you do that to her. She didn't deserve it."

"Hey, I kept my promise. Did you ever think for a minute maybe that's why I acted the way I did?" He tried to keep his voice low, but the anger was boiling. "Everyone forced me away from the only person I really wanted to be with. You were so afraid I'd screw up her life that I ended up screwing mine up."

"That's ridiculous. I didn't make you behave that way." Sam put his hands on his hips briefly, then started toward the bar. "I need a drink," he muttered as he pulled down a glass and filled it with scotch. He picked up an empty glass, motioning for Thomas to join him. The glug of Scotch pouring into the glass only served to accentuate the silence between them. Both men downed the drinks without a word.

"What's going on in here?" Dierden's voice grumbled. His hand rested behind his back as Dierden leaned against the wall.

Thomas knew a loaded Glock was grasped in his hand, ready for use. The irony of their situation was like lead on his heart.

Sam wanted to kill him for making love to his sister. An unknown criminal probably wanted to kill her for discovering the paperwork in his home, a result of their love-making. Two FBI agents were following them around with guns to make sure nothing happened. He laughed, wondering if Dierden had considered keeping Sam from killing them both before the other guy did?

"What the hell is so funny?" Sam spat, glaring at him over the glass.

The clattering of metal against concrete outside the house prevented Thomas from answering. All three heads whipped toward the door. Dierden's gun was in full view now as he moved to see where the noise came from. He lunged to grab Thomas' shoulder and shove him between the sofa and table, then surged toward Sam.

"Jesus! What's with the gun, dude?" Sam backed away from Greg as he advanced.

"It's okay, Sam," Thomas spoke. "He's just doing his job. He's here to protect us."

"Protect you? From who—me?" Sam watched warily as Dierden opened the back door quietly and slid outside. "I'm pissed, Tom. But not that pissed."

"Look, it's a long story—but they think someone's going to try to hurt us. Greg and Roy are here to protect Kathryn. And me too, but mostly her." Thomas was torn between saying too much and a need to explain.

"I need another drink." Sam poured Scotch generously. He held the bottle up to Thomas' glass.

Thomas covered the glass with his hand. He needed to be fully aware if something happened.

Sam frowned. "I also need a better story than the one you just gave."

"Later."

Roy and Dierden came in the door and closed it solidly behind them. They walked the entire house, peeking in on her parents without waking them.

When they returned, Roy spoke, "We had an intruder. I'm not sure if it was our guy or just some thief hoping he'd catch you gone for the holiday weekend."

Thomas had heard him speak so little that he was dumbfounded. He watched his lips move as the words sank in.

"The sliding door to the patio in Sam's room was open. I assume your voices startled the person or persons and they went right back out the way they came in. I checked all the doors when we got here, so I'm certain it was locked. Did one of you guys unlock it?"

"Not me. I don't even notice those things," Sam answered. "We've never needed to worry about locks before."

"That's what most people say. Frankly, I've never understood it. It's like playing Russian Roulette with thieves. The more you leave your doors unlocked, the more likely it is someone will come through that you don't want." Roy shrugged. "Stupid, if you ask me."

"Whoever it was, they're gone now." Roy moved the curtain to look outside again.

"I'm staying in here. Thomas, you've just lost your spot," Dierden spoke. He looked at the couch and grinned. "Guess you weren't really using it anyway, were you?"

Kathryn walked in, rubbing her eyes. Her hair was tangled around her head like cotton candy. "Why are you guys all awake so early?"

Before the others could speak, Thomas answered, "Sorry we're making so much noise. We didn't mean to wake you up." He held up his glass to punctuate his next remark. "Male bonding."

She glanced from Tommy to Sam. Sam tilted his glass to confirm. Her gaze moved toward the two agents. Fortunately, they had slipped their firearms back into the holsters at their backs. Still, the presence was noticed.

"Male bonding over guns and booze. Somehow I doubt that, Tommy."

He sighed. Nothing got past her. As he moved to her and took her arm, he became keenly aware he was standing among the group in his boxers. "Go back to sleep, Katy, honey. We're just—trying to out-drink each other. I guess we got a little loud."

She looked over Thomas's shoulder at Sam. Thomas glanced back, catching the glare Sam sent them both. He pushed her down the hall to her room. "You're not telling me the truth," she whispered. At the door to the pink and purple room, she turned back to face him, a challenge in her look. He groaned. He wasn't going to lie.

"There was someone lurking around. Roy and Greg chased them off."

"And Sam knew you were in my room? That's why there are daggers in his eyes?"

He shrugged sheepishly. "Yeah." He didn't mention the exchange he had with her brother. No need to fuel the fire.

"Great. Just great." Her voice choked. She obviously had not wanted anyone to know about him. To know that she'd just had her hands and lips all over him. Now he was pissed.

Fire shot into her eyes. "You called me honey back there." She pointed down the hall. "In front of them."

"Yeah, I did. So what?" He didn't register his voice rising.

"They'll think..." She hissed loudly.

"Think what?" he spat. "That I care about you? Damn it, Katy. I spent the last ten years trying *not* to care about you because someone didn't want me to. Someone in your family and someone in mine. Screw them. If I have to wait ten more years for you to realize you care too, we're gonna be too damned old to have kids. Is that what you want?" His voice thundered down the hall.

The crash of glass breaking jolted their heads up as they realized every word had been heard. Her mouth fell. She narrowed eyes on him coldly. *Did he really say that? Did he mean it? Wow.* He did.

"You *waited* ten years, my ass." Spit flew out of her mouth as she spoke. "Yeah, you cared. Cared for any girl who would let you touch her."

He reached out and shook her. "Did you ever think for once that you were told those damn stories for a reason? The same reason I was talked into a stupid promise? Nobody else had any faith in us. Well, I do, and you damn well better get some too."

The sound of Dierden's throat clearing behind them brought the argument to a halt. "This is all pretty interesting guys, better than *All My Children* actually, but we all want to go to sleep. It's four in the morning." He winked at Katy. "Pack it up and go to bed. You two can brawl all you want tomorrow."

"Good point. I'm tired." Thomas looked past Katy at the pink and purple room, then turned. "Don't worry, honey, I'll sleep in Dierden's bed since he's in mine." He paused then added, "At least for the rest of the night."

"Stop calling me honey," she shot back.

"Yes, dear." He smirked as she slammed her door.

Chapter Thirty-Six

Two hours, two beers, and lots of rock music on the iPod, passed easily. A nice little break from all the travel of the past couple of days. Eric stretched his arms and legs, then stripped down, put on his trunks, and pegged the engine into gear. He maneuvered the boat to a dock three houses down. He'd noticed the For Sale sign on the house earlier and, due to the proximity, it seemed perfect for his needs. Out of view due to the curve of the cove around them, yet easily accessible by foot in a few minutes. He tied up and slipped on the dark clothes over his trunks, then strapped the backpack on and holstered the revolver. He had no intention of shooting her. He just wanted to get in and check things out. See what he needed to see. He was a little concerned about the size of the group. Too many people tended to complicate plans.

Getting in and out of the house had been a piece of cake. Small town people never seem very fond of locks so they don't opt for deadbolts and alarms. The simple latch was no obstacle. He eased in through the back door, and worked his way down the hall to her room—easy to identify since it had large purple letters with pink dots that stated "Katy's Room." He had thought perhaps he'd snoop through her bags and computer, if he could find them. He'd check for emails or file copies that might indicate her involvement.

Once in the room, though, he realized his mistake. He hadn't thought it through well enough. The twin bed barely big enough for one adult was overflowing with skin. She was draped over some guy like silk sheets. As he stood trying to decide what to do next, the guy woke and moved his hand to his head. Eric sucked in his breath and blended into the dark purple paint behind the dresser as the man rose and pulled on shorts, then padded out of the room.

The voices down the hall grew louder and were subsequently joined by others. The party was getting crowded. Any minute and they could be in here, switching on the lights. He slithered out the door and down the hall. No way he could make it out the back door. He slipped into the next room. Bingo—a sliding glass door. He quietly eased it back and stepped outside, then slipped it back into place. Once out, he backed away—right into a flowerpot that sat against the steps to an upper deck. He turned and fled across the grass as the sound of clay hitting concrete thundered in the background. Voices came out the door, but he kept moving, sticking to the shadows of the houses.

Eric didn't look back until he'd made it around the cove and to the boat dock. He stepped into the water and worked his way to the boat in the dark, then slipped down into the hull and covered himself. He laid still for an eternity before he felt comfortable starting the engine and moving on. His pulse was exploding, his heart beat so fast, he imagined he could hear it. *She had bodyguards—and they were definitely feds. Smitty may not have feds on his tail, but she sure did.* She knew everything—and so did they. Holy crap.

Chapter Thirty-Seven

Kathryn sat on the stool by the kitchen counter, swinging her feet in rhythm to a song on the radio. Her hands gestured wildly as she told her mother about the girls on her soccer team. She couldn't help but feel pride in the little girls, knowing that someday they'd look back on this experience as she did. With nostalgia and pride.

"Those girls will remember this always, honey." Her mother smiled. "I'm so proud of you for volunteering." The simple word of love reminded Kathryn of her argument with Thomas a few hours earlier. *Honey.* He'd witnessed her mother say it to both Sam and herself on numerous occasions. Mom even called Tommy that a few times. And now he used it with her.

Ruby Delroy's eyes moved to the door behind Kathryn. "Good morning, Tommy. Did you sleep well?"

Kathryn's back stiffened but she didn't turn to look. She felt him approach.

"Yes, ma'am. It was a little restless at first, but I'm good now." He passed by Kathryn and gave her mom a quick hug. "You're up early," he said to Katy. "I half expected you to still be down there snoring away."

"Unlike you, I didn't sleep that great. I'm not used to that little bed any more. Mom and I were discussing my soccer team." She rubbed her shoulders as the neck muscle glitch reminded her how badly she'd tossed and turned. Thomas moved behind her and put both palms over her shoulders then started kneading at the knots. Her mother noticed but turned to open the fridge.

"I'm told I have good hands for this," Tommy said. "Let's get those kinks out." Kathryn shrugged at him in a slight attempt to loosen his hands. The familiarity was a little awkward but still his hands felt good—and her neck didn't. She let him rub as the tension started to melt away.

With her nose in the fridge, Ruby spoke matter-of-factly. "I was wondering when you two would finally stop tiptoeing around each other." Eggs in one hand, bacon in the other, the woman turned and grinned at them.

Kathryn's mouth fell as she feigned ignorance. "What does that mean?"

"It means exactly what you think it does, honey. I raised you, remember? I'm not blind. Or stupid." She placed the food on the counter and dug a skillet from the cabinet.

Tommy snickered. Kathryn reached up and pushed his hands off her shoulders. He patiently returned them and continued the massage. "Maybe you're not, Mrs. Delroy, but someone else in this room seems to be."

"Let her bristle for a while. It's only taken twelve years for you to make that move." Ruby pointed at his hands. "I don't guess we're in any big hurry around here, are we, Kathryn?" She wouldn't be so quick to approve if she knew the other moves he had made. The man had some pretty animalistic needs. Okay, maybe she did too, but Mom didn't need to know about that.

"Mom. Stop it. You're supposed to be on my side."

"I am, honey."

"She is, honey," Thomas repeated.

Kathryn let out a loud groan. "I'm getting dressed." She spun her chair around, dropped her feet, and pattered to the stairs. "Call me after you two have finished your plotting."

A thought occurred to her as she descended to the basement, and she called back up at them, "I'm taking the boat out after breakfast, if anyone wants to go. I need to get outside."

A little sunshine and lake water would get things back into perspective, she hoped. Hadn't Thomas encouraged her to take more control? At the moment, she wanted sunshine. Maybe she could come to terms with all the turmoil afterward. Not simply the mess between her and Tommy, but also with the pending danger they'd spent the last week hiding from. She noted the silence above her.

"Fine, but I'm driving," Tommy shot back after a few minutes.

Kathryn's nerves had reached an all-time high when they eventually were able to ease the boat out of the slip. Greg and Roy had insisted on going back over the entire property in daylight before she could go near a window, let alone leave the house. They then called in to their office for approval.

"I have to get permission to go outside?" She had asked. "Come on. For all we know the guy has no idea where I am and doesn't care."

Greg had given her an up and down glance that Kathryn assumed he practiced mainly for the intimidation factor. It worked. "Are you sure you want to take the risk? The man has killed with no qualms. He may not care, but if he does—well, is it worth it?"

She rolled her eyes when they advised her that the two additional agents would join them on the boat "as a precaution." Not because it angered her, but honestly, she saw no reason why the man would bother. They highly overestimated everything. It's not as if she had any influence on anything, *anywhere*. She was a nobody who had been in the wrong place. She doubted he even knew they'd seen the documents. She shrugged off Greg's paranoia in an attempt to maintain her composure...and live up to the new lifestyle she wanted to pursue. A lifestyle based on making her own decisions. Regardless, she was reminded, they had to pick up the other agents at the public marina across the lake at eleven.

"You know, guys," Thomas spoke over the engine as they pulled up to the marina, "Katy likes to be on the water by nine at the latest, and off by noon. She hates the afternoon crowds."

"That's right," she confirmed. "All the drunks wake up and get on the water late morning. From then on, it's a mess." She frowned at the two new additions in full gear that boarded the boat.

The furrows in her forehead deepened as they handed Kevlar vests to Greg and Roy.

"You're kidding me!" She shook her head at them. "We're going to be the only boat out here that has four armed secret service guys peering at the brush on the sidelines. We'll stand out like a pine tree in the middle of the water. Do you have any idea how ridiculous this looks?"

"Sorry, ma'am. We received word a few minutes ago that our man definitely made it into Houston Friday. Our contacts tell us he rented a car and we expect him to be looking for you. I doubt last night's intruder was associated but I don't believe in coincidences either." Dierden stared into oblivion. "You wanted to go out on the water. So stop complaining. Our job would have been easier just to stay put at your parents. I don't like this but we're accommodating you. For now." He took note of the calm water. "There aren't any boats out yet, so that's a plus. If it gets busy, we're out of here. Actually, the more I think about it…"

"Okay, fine. I get the picture. I just think you're overreacting." Kathryn tossed her hair back and opened her mouth to add more, but Thomas clamped a hand down on her arm.

His brows closed heavily over his eyes as he shook his head, warning her to stop. "Don't blow this, Katy," he whispered in her ear. "They were talking on the phone earlier. Roy thinks we should leave. If you want to spend some time with your folks, keep quiet and behave yourself."

She squinted through the sun at Roy—his eyes darted across the horizon. He had one hand on the rail and shifted slightly every few minutes to scan the coastline. The guy looked like a robot, tense and stiff.

*

As promised, Tommy took the helm and wouldn't let Kathryn intervene. Greg stood at his left, noticeably blocking Kathryn from view. Sweat trickled down the side of his face.

Thomas smirked. He had board shorts on. He'd yanked his shirt off after they got out on the water. The temperature was too damn hot and the wind felt good on the skin. They had to be miserable in those outfits they were wearing, not to mention they looked ridiculous. Stood out like a red dress at a funeral. But it was their job and he knew they took it seriously. He was thankful for their presence.

"Dierden, I'd recommend you guys take turns guarding and cooling off. Take off the vest for a second and get a cold one from the ice chest or something. It's hot as hell out here and if you don't budge a little on the rules, these guys might get heat stroke." Thomas said. "Look, we're the first ones out today, so no need to worry about anyone sneaking up or getting too close."

"It is pretty damn hot," Dierden crossed a thumb over his forehead to catch a drip, "but we're used to it and we'll manage. In fact, seems like time to head back, don't you think?" He unzipped the vest and Thomas noticed the slickened shirt underneath. The wind probably felt good as they bounced along.

"Okay. I'll turn it back." The extra Kevlar vest they'd brought slipped to the floor as the bow tipped into a curve and bounced across their own wake.

Thomas heard a loud *thunk* as if he'd hit something in the water. He glanced behind them for debris, then looked around the boat. *Thunk. Thunk.* On the last one, he noticed the small hiss before. He still didn't equate it to a gunshot.

"Shots fired. Get down!" Roy yanked his firearm from his side and shoved himself over Kathryn. Thomas killed the engine, slamming Dierden forward into the hull. He looked up to see him topple into the waves.

Thomas ducked just in time for another shot to skim over his left shoulder, lodging itself into the seat cushion that Kathryn had ducked under. The shooter had adjusted his sights and was now getting them over the hull and into the boat. Everything seemed aimed at *her*. They were sitting ducks. If they stayed in this spot, he'd eventually meet his target. If they started the boat and surged on, they'd have to leave Dierden behind.

Thomas moved his foot, sliding it over the clothes on the floor. Without hesitation, he grabbed the Kevlar vest, threw it around Kathryn's body and yanked her with him over the side of the boat and into the water to put the boat between her and the shooter. They plunged deeply but he held the jacket around her as their four feet kicked together to propel them to the surface.

"Are you okay?" he asked. She nodded. "Stay here, hold onto the side rail above you and keep that jacket on."

"Where are you going?" she gulped. He put a hand on her shoulder.

"Dierden's up there in the water. I have to pull him in before he gets hit. The others have their guns out and are returning fire but he's a sitting duck." Thomas worked his way toward the side of the boat, he kept his head barely above the surface and below the deck as he moved. The tie line was loose and he anchored a hand on the end. He grabbed the line and backed to the protected side of the boat, then started pulling. "Dierden! Grab the rope."

"I'm right here." A voice called behind him. Dierden had made his way to them without help and was tying the rope to the cleat above Kathryn. "Start the engine, guys," he called. "We can't stay here or we'll all be dead."

Dierden gestured to Thomas. Thomas and Kathryn wrapped the rope around their hands. Thomas closed the Kevlar around her, lifted her onto his chest and arched his legs up and hooked them into the guard rail, making himself into a human sling. Dierden looped the remaining rope over the back cleat, fastened himself in similar to Thomas and yelled. "Go! Go! Keep the boat faced due west until we get around the cove then turn it and head straight across the water. Don't stop for anything. Thomas. Kathryn. You hold on no matter what. If we keep the boat between us and him, you'll be fine."

"Got it!" Thomas shouted.

Kathryn echoed his response. Adrenaline surged through him and he held her tightly to the hull of the boat, cocooned within his arms and legs. She had wrapped her hands around the rope as well and her legs twisted around him. They were a knot of rope, bodies, and Kevlar. If it weren't for the gravity of the situation, he'd say something suggestive. They blazed over the water. The strain of holding on was putting tremendous strain on his arms and back, but there was no way in hell he would let go. He'd pull every muscle or break an arm first.

The firing stopped. Either they were out of range, the shooter had been hit, or he was moving to find a new spot. Whatever the reason, Thomas was thankful. The agent at the wheel eased the throttle enough to keep the boat swiftly skimming forward. Roy had binoculars and was scouring the hills above the lake for signs of their suspect. Trying to see through binoculars while sailing over the bouncing waves was a lesson in futility. No matter how the agent anchored himself in the boat, the movement rendered it impossible to see anything. He finally cast the binoculars into the side cubby with a curse.

They made it around the cove. Thomas' arms were burning. One of his feet slipped and dangled in the air. He turned his body to keep her tightly against the boat as he fumbled to bring his leg back in and anchor once again to the rail.

"Stop!" Dierden shouted and they came to a stand-still. "We have a few minutes before he can get over the crest of that hill. There's no way we can hold on long enough to get across the lake. Everybody in the boat. Now."

The agents leaned over the side and gathered both Thomas and Katy into the hull, then retrieved Dierden. The boat was throttled into action and they headed straight across the lake without stopping. It would be impossible for the shooter to reach them now. And unlikely he would see where they ended up once they were on the other side and had moved into the coves. Roy yanked his cell out of his pants and made a call. A place to pick up was arranged.

Within thirty minutes, they'd arrived at their pickup point. A car collected them seconds later. They barreled away from the lake with another car behind them. Dierden spoke. "Okay, everyone. It looks like he's found us now, so the game has begun. Kathryn, Thomas—any injuries?" They both shook their heads and huffed out a quick "no." "Good. Let's get out of here as quickly as possible, then we'll conference in with the office. We should be able to find him before he can cause any harm. No more public places though. Not until we can track him down."

"Hold on a second." Thomas held up a hand. "I want someone to go back to Katy's house and get her family out of there. *Right now.*" His voice strained on the last words. He glanced sideways—her face was ashen. She rubbed her wrists and stared sullenly out the window.

"It's already done. They'll meet us in a few minutes," Dierden continued. "He won't go after them. He's a weird guy—has principles about that. If a criminal can have principles."

"I don't care what his principles are," Thomas said sharply. "That's her family...and they might as well be mine. I grew up with them."

What was wrong with her, he thought. She hadn't said a word since he dunked her in the water. She trembled slightly, then tilted her neck as she stared into nothingness.

"Hey. Katy." No response. He put his hand on hers. "Katy. Look at me."

Her glazed eyes turned, then strained to focus on his face. "Hmmm?"

"Are you okay?" he asked softly. "Are you hurt?"

"No." She hesitated, her lips trembling. Water puddle in her eyes. "Thomas, I nearly killed us all."

Chapter Thirty-Eight

Eric hadn't anticipated the wind accurately. He normally was pretty good at that, but his target usually was grounded. The only wind factor to worry about involved how much it changed the trajectory of his shot. He neglected to also consider the effect on the waves. The boat bobbed along fairly smoothly, so he eased the trigger back for the first shot. He was completely confident that was all he needed.

The boat driver shifted the wheel right at the same time, and the hull lifted and turned. The shot missed, low. He fired off two more but missed again. The agents scattered and shoved his target and her boyfriend onto the floor. He could see a small thatch of hair on the vinyl seat, his only sign of her location. He tipped the nose back a hair and tried to launch the next shot over the hull and into the boat. It whizzed toward the guy's shoulder, but he couldn't tell if he made contact. He moved the sight on the gun to observe their actions. The agents were scanning for him now. He fired a few more rounds, then dropped down. Grabbing his gear, he headed for the hilltop. He needed better position.

Speed was critical. He had to get there before they made it around the point. If they reached open water, they'd be out of range. The boat sprang forward, whizzing across the water. They were in a race now, the engine against his feet. Rocks flew out below him as he scrambled. The path split—one went straight up the hill, another criss-crossed through the trees. He looked over his shoulder. He didn't dare risk the open path, though it was faster. He sprinted through the trees, gun raised over his shoulder. He dropped the pack and everything else. Too much trouble. As he crested the hill, he sunk to the ground and raised the sight to his eye. He moved it back and forth, focusing for the boat. Damn it! Too late. They were out of range.

Eric flipped open his cell. As much as he hated to make the call, he had to inform Smitty of the status. It would delay the other project. He was confident he could still contain this. Or at least he hoped so. Still, the wave of panic that rushed over him earlier returned. God, he hated this job.

"It's worse than I thought," he said when Smitty picked up.

"Worse how?"

Eric explained the details as Smitty's anger lashed out in a series of expletives. He reached in his vest pocket for spare ammo to reload while the tirade continued. His fingers crumpled on a piece of paper and he drug it out and tossed it on the ground. A plastic wrapper of some sort. The conversation concluded with a threat and a directive to maintain the security of this information "at all cost." There was no mistaking that his life depended on it.

Eric flipped the safety on, reloaded his weapon, then snatched the wrapper. He started to crumple it up for trash, then noticed a note attached. He lifted it and read.

Eric, thought you might like these better than the peanuts on the plane. Brenda.

She had bagged the bar snacks from the counter for him and attached the note. *Weird.* They had a long discussion in bed about the peanuts on airplanes and how much he hated them. Thoughtful of her to drop that in his pocket. He hoped she didn't see what else was in there. Not that it mattered—it's a hunting vest in Alaska, so she wouldn't have thought it odd anyway.

Chapter Thirty-Nine

"It's about damn time you realized that," Thomas snapped at Kathryn. She was losing it, he could tell. He'd never really seen her go totally comatose, but this was pretty close. "Any other fancy stunts that you want to pull—or hoops you want us all to jump through before you're ready to listen to these guys?" Her eyes narrowed and he saw the glow start to come back. Good.

"Excuse me? Aren't you the one that said I needed to be more assertive and ask for what I want?" she snapped.

"Well, you've been calling all the shots so far," he snarled. "And these idiots have let you just because you're too pretty to say no to." He waved a hand at the agents causing Roy to snort angrily.

"I have not."

"Yes, you have. Starting with soccer practice, then a weekend at the lake, even the stupid boat." He slapped his hands together hard. Everyone in the car jumped. "So, here's how it's going to be now, honey."

"I told you—" she started.

"Yeah. Yeah. Don't call you honey. Forget it, girl. I'll call you whatever I want." His pulse was about to explode as he spoke. "He wasn't after all these guys. He was after you. Get it? Because you keep putting yourself in places that make you a sitting duck, I nearly lost you. *We* nearly lost you. And maybe one of the rest of us could have gotten hurt too. Who knows. Yes, I said to go after what you want but that didn't include dying in the process."

He turned to Dierden. "From now on, you call the shots—period. Not her." He jerked a thumb at Kathryn. "I am not going to lose that woman—do you understand? If anything happens to her or her family, I swear to God, I'll kill all four of you myself. I don't know how but I will." His voice reverberated in the moving vehicle.

"You can't really lose—," she muttered faintly.

He sent her a silencing glare. "Shut up, Kathryn. Stop fighting me and let these guys do their job."

She opened her mouth to reply, then closed it as he lowered his brows even further. He'd lost his temper with her twice in two days. He bit his lip and stopped talking. He had already said too much. He clenched his fists then jammed one into the car door for good measure. He wanted to strangle her. Well, not really. He wanted to hold her. Tightly. He closed his eyes and leaned back in his seat. The tension in his neck had given him a headache.

"Well, you did say I needed to ask for what I wanted more." Her voice was petulant as she said it.

"That was when it wasn't life-threatening. I didn't know you would go that far."

Forty-five minutes later, they pulled into a parking garage in Austin, circled to the fourth floor and parked. A walkway extended off the lot into a neighboring building. The agents escorted them across to a room adjacent to the walkway. When Kathryn walked through the door, she was rushed by her parents and Sam. The embrace was so tight, she couldn't breathe. The air in the room blasted her and looking down, she realized she still wore the black bikini and lifejacket covered with Dierden's vest. The vest was so big, it met her hips. She was cold, yet glad to see everyone safe and unharmed.

"God, Katy," Sam exclaimed, "Why didn't you guys tell us about this?" He stood nervously moving his legs back and forth as if running in place.

"I couldn't—and we didn't want to alarm you." She reached for Thomas' hand, threading her fingers through his. "Besides, what difference would it have made if you knew? We didn't even know what this guy might do. We still don't." She tugged Thomas to her side, her fingers clenched tightly around his. She looked at everyone standing around. All here because of her. Because she'd left that stupid note. Thomas stood with his chest against her shoulder, his hand warmly engulfing hers.

"I'm sorry," she said, her voice carrying softly in the tension of the room. "This is all my fault." She slid her eyes to Thomas and repeated the words. "I'm sorry."

"Don't blame yourself. It's as much my fault as yours." He stroked a thumb against her hand and flashed an attempted smile. *He could smile at a time like this? She nearly killed him, and put everyone in this room in danger.* She'd chosen to be selfish and it paid serious dividends. Painfully serious.

Ask for what you want, he'd said. That's kind of like that stupid "Go For It" phrase. Sounds great in theory, not so cool in practice.

"No, I'm the one that left the dumb note."

He paused and shrugged. "You're right. It's your fault. Hell, the guy doesn't even know who I am." He paused. "I'm out of here, honey. You're on your own." He opened the door and walked out. Her mouth dropped as he left. Everyone in the room stared at the door, dumbfounded. Seconds passed.

"Hey!" Kathryn yelled. She yanked the door wide and stomped out after him. The door closed behind her as she looked down the hall.

"I was hoping that would get you." He spoke from behind her. She whirled around to see him grinning a huge, toothy grin as he leaned against the wall behind the door. He straightened and held out his arms.

A laugh erupted deep from within her chest and she jumped up and wrapped her arms and legs around him as she rested her forehead against his. He put his hands under her hips holding her in place.

"You know you wouldn't dare leave me alone," she challenged as she pulled on his tousled hair.

"Yeah. That's true, but the question is, do you know it? Are we done with the pity party now? I think I liked the new selfish you a little better, just please don't overdo it anymore." He hugged her tight and whirled her around, kissing her lips deeply. "And don't ever scare me like that again, Katy. I almost had a heart attack."

"I can't believe you thought to get the vest and get over the side of the boat." She said with excitement. "That was awesome. So— James Bond. Way to go!" She held up a hand as if to "high-five" him. Instead, he clutched her fingers and kissed them individually. The smell of his skin and the adrenaline rush overwhelmed her. She started trailing kisses down his neck, clutching into his skin, easing her hands up under his shirt.

The door flung open and the sound of someone clearing their throat brought her back into focus. She opened her eyes and turned to see Sam and Agent Dierden watching her attack Thomas. Dierden controlled a twitch at the side of his mouth. She loosened her legs from their vice grip around Thomas' waist and let them drop to the floor. She vaguely noticed his hands slide from her ass to her waist as he chuckled quietly.

"I was just kidding, guys." He held up his palms innocently and pushed her back toward the door and into the room of people. "Someone needed to give her a quick nudge in the right direction—you know, a wake-up call." His smug grin let everyone know he'd accomplished what he set out to. She had needed that—a good kick in the gut—a reminder to stay on track.

Fault was irrelevant at this point. Feeling regretful served no purpose. Yet, a casual indifference to the severity of their situation had to stop. His fingers dug into her shoulder teasingly as they returned to the room and she was thankful for the warmth of the body against her back as the short meeting spelled out their next steps.

Thirty minutes later, a plan was in place. Sketchy at best, but enough to get everyone safely away and know what to do next.

Dierden stayed behind to conference with the Washington and Houston offices. Roy escorted Kathryn and Thomas. Thomas' friend, Trevan, had joined them. He was the contact that scooped up her family after the reported shooting. He would get them to safety.

Kathryn was assured that she was the only target, other than perhaps Thomas, if the man discovered he'd been there and saw the information. Her family's movement was just precautionary. Regardless, she was relieved.

Kathryn sighed loudly as they sped away from the city in a white Explorer. They had changed vehicles at Roy's insistence. The guy seemed a little paranoid but in his business that wouldn't be unusual. Both Thomas and Roy looked at her strangely.

"Want to enlighten us, Katy?" Thomas asked.

"I just had a thought. We went from *team* building to swat *team* in just under a week. Doesn't that seem a bit extreme?" She forced a smile, "I guess all that training paid off in a weird way." It was better to smile than lose it at this point, yet she registered her hands shaking in her lap.

Chapter Forty

Kathryn sat in the vehicle next to Thomas as they sped along to an unknown location the agents had chosen. She noted his clenched jaw at her forced humor.

The car was so quiet, she could hear his teeth gnashing. Her hand, clasped tightly in his, flexed. He was crushing her fingers, the strength of him painful on the thin bones of her hand. His leg against hers was warm.

She shivered, the full weight of their situation sent a freezing blast through her. He had saved her life. She glanced nervously at his profile. This wasn't the boy she'd teased with for years. A man whose only skill seemed to be mastering the art of flirtation and taking it as far he could.

This was a man of strength and awareness. He had seen the danger before she did. He understood the seriousness and plunged them to into the water, to safety. Common sense prevailed—for him.

What had she done? She had talked federal agents into shirking their duties for fun. She had jeopardized their safety. Jeopardized their jobs. She had trivialized the situation and put everyone at risk. Her small moments of selfishness could have carried a tremendous burden. A week ago, she was afraid to ask for what she wanted. Today, she had forced everyone to follow her desires—and they could have died.

"I'm a little cold," she said, breaking the silence. Thomas released her fingers and gripped the flesh on her leg and squeezed. His lips twisted up gently.

"No surprise since you're still wet, you were almost killed, and you're half-naked. A combination of cold and shock, I'd imagine."

He tapped the agent driving on the shoulder. "Pull over up there, please."

She didn't see where he was pointing but the agent nodded agreement. The vehicle rolled to a stop in the parking lot of a department store. The agents all tumbled out of the vehicle, creating a wall for them. Thomas led Kathryn into the store, completely comfortable with the fact they were both in swimsuits and flip-flops. "Juniors or women's?" he asked.

"Doesn't matter. I can wear either."

He made a tsking sound. "Just tell me what you want."

"Juniors."

His jaw set as he yanked her toward the department. "Thanks."

She quickly picked up a pair of jeans and a shirt and headed for the sign that stated in black letters, "Try-ons." His hand jerked her to a standstill.

"You need to try them?" He obviously didn't shop for women's clothes much.

"Yes. Just give me five minutes." He didn't let up on the padlock he had on her hand. "Tommy. I doubt anyone followed us into this store. And I don't see anyone lurking between the hangers." She motioned with her eyes for him to look around. There were customers browsing but not a soul paid any attention to them. She noticed a couple of stares at their dress—or lack of it—when they walked in. That was it. With clothes in hand, she pulled him toward the open door. His fingers held firm. A turn to face him, startled her. The expression was one she hadn't seen on his face before. She'd seen anger and laughter. Teasing and Flirtation, sure. This was something new. Greg and Roy hovered behind him, standing like sentries.

"Katy." His voice was almost pleading. "I can't let you go."

He couldn't let her go in a dressing room alone? Then he said it again softly and she thought for a second his eyes misted over. Seriously? He looked back at Greg and Roy, then followed her through the door. Okay, no problem.

A woman scurried over from the register. "Hey. You can't go in there," she called after Thomas. Katy watched Greg and Roy cut the woman off just before Katy slid the curtain closed in the small booth. Thomas stood outside and waited as she slipped into the clothes.

Can't let her go, she thought. A couple of weeks earlier, she was just another conquest. Now he talks about having kids and tells her he can't let her go? The flirting hadn't surprised her. The sex had been phenomenal—but then, he was well practiced right? This, however, was not the way a fling went. Was it? He was almost smothering. It was so...not Tommy. His behavior on the lake and now was out of character. It was protective. Controlling. It was almost like a relationship. A lump formed in her throat.

The shoulder on the other side of the curtain was comforting. The well-defined muscle structure brought memories of his skin. Skin she had stroked with hunger during the night. It had a distinct and familiar scent that was unforgettable, even addictive. Now, that shoulder was square and stiff as he stood guard outside her dressing room. But then, it always was.

There had never been a time when Thomas hunched or cowered in her presence. Never a time that he didn't face life head on, sometimes almost bullish. He was, she realized, dependable. Maybe not a good risk for a relationship, but certainly someone that could be counted on in a crisis like this. What happened when the crisis was over?

She slipped out of the clothes and back into the bathing suit. "Tommy, they fit." He turned toward the curtain and put a hand in to take them. His hand touched her side, sending tingles along the edges. She met his eyes through the opening. "Would you mind taking them to the counter and then bringing them back? I'd like to wear them out."

There were shadows in his eyes. He looked almost haggard.

"No problem," he answered, holding out his free hand for the garments.

"I'm not stupid or blind," she blurted.

"Huh?"

"I care."

He kept his eyes down. "Do you now."

"Of course I do. I've known you forever. How could I not care?"

"That's it?"

"Tommy." She hesitated. "Don't try to make me fall in love with you. I'm not very good at breakups." His jaw twitched.

"Don't get ahead of yourself, honey." He pulled the clothes from her fingers, took them to the register, then returned and tossed the garments to her. He yanked the curtain closed for her to dress. Seconds later, he yanked it back open as she was slipping her leg into the newly purchased jeans. "Katy, do me a favor and explain yourself."

"Explain myself?" she looked down the hall. "I'm getting my clothes on. What is there to explain about that?"

"Not that. What you said a minute ago. What does that mean? You care."

"Of course I do."

"Of course I do," he mimicked. "That's not good enough. I want more than that. I want to hear more." He grabbed her wrist as she stood with one leg raised, her foot partially inserted into the jeans. She teetered, unlike a stork, then fell against him. His breath was hot on her face as he spoke. "What did you mean by saying 'I'm not good at breakups'? Do you really think this is meaningless?"

Her wrist burned from his tight grip. She couldn't move away. Her legs were completely wrapped in denim at her feet. "I. Don't. Know. You always..."

"I always what? I always nothing. I want to know what you're telling me—and don't give me anything cryptic, like 'Don't make me fall in love with you'. That's crap. I haven't made you do anything and I certainly can't tell you how to feel. Or make you feel something you don't. That's all you. It can't be anything else. So, tell me, what is it?"

"Okay. I'll tell you what you want to hear but can I get my pants on first?"

"Don't tell me what you think I want to hear, tell me what you mean." He released her hand and stepped into the small booth and drew the curtain behind him, plopping down onto the bench. Kathryn's hands shook as she wiggled into the jeans and zipped them. *Tell him the truth? Could she do it? She wanted to. Would he bolt? How many times had he heard it before?*

"I already fell," she admitted.

"Fell?"

"In love with you." She picked her bikini top off the floor. His hand grabbed her chin and pulled her face up to his. "Are you happy now?" She asked. Endless seconds passed before his mouth opened.

"So, now we break up?" he asked.

"Yeah. Isn't that how it works with you?"

"Katy. Haven't you heard anything I've said?"

"Sure, but I've also watched you say things to a lot of girls over the years."

"You have, have you? Well, maybe what you thought you saw wasn't the truth. God, you're a pain in the ass." His voice reeked of frustration.

"We've only seen each other a few days. You can't get physical like that and just instantly know."

"Did you ever think that it wasn't about that—the physical part? Not that it wasn't great, but I can't go for years wanting someone, finally get a chance to be with them, find out it's better than expected, and just give it up. Besides if you think about how long we've known each other, this has been a pretty long-term relationship."

"You wanted me?"

"Shit, even your mom knew it. Why can't you see that? Look, I'm not the emotional type and you're probably not going to hear this often enough—but I fell too. Okay. Hard. Now, let's get out of here."

He grabbed her hand and pulled her out of the dressing room. *So, that's how you say it, Tommy? That's how you tell someone you love them?* She was disappointed. She'd always thought when the right person said it, her heart would soar or something. Maybe lightning would hit or she'd feel goose bumps. Instead, she felt cheated out of an important moment.

"Well, you don't have to be so happy about it," she spat. She realized she should be glad that he'd said as much as he did. She wasn't. *Not the emotional type,* he said. Well, that was not enough for her. Everything about love is emotional. Everything about life has emotions involved. He acted as if it angered him. It was an inconvenience.

He stopped, turned around in the hall with his hands on her shoulders, and planted a firm kiss on her lips. It wasn't just firm, it was melting. His tongue slipped inside her mouth, searching, and his hand slipped up to lightly brush her cheek. It was a kiss that he'd perfected—one of the ones that started her hand slinking inside his shirt again.

He moved back. "When we get out of this mess, I'll show you how happy." He looked down at her hand and smiled. "I love it when you do that."

Okay, she thought, *that'll work.*

Chapter Forty-One

Thomas sat in the lobby of the hotel, reading a paper, or at least looking at it. His thoughts were a million miles away.

If someone had asked him five years ago, he'd never have said things would be like this. He could not have imagined it or anticipated it. His philosophy had always revolved around the idea that people's lives reflected the effort that they put into them. He had done everything to right his wrongs—had followed his father's dream for a legal career, he followed Sam's desire to not ruin Kathryn's life. Yet, after the past weeks with her, he questioned the logic in doing what they wanted versus what he had thought at the time. Sometimes instinct wasn't so bad.

Still, a lot of good came out of the time in between. Her education, for one. And his. Their successes in business, perhaps. Other people. Then he remembered that she almost married David. What a jerk. Okay, maybe the other people in between were a mistake—a substitute.

"I had an idea." She came up behind him. She had on a blue T-shirt and jeans shorts and held out a coffee cup.

"Yeah. What's that?" He took the cup and leaned back in his chair to look up at her.

"This guy is going to keep coming back until he gets us, gets me. He will follow us and keep asking questions until he finds us, right?"

"Yeah. Most likely. You're pretty well known around here, so that's not too hard."

"Exactly. What if we took the initiative and used that?" She pulled a chair out and sat facing him. "What if we found him first?"

"You mean go after him while he's looking for us?"

"Yes!" She slapped a hand on the table next to them. "We tell everyone everywhere—and pass out pictures. His face could be plastered all over town. He wouldn't be able to go out without being noticed. He couldn't hide. We'd have the advantage."

He studied her. "So we tell everyone about the information too?"

"No, we just say he's wanted. And he's here to harm me—us. Then we set up a mechanism to feed him what we want him to know and only that. We lure him to Greg, Roy, and the rest of their team."

"I like it."

"Yeah, me too." She smiled, a little smugly. A flash of fire in her eyes sent a little shot of warmth through him. "And it gets us back to normal faster."

"I don't think we're ever going to be normal, hon—God, you're sexy when you're planning a take-down." He grinned. "Come here."

She frowned. "You're making fun of me."

"No." He wrapped his hand around her wrist and pulled her to him. She resisted. He pulled harder and she almost fell into his lap. "I like the plan. A strong offense is always a good tactic. I like the planner better." He slipped his thumb into the waistband of her shorts and squeezed her hip with his fingers. "So, how do we do this, coach?" He nibbled at her ear as he spoke.

"You're teasing me," she answered, her voice low. She looked around the hotel. He followed her glance.

"No. What are you looking at? Are you afraid someone might see us?"

She met his gaze. "I'm not afraid."

"Of that, being seen with me? Or of him?"

"Of that."

"Good. Now we're making progress." He hooked the other

thumb on her jeans and pulled her tighter against him. "Let's work on the plan. I think we need a command post. A place to spread out and talk this through. Let's go upstairs. I know just the place."

"You do, do you?"

"Yeah." He stood up with his hands on her hips and let her legs fall to the floor. A gentle shove toward the elevator had her moving in the direction he wanted to go. Their entourage followed but the elevator slid closed before they made it. When the doors opened on their floor, his mouth and hers were together, her hands were in his favorite place against his skin, and his had slipped into the back of her shorts. "Let's go do some offensive strategy planning." He mumbled as he moved his hand to pull his room key from his pocket.

"Tommy, what would you consider your best strengths?" she asked, with her hand resting on his back.

"You're serious? Or are you trying to bait me?"

"I'm serious—if you had to tell someone what you could do best if needed, what would it be?"

"I can only pick one thing?"

"No. No. You can pick as many as you want." She followed him in the door and sat at the desk by the window. "What can we use? If we're going to take the offense, then let's do it. For example, I can run pretty well. I hunt with my family so I'm pretty good with a gun. I can fish. Handle a boat. Pretty much anything outdoors."

"I get it. But you underestimated a few of those things, don't you think?"

"How so?"

"You run faster than, well, most of the country. You hunt and fish like any man would. And the rest—well, let's just say you're an outdoorsman's dream girl."

"Maybe I should go looking for an outdoorsman then?"

"Funny. No. Don't even think about it. You're better off with someone that can—you know—multi-task."

"Multi-task?"

"Outdoors and Indoors. You know. Talented in more than just the outdoor stuff."

"And who would that be, Tommy?"

He grinned. She ignored him and continued talking.

"How well I do those things is less important than what I can do right now. Besides there's a few others. I'm a programmer. Not a hacker, but I can write and rewrite code. And a decent project manager. What about you?"

"Okay, I'll bite. I know the law. Inside and out. Especially contract law. Most of the things on your list, I can do reasonably well. Except for the programming and project management stuff. I can't outrun you but I'll keep up in a dead heat. Are you writing this down?" He raised a brow when he saw the pad in front of her.

"Yes. Of course." She made some lines like a grid on the paper as she spoke. "Who else can we use?"

"For what?"

"Our offensive plan."

"I thought you were kidding. You're going to have to fill me in a little better before I can answer that. You obviously have thought this through a lot more than I know about. Tell me what you've got in mind, honey."

She looked up for a minute and then put her head back down. Her hand scribbled away at the paper pad. Her concentration amused him.

For the next couple of hours, Thomas listened as Kathryn gave him, bit by bit, a thorough description of a mechanism to bring an end to their hiding. The only problem was it involved baiting the man—with her. He didn't like it. Not one bit. The agents in the next room wouldn't either.

"No," he said after she breathed the last word.

"What do you mean no?"

"It's not safe. If even one thing goes wrong, you could be killed or hurt. If it all goes exactly as hoped, that could still happen. That's too big of a chance to take."

"It's not any bigger than the one we took on the boat. Besides, we could get killed driving to work in bad traffic, too. That doesn't stop us from getting in the car. When you have something that has to be done, you do it. You assume the risk and do it."

He shook his head. "Not the same and you know it. I'm not taking the chance."

"*You're* not taking the chance? Are you?"

"Yes. We're not doing it. I'm in this too."

"It's not *you* he's after. He doesn't even know about you. I say we do it and get this silly charade over. I need to get on with my life—get back to normal. I'm *not* going to spend the rest of it looking over my shoulder, wondering if there's a gunman or slasher out there looking for me somewhere."

"No."

"Yes." She stood from the chair and headed for the door. "I'll run it by Greg and Roy."

"Katy," he snapped. "Don't." He was not going to dangle her life like a carrot in front of this maniac. He knew what was in those contracts and understood the risk greater than anyone. He hesitated to mention it but he knew. The information was all on his laptop, which they had yet to return.

"I have to." Her back was to him with her hand on the doorknob, ready to fling it back and leave. Yet she didn't open it. "I have to know if this is going to work."

"Going to work?" he questioned. "Your plan? You have to know if this plan is going to work? And you'd risk your life on it? That's crazy. I can't let you do that."

"Not the plan. Us. And yes, I would." She opened the door and slipped out. He stared at the door as it slammed shut behind her.

*

In that insane, volatile moment when Kathryn raised her hand to tap on the door of two FBI agents, she realized what it must be like for a victim to be irrationally and perversely attracted to their stalker or abuser. As she showered earlier and thought through the plan that she hatched, it forced her to attempt to think like him. What makes him tick? Why does he do what he's chosen to do? And why would it be so important to silence a single woman from across the continent just on the off chance she saw something?

Exposure? Fear of capture? Fear of jail? No, she doubted that. Money? Perhaps. Almost all things eventually revolve around money in some way. But that too, didn't seem to be enough. There had to be more to this. He had to *identify* with what he did in some way. So much so, that it was critical to be successful. She wanted to know more about the man. Needed to understand his motivation.

When the door opened, she was faced with three—not two—men in dark golf-style shirts and shoulder holsters. The number caught her off guard, but only for a second.

"I want to know him," she stated simply.

Greg was surprised. "Know who?" He glanced at the other man in the room. "Him?"

"No. The guy that tried to kill me." She frowned. "I want to know what this is about. What is so important that I would matter. What's in the data? What kind of guy is he? How long has this gone on? Who else is involved?" She waited nervously at the door for an invitation.

"Come in, Ms. Delroy," the new guy said. "Let the woman past."

Greg stepped aside and Kathryn breezed in and planted herself on the end of one of the two unmade beds in the room. She looked at the blankets thrown on the floor and clothes piled in small mounds.

"Does the FBI make you double up? Seriously? They can't spring for separate rooms?"

"Government work." Greg shrugged. The other two men glared at about the same time the door to the bathroom opened and a girl with short-cropped bleached hair stepped out.

"Do you have any—" The girl stopped when she saw the group and registered the guns, dress, Kathryn, etc. "Whoa."

Greg grabbed a bag from the floor by the bed, retrieved two shoes that were tangled in the blankets lying on the floor, and grasped the young lady's arm. "Time to go, sweetie." He opened the door and ushered her out. The girl's startled expression was her only response. She didn't utter a word as he whisked her into the hallway. A few seconds later, he was back in the room—alone.

"Ms. Delroy," Greg said, "this is Special Agent Forest Ewan. He's from our Washington office and came in last night." He motioned to the remaining new face in the room, ignoring any questioning glances.

Kathryn, dumbfounded, held out a hand to the man. One shake, then he let go, barely meeting her smile. Ewan was older than the others with a stockier build and shaved head.

"To answer your questions, Ms. Delroy." Ewan cast an admonishing glance toward Greg. "No, the FBI doesn't make our staff double up. You're important because he thinks you know too much. He thinks you've seen the data and if you have, you're a risk to his success. The data documents his jobs. All things that he was contracted to do— things that most people would consider unethical or illegal."

"Are you telling me they're not?"

"No. I'm telling you that, in his head, they are essential to our way of life. He considers himself protecting others. Either for national security reasons, or financial reasons. While the things he does are wrong, even criminal, he justifies them in his own head."

"So, he's basically a psychopath."

Ewan laughed. "Not necessarily. He's shrewd. He's smart. And he's dangerous. Very dangerous. But he has some ethics, if a guy like that can."

"And what would that be? Don't torture his victims first? Or don't let them see him kill them?" Her voice dripped with sarcasm.

"He doesn't kill innocent people and he doesn't kill unless there's no other way to attain his goal. He won't touch kids. Not ever. And he doesn't believe in casualties. His clients normally like his ethics."

"You're kidding, right? How would you know they like 'his ethics'? Have you talked to them personally?"

He was stunned into silence, briefly. "Of course not."

"Then how do you know this? How can you pretend to understand his thoughts or perverted ethics?" she challenged.

"It's my job. I've been trained to profile suspects like this, ma'am. We have a team of other profilers that have been consulted. The man has been on our radar for some time but he's pretty good at evasion."

"So, you don't *really* know him. You've never met or talked to him. You *think* you know what he looks like, but even that is questionable because I've seen several photos and they all look pretty different—and you think he has *ethics*." Kathryn couldn't hide the ridiculousness in what she'd just heard as she spoke. It was obvious they didn't know anything at all about the man. Or they did, but they weren't going to tell her. She suspected the latter. "Unbelievable," she hissed.

Greg and Roy exchanged glances behind Ewan's back, obviously registering her credibility. She wondered why they didn't speak up. They'd been with her most of the time. They surely knew as much about this guy as anyone or they wouldn't have been assigned to protect her from him. Why, out of the blue, did this newbie show up?

"I want to see the data on him." She said.

Agent Ewan laughed. "And I want to win the lottery. Not gonna happen, cupcake. This is a federal investigation and you aren't in charge. We can't afford the risk of information leaking."

"*You* can't take the risk? You, Mr. Ewan, haven't even been involved until ten minutes ago. I hardly see why you're at risk. I want my life back. I am willing to take any all steps to do that."

"Are you also willing to die?"

Chapter Forty-Two

Frustration sometimes renders a man immobile, unable to register what to do next. Thomas had such a moment as he watched Kathryn march out of the room to pitch her plan to the FBI. The plan made sense in a way, but there had to be a better alternative. One that didn't put her right in the middle of the fray. He didn't want to go through the panic he experienced on the lake again. He was certain they'd turn the idea down. They were professionals and likely wouldn't take the chance. How would they protect her if she were out there on her own, baiting the maniac to come get her? No. Surely they wouldn't let that happen. This man could not get the opportunity to take Kathryn away from him again. He strode to their room and banged on the door until it was opened.

"Roy." He nodded at the man opening the door as he barged in without invitation. "Greg." He turned to the new face and introduced himself. He grinned at Kathryn, "I leave you alone for a second, and you're in a hotel room with three guys. Some loyalty."

"Make that four now and, last I checked, I didn't have a leash around my neck," she retorted.

"That could be arranged."

"Not willingly."

Ignoring the remark, Thomas turned back to the group, "The idea is crazy. Don't listen to her." A quick glance at their blank faces assured him she still had to make her pitch.

"I haven't told them yet," Kathryn acknowledged.

He thought it would be effective to grab her and drag her back to his room—at least there he knew what to do, where she was.

The reality was that as much as he liked the idea, she wouldn't care much for the caveman routine. She wanted to take the offense, she wanted to force this guy's hand and in doing so, get the upper hand. That was the kind of thing you see in the movies. It wasn't real life. Yet, she wouldn't accept it if he didn't support her.

"Kathryn has an idea she'd like to run past you." He broke the barrier for her, and then lowered himself onto the tangled linens at the end of the nearest bed.

She cleared her throat and started detailing what he'd heard earlier. When she was done, he expected the men to shut it down immediately. They realized the pending dangers of such a plan and the possibility of so many things that could go awry. Yet, they all looked at each other, nodding their heads. It was as if she'd handed them each a hundred dollar bill. They were stunned but they loved it. He hated them.

"You're going to let her do this?" Thomas asked.

Agent Ewan cleared his throat, looked from Roy to Greg, then spoke. "The plan has merit and we had actually already discussed something similar."

"Merit," Thomas repeated. "Sure—if you don't mind the risk of killing someone that has nothing to do with this man's crazy plots."

"No one is going to get killed."

"You can't guarantee that. Not any more than you could keep her safe on the lake."

"He's right," Dierden interjected. "There aren't any guarantees. It would be better to use an agent in your place."

"Yeah, sure. That worked real good at my apartment, didn't it? This guy knows who I am. He's seen me up close. You can't fool him."

Thomas swallowed his disbelief. "It's too dangerous. She's not going to do it."

"Thomas," Katy interrupted, her voice escalating. "I'm standing right here. Unharmed. And I can speak for myself."

Somehow the conversation whirled around him, taking on a life of its own that propelled it forward. He was powerless to stop them, no one would listen to his protests. So, he watched and listened as they talked it through. In the hours that followed, a detailed plan was hatched and nurtured to maturity. They drew up a map of the community and plotted the plan on it. Who to talk with, what to say, where to stage the events that would need to occur—and what to do if he didn't take the bait. The bait that everyone kept forgetting was a human life he had no intention of sacrificing or jeopardizing as easily as they suggested. Agent Ewan took keen interest in the details. Roy and Greg shot hesitant glances at Thomas periodically, expecting more protests. Kathryn remained caught up in the process, her eyes flashing with excitement. Thomas' heart sank more and more as the plan grew.

When he could stand it no longer, Thomas spoke. "You realize you're forgetting something fairly important. The guy's assuming Kathryn knows something, which she doesn't. If he knew she was oblivious to the contents of that folder, would he even bother with her?"

Ewan stared at him, his eyes narrowing. "No, this guy wouldn't take the chance."

"You said he had certain ethics about that."

"Yes, he d-does," Ewan stuttered as he spoke; he seemed to pick his words carefully. "Maybe he wouldn't care. I don't think it would be wise to take that chance though."

"Yet, you think it's okay to take a risk like you're planning right there." Thomas motioned at the map they'd drawn and the notes they'd penned on their pads. "You seem pretty comfortable with throwing Kathryn in front of this guy—knowing he could hurt her seriously. Knowing it's her life at stake here, not yours. I don't like it. Not one bit. Can't you get the agent from her apartment to sub in?" He gritted his teeth and shook his head.

"Like she already said, the guy obviously knew the difference at the apartment since he didn't bother with her. He came straight here."

And the snowball kept rolling. He had no earthly idea how to stop it. They'd all gone crazy.

*

So crazy that three days later he found himself scaling the side of a rocky incline, staring at Kathryn's backside. The sun was a mere flicker through the trees as it teetered lazily on the horizon, threatening to drop them into darkness within minutes. They needed to move quickly. The plan had worked great so far, much to his disappointment. Reports came in from a few of their contacts that the man had been around asking questions, getting the answers they wanted him to have.

The scruffy socks around Kathryn's ankles kept her legs from getting scratched by the brush they'd worked their way through. The back pockets of her hiking shorts stretched comfortably across hips he knew to be strong and incredibly agile. The backpack filled with supplies, and the shotgun over her shoulder had little impact on her ability to move up the hill with ease. He watched the muscles in her calves and thighs flex and roll as she dug into the hill above him.

"What are you looking at, Tommy?" She glanced back at him and bristled.

He grinned cheerily. "The view, honey. Just the view. It's beautiful up here. All this Texas pine—and dirt." His foot slipped, sending pebbles scattering and rolling down the incline behind them. He landed with a thump on the ground, a dust cloud puffed up around him. A rustling of leaves caught his attention and he looked to his side to see a coral snake curled up facing him, its beautiful red, black, and yellow stripes doing nothing to blend into the dismal surroundings.

Red on Black—Friend of Jack. Black on Yellow—Kill a Fellow. Jack wouldn't like this little guy, less than eighteen inches long, still deadly. Nope, definitely no friend of Jack.

"Yeah, great view. You curled up on the ground with a beautiful snake ready to sink her teeth into you. Funny, I think I've seen this view more times than I can count." Kathryn reached down, the butt of her shotgun firmly in her hand, and flicked the little beauty into the trees. "This reminds me of the time I saw Cassidy Kincaid outside your window on a Saturday night, trying to slither inside to see you."

"Very funny. I never dated Cassidy. She barely spoke to me after my junior year." Thomas stood and whisked the dirt from his T-shirt and shorts, scruffed the twigs from his leg, and stepped forward up the hill.

"That's because I pelted her with mud and told her you gave Sam the impression she was way too prissy for you."

He quirked an eyebrow. "You did that?"

"Yeah. That was right after the time you and Sam told Grant Carden that I wasn't into boys. Remember that one? The guy stared at me weird the rest of the time I was in school. What I did was simply payback."

Thomas laughed. "Payback. How else were we supposed to keep him away from you? We couldn't tell him you had an STD. You never even dated."

"I dated. And that's gross and so juvenile. If you had told anyone that I would have come after you with this shotgun." She lifted the barrel briefly.

"Really, who did you date?"

"I had to sneak out. I never told Sam because he was horrible to everyone I spoke to."

"Who?"

"Mom knew, but she kept it quiet as long as I came home on time and nothing bad happened."

"Who was it?"

Kathryn pushed through the brush ahead of them with the ease of a person that spent a lot of spare time outside. "Ah, here we are," she said between short breaths.

He stepped through the brush behind her and looked down the hill. Dierden and his buddies were probably in place now. He didn't like them so far away. He turned back and lifted the pack from his back along with the heavier nylon bag that carried the tent. They worked together swiftly to set up their meager camp. She silently erected the tent and he made quick work of clearing the ground and getting a small fire started. He tested the tent inside and out and carried their supplies in as they had discussed.

When all was done, he strode toward her in the clearing by the fire and put his hands around her face. "You're not going to tell me, are you?"

"Tell you what?"

"You know what." He stroked her cheeks with his thumbs.

"No, I'm not. It doesn't matter. It's all over and done. Thank God we're not kids anymore. I brought some hot dogs and marshmallows. Let's make use of that fire and...keep your eyes open."

She raised up on her toes and kissed him, full on—nothing held back. *Keep your eyes open. How was he supposed to keep his eyes open when she did that? Hell, hers weren't even open.* The silky eyelashes lazily slid back to reveal the emotion he wanted to see just before she dropped down and turned to get the food from her pack.

Chapter Forty-Three

Eric watched them with envy. He imagined they'd sleep pretty cozy in that tiny tent for two nestled against the rock. It had taken longer than expected to trek up the hill and find a spot to wait, just out of sight. Fortunately, the locals knew the area well, and were free and willing to tell him where his old buddies had decided to camp. Small towns, he grinned. If you pretend to know someone, they'd tell you the person's life history, even where they ate their meals and who they slept with. It had taken half the day to get their whereabouts, and getting into this brush had been a nightmare in the dark. Fortunately, he brought his night vision hunting glasses. Without them, the dark would be unmanageable. Even with the time it took to pump information from unwitting stops along the way, it was faster than he thought and he felt confident he could resolve this by morning.

Eric had traveled across a continent after this girl, only to find the same couple he'd watched in Kenai. They were good together; he liked watching them. She clawed into him hungrily like a cat; he obviously couldn't get enough of it. It made Eric lust for another romp with Brenda, and it made him loathe his job. The more he watched them, the itchier he became for the feel of feminine soft skin. The feel of someone who wanted to touch him back and not fear him.

"What the hell?" he muttered at the red and yellow colored heat flecks of a form moving in the dark several yards outside their tent. He'd seen a slew of small animals already—but this was human. And slithering toward them out of view. Someone else tracked them? He pulled his scope from the front pocket of his vest and brought it up to his eye. A quick twist of his fingers brought the trees into focus. The light of the fire gave just enough subtle enhancement to show a vague outline of the person. The couple talking over the fire didn't even notice the presence of the man in the trees. They were completely captivated with each other. A spark flew up from the fire, sending red flashes into the night and he got a good view of the face in the trees. The face of a man that had been his contact for years.

Smitty.

"That son of a bitch." Eric glanced from the man to the couple and back. He was going to kill them *both*. The man didn't even know anything about them and he was going to eliminate them from the planet. A chill settled into his shoulders as he realized that as soon as they were dead, Smitty would come after him too. He couldn't afford not to. Too much was at stake for the people on those contracts. People that knew only one face. Smitty's.

Smitty's steady arm rose from his side, his fingers grasped tightly around the handle of a firearm as he propped it against the trunk of the tree that shielded him from their view. This man and woman sitting by the fire, enjoying their s'mores, enjoying each other—would be history in a few short minutes.

With clarity, and a huge desire for redemption, Eric placed his thumb over the trigger of his rifle, aimed the scope at the tree in front of Smitty, and ever so gently eased the trigger back. A short, quiet, zip quickly dissipated into the night sounds of crickets and owls. A small piece of bark splintered from the tree and fell to the ground. Smitty's startled face turned in his direction then dove into the darkness.

The couple bolted to their feet and looked behind them. The young man placed himself between the girl and the trees, wrapping her behind him with his arms. He shoved her toward the tent, grabbing a rifle from the ground as they quickly back-stepped into the flap of the tent.

Don't go in there you idiot—you're a sitting duck. I could pick you both off in two easy shots. He willed the young man to have more common sense. He switched to the night vision goggles. Their forms crawled backward in the small nylon structure against the rock, grabbing things from the ground—things he couldn't quite identify. Then, suddenly the heat of their bodies disappeared into thin air. Eric blinked and looked again. Nothing. He looked for Smitty's body heat in the trees. The man was running away, around the hill, with no regard for silence.

Suddenly, with all the hatred that had welled up over the years, Eric knew what he had to do. He slathered the black grease in his kit over his face, grabbed the goggles, rifle, and extra ammo then scaled down the hill toward the couple's camp.

*

"Tommy, it was just a raccoon," Kathryn assured him.

Still, he kept shoving her backward deeper into the shaft of the cavern that their tent had butted up against. The backpack over his shoulder slipped slightly and he reached up to adjust it, then returned his hand to the damp, cold wall as he felt his way deeper into the safety of darkness.

"I doubt that. Only a rabid raccoon would come that close to a blazing fire with people around it. Besides, you agreed we weren't taking chances, remember?" He tightened his grasp on her hand and continued forcing her backward, his thighs pressing hard against her legs.

"Hey. Can you ease up a little? You're hurting me."

His grip on her wrist relaxed. "Oh, sorry. Stop for a second." He slipped the pack down, pulled out a flashlight and flipped it on. "Okay, let's move. Can you imagine what the Indians felt like when they first found this place? It's pitch black—you'd starve to death trying to find a way out."

"Or die if you fell down one of the cavern holes."

"There aren't any. I've climbed every crevice of this place over and over again. We used to hang out here as kids. My parents would have killed me if they'd caught us. They hardly noticed I was gone." He forced himself to calm his nerves and pulled her after him, deeper and deeper down into the cave. When they reached the clearing where it opened up to see a ceiling of stalactites dangling overhead, Kathryn let out an admiring gasp.

"Wow," she whispered.

Thomas scoped the light across the ceiling to give her a better view. "Pretty awesome, huh? You've seen it before, haven't you?" Even with his voice just above a whisper, it echoed in the small space.

"No. I've been in the mouth of the cave—never this deep. I wish I could see it under better circumstances. These stalagmites are huge." She reached a hand toward one in a loving gesture.

"Don't touch it; the oil from your skin will kill it, remember? Didn't you learn that in grade school?"

They stumbled quickly forward, descending behind the yellowish gleam of the flashlight on the slippery ground in front of them.

"We'll come back," he promised.

"I'd like that. It's so beautiful." Katy whispered against his arm.

A loud, gruff voice boomed at them from the darkness just ahead of their flashlight's reach. "Maybe you could just stay permanently."

Thomas stiffened and pushed Kathryn behind him. When he lifted enough light to identify the silhouette, he relaxed. "Ewan. What are you doing here?"

"Looking for you two. You move a lot faster than I expected. I thought this was going to be simple." The man's frame eased out of the shadows, a dark menacing silhouette with a visible handgun. "This place is quite the tomb, wet, damp, and cool. Kind of perfect if you think about it. I doubt anyone's been here in for years."

"You can put the gun down. It's just us," Kathryn assured him. "I think we scared up a raccoon and Thomas panicked."

He didn't lower the gun and Thomas noticed a hardness settle into his features. "A raccoon?" The flashlight lit his face up with an almost red fiery glow that made Ewan look more than menacing. "No, not a raccoon. It's a shame, really."

"A shame?" Thomas asked. "What?"

"That you guys had to choose that cabin to shack up in. And that you couldn't leave the contents alone. I hate it when these things get messy and I have to clean up Eric's messes. You just can't count on someone else to do things well. What's that saying? *If you want it done right, you have to do it yourself?* Well, I guess I'm stuck now."

"I don't get you. Stuck with what?"

"You. Her." He motioned at Kathryn. "I can't let that information get out. It would ruin me. It would only be a matter of time before people connected me with the person on those contracts."

A sinking feeling hit Thomas. Hard. He glanced at the radio clipped to his belt.

"Don't bother. You know you won't get any signal down here. No one will hear you." Ewan nodded. "Feel free to try but I'd have to stop you. Not that it matters. I have to stop you anyway."

"No you don't. You don't *have* to do anything at all. We have no interest in this. It's not our problem. Not our battle to fight." *Shit.* He realized he shouldn't have said that after it slipped out.

"Ah, but that's just the dilemma, you see. If the battle must be fought...and won, then we have to be able to move freely, inside and out of the system. We can't be confined by governmental policy or agency rules. That's the beauty of this. We do what the agency can't. We make sure the tough things get done. And sometimes there are casualties."

Thomas scanned the dim edges of the cavern searching for a path to get them away from this lunatic's reach. He'd chastise the both of them later for not recognizing that a new face was always a bad thing in dangerous situations. Roy and Greg had accepted the man so obviously he'd had no choice to do so as well.

Fortunately, he'd done his homework and left little to chance. Not only did he have a photographic memory, he also had a serious addiction to detailed plans. And there had been no way in hell he'd let her walk into this particular situation without adequate preparation.

While she'd been at breakfast with Dierden and then showering, he'd made an excuse to go "work out." His work out consisted of high-tailing it into the hills and renewing his memory on the cave that he and his friends had used for a hide-out in grade school and junior high.

"Ewan, don't move."

"You're not calling the shots here, smartass."

"Not trying to. That cavern behind you that's pitch dark..." Thomas watched as Ewan shot a glance over his shoulder. "It drops about twenty feet into a rocky hole. You step too far backward and you'll end up hamburger."

Katy nailed him in the stomach with an elbow. He shot her an assuring glance. There was no way he could tell her what he was up to, though he wished he could. Then it might have a snowball's chance in hell of actually saving them. She thought he'd just made a mistake.

Ewan peered once more into the dark but saw nothing. "You're lying." He said as he tried to focus farther than the ten feet of dirt that showed beyond the flashlight. Thomas looked nervously over his shoulder.

He softened his voice intentionally. "Maybe so, but do you really want to take the chance? Besides, wouldn't it be better for me to *not* tell you?"

There were three paths out of their current location. One was Ewan's entry point and now blocked, unless Thomas felt lucky and could pass an armed assailant. The second went right back through their tent and in another few minutes would be swarming with FBI agents that could possibly be part of this convoluted mess. The third looped around to the backside of the hill, exiting on a rock ledge above the lake, but Ewan wasn't aware of it. Yet. He hadn't told them on a hunch, and now he was glad for it.

"Why don't we just test out your story...you check it out first."

"First?" Thomas suppressed the desire to fist pump. The guy was falling for his plan. His backup plan.

"Yeah, you say it plummets to a pile of rocks, right? I think you're screwing with me, so we'll just check it out. Actually, you'll do it." Ewan gestured with his flashlight. "Go on."

Kathryn tugged on Thomas' shirt sleeve, not taking her eyes from Ewan. "Aren't you worried that he'll escape rather than fall to his death?"

"And leave you behind? Not likely."

Thomas knew that Ewan was calculating the risk. Guys like him wouldn't leave anything to chance. He guessed that Ewan thought Thomas *might* fall to his death, and if so, resolve one of his two major problems. Then he'd just have to deal with Kathryn. And the fall, along with the gun in his hand would finalize that just fine. Or at least, Thomas hoped that's where his thoughts rambled.

"Thomas, you stay right here." Kathryn clutched his bicep. He felt the desperation in her voice, but he had no intention of enlightening her at the moment.

"Let go of him, cupcake." Ewan aimed the gun in his grasp at her arm.

"Are you nuts? He'll never survive a fall like that."

Ewan laughed. "Like I really give a shit. You really believe you're leaving here, don't you? You don't get it. Let him go. If the fall kills him, big deal. It's easier that way. Neither one of you is leaving and you might as well accept that and make it as painless on yourselves as possible."

As he glanced once more toward the dark abyss, Thomas suspected Ewan was struggling with the decision to send Thomas. The man squared his shoulder and lifted his gun an inch or two.

"Tell you what. Why don't *both* of you go? I'll be right behind you so don't get stupid and think you can escape."

Thomas snuck a glance at Kathryn. "Way to go, honey."

"Move it, I'm running out of time." Ewan waved the Glock at them. "And I'd appreciate it if you'd drop that shotgun and the handgun first."

Kathryn slid the leather armband from her shoulder and leaned the rifle against the cave wall and stepped toward the opening. Ewan switched his aim to Thomas and waited while Thomas carefully lifted his nine millimeter from his side pouch and laid it on top of a rock ledge near the shotgun.

"Good, now get going." Ewan stepped back and let both of them pass, keeping his weapon locked on their silhouette. He lifted the flashlight to cast a shadow around them but its glow was quickly lost in the depth of the cave.

Thomas pushed Kathryn behind him and stepped forward to where he thought the ledge was, then turned. They were in complete darkness except for the orange-yellow glow at their feet, and could only feel along from this point. He held her arm tight and again softened his voice to a mere whisper.

"You really don't want to do this, man. We aren't important enough to waste the effort on. Why don't you at least let Katy go? She hasn't even seen the data so what's she going to do?"

"Just fucking do it!" Ewan roared. His voice echoed in the caverns.

And the roof caved in over them in a large black cascade of furry bodies and squeals. *Bats.* Kathryn screamed and hunkered down. Thank God they were still there. Ewan fired a single shot as Thomas charged him. The bulk of his weight sent the flashlight sliding over the rock floor but only dislodged the weapon.

"Run, Katy!" Thomas yelled.

Thomas rolled his body over Ewan and pinned the weapon with his knee. He was considerably bigger than the man, so he felt confident he could keep him down until she was far enough away. He had forgotten one small key point. The man was a federal agent, or something of the sort—and much better trained for armed combat.

With a simple toss, Ewan shoved Thomas to the ground and rose. He scrambled to get his weapon righted and lifted it toward Thomas' head.

"I wouldn't do that if I was you."

Kathryn and Thomas whirled at the sound of another voice behind them. The man that emerged from the shadows bore amazing resemblance to a bar patron in Alaska they'd seen in Kenai. The man nodded at them as he stepped forward with a rifle raised at shoulder height, its sight narrowed in on Agent Ewan. "This ends here, Smitty."

"Smitty?" Thomas questioned. The two men ignored him as they glared at each other.

"Don't be an idiot, Eric. You can't get out of this. You know that—it's gone too far. They know too much. I've already fixed the data and all that's left is—cleanup." Agent Ewan stepped forward with both hands now on the handgun. He nudged sideways to get Thomas and Kathryn out of the way as he aimed at the other man.

"These people don't need to be involved." The new man motioned with a shrug. "I wonder what your agency would think about a decorated FBI officer going outside the law, or even his commanding officers, to mastermind the political influences of this country? Or perhaps how he manipulated a war by certain 'influences' with the right people? All for financial gain."

"It wasn't financial gain. Sure, there was reward but this wasn't about that. Besides, no one would believe you. Not after all that's happened," Agent Ewan fumed.

Thomas was having trouble keeping up with what they said. Ewan was the guy? His real name was Smitty? The other guy? Who was he?

"You forget that I'm dead. You identified me. If I'm resurrected now, they'll question your story. You really think you'll be able to convince them I'm the only person behind this? It was easy before because you were higher up the food chain. Now, I'm not so sure they'll believe you when they find a hotel room with your name on it, filled with evidence."

"My room is clean."

"Yeah, that's what I said, remember? You fucker."

Kathryn whispered to Thomas' back, "There are two of them?"

Thomas shrugged and backed Kathryn into the wall. He whispered into her hair. "If you see an opportunity to run, take it. I'm not sure what's going on, but we're sunk." He gave her hand a reassuring squeeze as he stifled the panic rising like a volcano in his gut.

Thomas turned toward Ewan and spoke loudly, "Roy and Greg ought to be here soon. I'm sure they've noticed we're gone by now."

Eric's startled expression didn't go unnoticed. Agent Ewan chuckled a short, arrogant snort. "Not likely. I sent them on a wild goose chase after a stranger I saw on one of the other trails. A trail that ends down at the foot of the hill five miles away. By the time they make it back, you'll be dead. The unfortunate victims of a crazy, rogue agent that we've tracked for years." Ewan gestured at the other man.

"You piece of shit. You're not going to do this to me again." Eric fired his rifle, dislodging the handgun from Agent Ewan's hand. Ewan snapped his head up in disbelief, then reached toward his ankle. The rifle on Thomas shoulder was yanked up. A shot rang out from it, reverberating painfully in the cave's closed space. Thomas and Kathryn both jumped at the sound and looked at the stranger that had leaped to their side without warning.

Thomas slammed his hand into his pocket, reaching for the blade he'd shoved into it earlier. It was a futile effort, because this guy was a pro. The man was shorter than Thomas, but his strength pressed into the two of them, capturing them against the coldness of the cave walls. Kathryn sucked in her breath loudly, causing the man to glance between the two of them.

"Listen. You have a choice here," the man snarled, holding the shotgun under Thomas' chin. He slipped a blade in his other hand to Kathryn's throat. "My name is Eric. Special Agent Eric Simmons. CIA. I've been 'out of play' for eight years. Since that son-of-a-bitch led me on a wild goose chase, then threw me to the wolves." He gestured at the body on the ground that was slowly oozing blood on the moist rock below them. "Here's how we're going to do this. I'm a man of my word. I never go back on a contract—a promise, so to speak. That man has a fatal wound from this rifle, your rifle. He chased you into this cave and told you how he'd planned all those jobs, using his position in the agency as a mechanism to carry out those contracts. He then tried to kill you, but you managed to get a couple of rounds off first." The man stepped back and eased his pressure on Thomas and Kathryn.

Thomas hated to bring it up but there was a minor detail that had been ignored. "There's also a bullet in him from your weapon. How will we explain that?" Thomas asked.

"You won't have to." Eric eased himself stealthily back over the body. His eyes stayed focused on them while he sliced the man's arm open and pulled out a bullet. He dropped it in his pocket and shredded the arm with the knife. "You struggled and got a good cut out of his arm before she," Eric pointed at Kathryn, "got a lucky shot off and killed him."

Kathryn and Thomas stared dumbfounded at the man as he emptied the shotgun into the walls of the cave, then dropped it on the ground. His gloved hands left nothing but smudges on the stock.

"I've seen enough to know she's a crack shot, so the story's believable. This man framed me to look like I did his work. The only reason I wasn't dead was in that envelope. My insurance, you might say," Eric told them. Thomas' eyes widened. The man's desperate explanation seemed more of a plea. A plea for closure and escape. "You walk out of this cave heroes."

"And you get away. What makes us believe you won't come after us again?" Kathryn's soft voice confirmed.

"No." He frowned at her. "I get my life back. You tell it like I said and you'll never have to worry about anything again. You killed the bad guy, found a terrorist that had hidden under the CIA's nose for years, and I—never existed. An agent that died years ago in the line of duty, probably at the hands of this maniac." He gestured again to Agent Ewan's body.

They stood staring at each other as seconds ticked away. Eric stepped toward them. "You have my word. My word is my contract. Your only other choice is to die right here. If that happens, I'm still on the run, hiding—and you're dead. No more boats, and fishing...no more nooky in strange cabins and tents."

He glanced from Kathryn to Thomas. "You have a future if you do this. A future that, by the looks of the two of you, will be pretty full. Your choice, folks."

Thomas stepped toward the man, stopping abruptly when the man lifted his rifle and stuck it in his face.

"You have a deal, sir." Thomas thrust his hand to the man and waited. The man started to raise his gloved hand to grasp the extended appendage and seal the commitment. Thomas shook his head and stared into the sad, desperate eyes. "No." He pointed to the other bloodied glove. "That hand."

The man's hand, the one Thomas referred to, was grasped around the butt of his rifle. Lowering it would make him vulnerable. He shifted a glance to Kathryn nervously as he considered the weight of Thomas' suggestion. The blood on Thomas' hand would only solidify the story. Yet offering it left him wide open for attack. He raised the other hand to the rifle, switched his grasp, and took hold of Thomas' fingers.

As Thomas felt the wet, warmth of Ewan's life paint the inside of his palm and drip through his fingers, he gave the man a nod.

Chapter Forty-Four

"Have you forgiven me, Mrs. Delroy?" Thomas teased. From his sprawled position, with Kathryn draped across him, he watched Kathryn's mom and Sophie Prater, Trev's wife, busy cataloging wedding gifts from the reception. Sophie unceremoniously removed cards, read them, then ripped the paper free and tossed it on the floor. Mrs. Delroy documented the process and stuffed the paper and miscellaneous trash into plastic bags.

Without lifting her head, Mrs. Delroy responded, "What was there to forgive, Tommy?"

"Oh, I don't know—running off to Vegas and marrying your daughter without so much as a word. Moving in with her and stealing her away from you all in the space of a month. Cheating you out of a good cry at your only daughter's nuptials."

"I've had a year to get over that, young man. Besides, you made it right today. A beautiful ceremony, don't you think?" She grinned.

Sophie ripped paper from an almost crate-sized box and unveiled another gift. "A cooler full of imported beer from Greg Dierden." She frowned. "What kind of guy gives that for a wedding gift?"

Kathryn lifted her weary head from Thomas' lap and grinned. "The kind that drank three twelve-packs at our lake house while trying to learn to wakeboard. That's payback."

"Or bribery for another round," Thomas added. He stroked the wisps of hair back from her temple. Little white flowers tumbled out of the strands and fell on his pants. She was exhausted. A rushed marriage in Vegas, followed by a family one ten months later had brought out the best and worst in both of them. Katy's mom had chastised him severely about the Vegas trip, but Katy stifled that pretty quickly by informing her that they'd have a true ceremony for the family later.

Two months to the day after they'd walked out of the cave with blood dripping off his fingers, they booked the trip to Vegas and left. Trevan and Sophie met them and stood with them, the only faces there on their behalf. It was simple, quick, and he'd never been happier.

Trevan lounged in a big brown faux-suede chair, with a white plastic toothpick shaped like two hearts, hanging out of his mouth. "I liked what your dad said, Thomas."

"Yeah, can you believe that? I always knew something had gone wrong when I was in high school. I just never understood it. He never explained—just turned into a real ass. I thought it was me. I guess you never really know, do you?" Thomas slipped Kathryn's shoes from her feet and plunked them to the floor.

Sophie piped in. "I can't imagine how they felt—having to get married that young, then losing the baby within a few months. No wonder he had trouble with it."

Thomas grimaced. "I can't believe my mom never said anything. I never knew I almost had an older brother. I knew they married young and I pretty much gathered Dad felt cheated to some extent. I had no idea that it wasn't him, it was Mom. I can't blame her. Pregnant at seventeen with a husband, a job, and night school to try to get a college education. No wonder she miscarried."

Mrs. Delroy watched Thomas' face as he slowly mouthed his thoughts, then she spoke with softness in her voice. "She talked about it once with me. Only once. She wasn't one to open up, but I don't think she really felt cheated. It was more like overwhelmed and maybe a sense of guilt. I think she worried that she had held your dad back from what he could have been. When you were approaching your senior year, your dad started wanting more out of life—mainly for her. She was the salutatorian of her class, and all she achieved was marrying her high school sweetheart. She misunderstood it and thought he resented their mistaken marriage...or at least that's what it sounded like."

Thomas' mouth dropped. "She told you this?"

"In a way, yes, some of it I just picked up on."

Kathryn raised up on one arm, pressing her elbow into Thomas' leg. "I think it was sweet the way he said that he'd met the love of his life at seventeen, but life was bigger and harder than they expected. That was a good way of expressing it—and when he said he wanted more for you—he wanted you to know that love and also feel the confidence of reaching your full potential...I almost cried."

"So, Thomas," Sam said as he came from the washroom and reached into the beer cooler/wedding gift for a bottle of beer. A quick hiss exhaled from the bottle as he twisted the cap free and tossed it into the trash. He'd listened in on the conversation afraid to comment. "Does this mean I'm forgiven for meddling in your life and plotting with your dad?"

Two voices, Katy's and Tommy's chided in unison, "No!" Tommy glared at Sam. "Give us another ten years to make *your* life miserable."

"Fair enough." Sam leaned against the wall and took a swig from the bottle.

Trevan pushed his lanky build out of the chair, strode over to the cooler and carried it back to the table between them. "Want one?" he asked as he pulled a Modelo out for himself, not caring if it was intended to be shared or not. He tossed one to Thomas and they both popped them open.

"Great gift." Thomas held the bottle up in a toast.

Kathryn laid across him, her legs propped on the end of the sofa, her beautiful toes painted a shimmering pink. The white satin lay in folds around her, draping gently on the carpet below the couch. He was keenly aware that it was his wedding night—for the second time in a year—and he had a room full of people. He gave her a look that was laced with a plea to get rid of the crowd so they could take advantage of this beautiful hotel suite his dad had rented for them. A surge of lust passed over him as he remembered the little blue box that she had hidden in her lingerie drawer.

She didn't know he'd peeked a couple of nights before when he was putting away the clean clothes they folded. The box held a white lace thong and bra that currently had to be under the yards of satin he planned to remove from her as soon as possible. He was anxious to get started on that exploration.

"Sophie," Kathryn started, "you don't have to do that tonight. There's no rush."

"We only have a few more gifts left and if we don't do it now, it won't get finished. Some of us have to go to work on Monday. Not everyone is hopping on a plane for a two-week honeymoon full of sunshine and sex—not in that order, of course." She flushed as she realized she'd said that in front of Kathryn's mom. "Sorry, Mrs. Delroy."

Sophie concentrated on ripping a card from a blue and white package in front of her. She observed the address. "This one's from someone named Eric in Kenai, Alaska." Sophie tossed the card on the table without reading it, and reached to rip the paper from the box.

Trevan and Thomas leaped to their feet in unison and yelled "No!"

Katy tumbled to the floor in a heap of silk and roses. The color drained from her face. "Don't open that!"

It was too late.

As Sophie peeled the paper from the side of the box, Trevan barreled toward her, tackling her and wrestling the box away.

He darted his eyes at Tommy and yelled, "Get the window!"

Thomas flung the sliding window to the balcony of the suite open just in time for Trev to pass the box out the window as if it were a football. Kathryn jumped to her feet and followed the two men to the balcony. The box floated heavily to the ground, crashing and spilling its contents on the sidewalk.

"Trevan Prater!" Sophie blasted. "What the heck is wrong with you guys?"

"Sorry, babe. It's just—well." Thomas watched Trevan stumble with the explanation for a second, then cleared his throat. "Give me the card." He held his hand out and waited.

The card had glitter-spattered wedding bells on the front. Thomas read the words for everyone to hear. "Thomas and Kathryn, I hope you'll enjoy these crystal candlesticks. Best wishes on a long and happy marriage. I will always think of you as my two little guardian angels—and hope you'll think the same of me. Take Care and Stay on the Road (You know—don't get stuck). Eric."

Ruby Delroy glanced from her daughter to Thomas and then to Trevan Prater. She didn't try to mask the confusion on her face as she spoke. "Wow, that was a mean thing to do with such a nice gift. Remind me not to buy you two candlesticks."

*

Eric would have laughed if he'd seen their reaction. He and Brenda had purchased the gift in Seattle just before hopping a plane to Hawaii. The nice lady that had assisted him with Brenda's gift remembered him and very sweetly fawned over them as she helped them select "the perfect wedding gift for their niece and nephew." Judging by the way he remembered the young couple's passion for each other, he thought the candles would add a nice romantic touch to their bedroom—along with the massage lotion he tossed in as a joke.

Squinting into the Hawaiian sunset with Brenda at his side, he heaved a relaxed sigh. He hoped they had liked the gift—it would be the last word he sent to anyone from his past. Now, it was time to have a future.

About the Author

Shelley grew up on a farm outside of Kansas City, Missouri. She's a graduate of Oklahoma State University with a bit of post-graduate work at OSU and University of Wyoming-Casper. She now resides near Houston with her family.

In the mood for more Crimson Romance? Check out *Nature of the Beast* by Stephanie Freeman at *www.crimsonromance.com*.